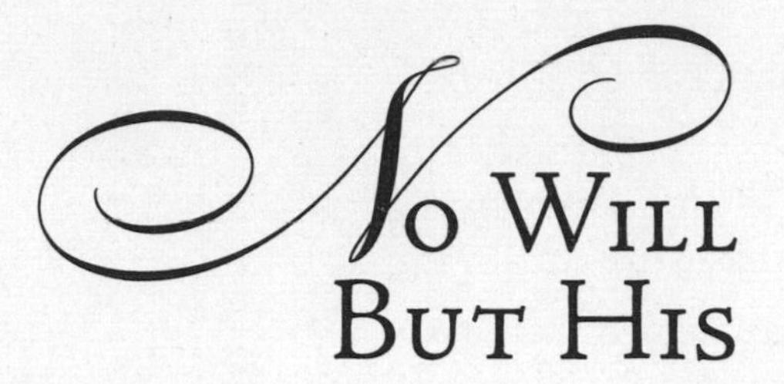

GAIL BORDEN
PUBLIC LIBRARY DISTRICT
ELGIN, ILLINOIS

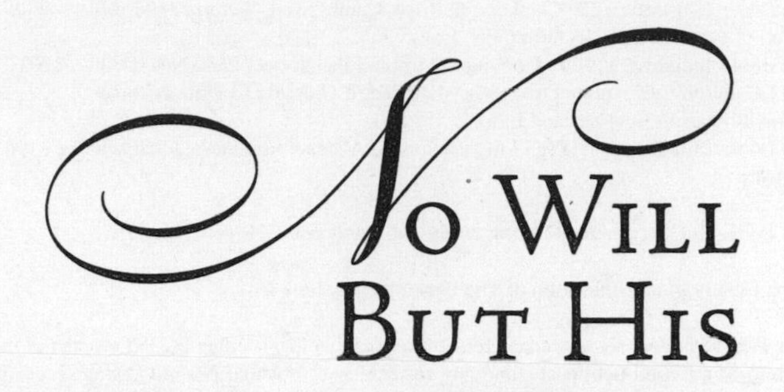

No Will But His

A Novel of
Kathryn Howard

Sarah A. Hoyt

BERKLEY BOOKS, NEW YORK

THE BERKLEY PUBLISHING GROUP
Published by the Penguin Group
Penguin Group (USA) Inc.
375 Hudson Street, New York, New York 10014, USA
Penguin Group (Canada), 90 Eglinton Avenue East, Suite 700, Toronto, Ontario M4P 2Y3, Canada
(a division of Pearson Penguin Canada Inc.)
Penguin Books Ltd., 80 Strand, London WC2R 0RL, England
Penguin Group Ireland, 25 St. Stephen's Green, Dublin 2, Ireland (a division of Penguin Books Ltd.)
Penguin Group (Australia), 250 Camberwell Road, Camberwell, Victoria 3124, Australia
(a division of Pearson Australia Group Pty. Ltd.)
Penguin Books India Pvt. Ltd., 11 Community Centre, Panchsheel Park, New Delhi—110 017, India
Penguin Group (NZ), 67 Apollo Drive, Rosedale, North Shore 0632, New Zealand
(a division of Pearson New Zealand Ltd.)
Penguin Books (South Africa) (Pty.) Ltd., 24 Sturdee Avenue, Rosebank, Johannesburg 2196,
South Africa

Penguin Books Ltd., Registered Offices: 80 Strand, London WC2R 0RL, England

This book is an original publication of The Berkley Publishing Group.

This is a work of fiction. Names, characters, places, and incidents either are the product of the author's imagination or are used fictitiously, and any resemblance to actual persons, living or dead, business establishments, events, or locales is entirely coincidental. The publisher does not have any control over and does not assume responsibility for author or third-party websites or their content.

Copyright © 2010 by Sarah Hoyt.
Cover design by Judith Lagerman.
Cover illustration © Frederick Richard Pickersgill / Private Collection / The Fine Art Society, London, UK / The Bridgeman Art Library International.
Text design by Tiffany Estreicher.

All rights reserved.
No part of this book may be reproduced, scanned, or distributed in any printed or electronic form without permission. Please do not participate in or encourage piracy of copyrighted materials in violation of the author's rights. Purchase only authorized editions.
BERKLEY® is a registered trademark of Penguin Group (USA) Inc.
The "B" design is a trademark of Penguin Group (USA) Inc.

PRINTING HISTORY
Berkley trade paperback edition / April 2010

Library of Congress Cataloging-in-Publication Data

Hoyt, Sarah A.
No will but his / Sarah A. Hoyt. —Berkley trade pbk. ed.
p. cm.
ISBN 978-0-425-23251-4
1. Kathryn Howard, Queen, consort of Henry VIII, King of England, d. 1542—Fiction. 2. Great Britain—History—Henry VIII, 1509-1547—Fiction. 3. Queens—Fiction. I. Title.
PS3608.O96N62 2010
813'.6—dc22

2009043936

PRINTED IN THE UNITED STATES OF AMERICA

10 9 8 7 6 5 4 3 2 1

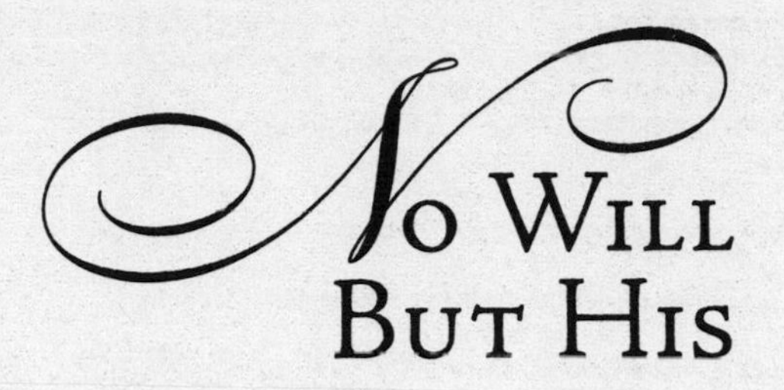
No Will
But His

The Back Stairs of Hampton Court

"Are you brave or foolish, Your Majesty? Brave or foolish?" Thomas Culpepper's fine, long fingers quested beneath the bodice of my dress, caressing along the rounded slope of my breast till they found the nipple and played upon it as a musician upon a virginal. His blue grey eyes sparkled like a cloudless summer's sky down at me as he demanded, his voice thickened by desire, "Brave or foolish?"

I smiled at him, but I said nothing. It has ever been my belief with men that it is far easier to allow them to make up their own minds and tell themselves whatever pretty story they want about your motives.

They can think you love them or hate them, that you're broken-hearted at leaving them or else that you have turned your heart to another. There is naught you can do about their fanciful imaginings, and it saves time and many tears if you simply let them believe as they will. Then they tell themselves their pretty stories and your soul remains unstained by the lie.

As I looked at Master Culpepper from beneath my half-lowered eyelids, I thought it was a good thing he had auburn hair and those fine eyes, and that his features—I thought—resembled what my husband's had been before he'd grown so fat. Any get of Thomas could pass as the get of Henry, the king of England.

"Don't you know, madam, that the wrath of kings is death?"

I smiled at him, my sauciest smile, and endeavored to appear light-hearted and fanciful and interested in nothing but my pleasure. Or perhaps half mad in love with him, which Thomas would probably fain believe I was. He'd grown very vain.

"You speak too much, Master Culpepper."

"Should one not speak?" he asked. "When such a grave matter is afoot?" His hand, more forward than his brain, quested still in the warm reaches of my bodice, and by that questing hand I knew I had him. He might think, and he might talk, but his body would no more let him walk away from me than it would let him ascend to flight like an angel bound for heaven above.

"My quarters are warm, and all my servants abed, save only Lady Rochefort and Mistress Tilney who is utterly devoted to me—and both of them would die before they betray me."

In his eyes for a moment there was a flash of fear. Then it was gone. "Madam!" he said, desire in his voice strong enough to drive away any fear. "Madam."

"Dare you not, Thomas Culpepper? And I thought you a brave man." Which by all accounts I should well think him—in the field of joust and in dispute, he stood with the most gallant courtiers.

"Brave I am, and I'll dare if you will, but . . ."

My finger rested on his lips, stilling them. "Hush then, and dare you all."

In his eyes I read lust mixed with a little fear. He would never be allowed to see the fear in mine. I kept my gaze level, my smile broad. He would never be allowed to know that as I stood here, in my velvet gown, my sparkling jewels, I walked a narrow path between two deep abysses.

The king, my husband, lay ill abed. At this very moment, already, he might be dead, taken by the same illness that had caused the wound in his leg to stop flowing and turned his face black with foul humors just two months ago. That same illness had returned, that same blocked humor. And now he would die. And if he died—

If he died, he left nothing. Two daughters and a small son who, though he might be a lusty infant, would still be a pawn of every pretender, every hand against him.

We would find ourselves again as in the time before the king's father when my grandmother said every man had been against every other and no one safe. And I, the relict of the sovereign, would be the first to lose life and limb in such strife.

Only one thing would protect me, and hold me on the throne, and that was that my womb should ripen with a child. But that was impossible as my husband did little that could lead to such an auspicious result.

And so, at this moment, in my peril, I must seize upon another who might impregnate me and whose son I could pretend to be Henry's. Of course, discovery of my treason would lead to death, but so would Henry's death without having seeded my womb.

I half closed my eyes and wondered how I—who had wanted nothing more than to keep myself free from any man's single, brute power over me—should have come to this.

But I said nothing. I closed my eyes and allowed Thomas to think it was just my desire for him making me hoarse, as I said, "Speak no more, Thomas. Only make me yours."

The Rose in the Bud

One

"So *this* be your get, Edmund Howard!" the old lady said, and the way she said it made it clear she disapproved.

She looked very great and more important than anyone Kathryn had yet seen—tall and well arrayed in shining satin and splendorous brocade. Her face set in a mask of disapproval as—her back very straight, her eyes hard—she walked down the line of Kathryn's siblings and looked them over with the kind of speculative glance Kathryn had seen the Howard housekeeper give a side of beef in the market or a row of ill-plucked chickens.

Her eye ran over Kathryn's brother Charles, just fourteen and looking very much like someone had taken an end of him and stretched him up, without making sure that his limbs and form should match his new, greatly increased height.

Like all of Edmund Howard's children, he had been dressed in new clothes, or at least as new as their father's diminished fortune could command. The hose were somewhat faded, but they matched the doublet, which was a new and brilliant shade resembling orange peel. Even then Kathryn thought that it was a right pity that Charles's hair, too, should match the doublet and, as he blushed under the old lady's look, so should his face, which became right ruddy under a smattering of freckles.

"Umm . . ." the lady said, and passed on. Her walking stick tapped the ground in rhythm, as though she were keeping pace with her thoughts. *Tap, tap, tap.* And she stopped in front of Kathryn's brother Harry. He was, like Charles, ruddy and red-headed, but the hand of God had as yet to take hold of him and stretch him to a man's height with a boy's frame. Instead, he was almost as short as Kathryn and twice as round, the freckles on his face making it look like an apple that has got speckled from waiting too long in the cold cellar.

The stick stopped tapping the ground for a bare moment, then resumed its tapping again. *Tap, tap, tap, tap,* it went, as the lady said, over her shoulder in the direction of the bowing and cringing Edmund, "That will never do, Edmund. You'll never raise him. He's too fat to be healthy and too ruddy to be gentle."

Kathryn didn't hear what her father muttered, but it had that tone of cringing apology that she remembered from when Mother was alive, when she used to ask him what he had done with this or that money that she'd entrusted to him. Father among men was one thing—wise and reserved, the hero of Flodden Field. But Father with female relatives . . .

The lady didn't pay any attention to him, anywise, but tapped her way to stand in front of Kathryn's brother George. George did not have the carroty hair that had, mayhap, come from the Culpeppers, the family of Kathryn's mother. Instead, his hair was a dark auburn, like Kathryn's, and his eyes, like hers, were broadly spaced and dark.

He was a year older than Kathryn, and she remembered that their last stepmother had accounted him a right proper and pretty child, and petted him much and made much of him, even though she had brought eight children of her own into her marriage with Kathryn's father. Kathryn had been jealous of him, then. Since her mother had died, no one had made much of her. But Kathryn's nurse had told her envy was a sin and that if she persisted, the devil would come and take Kathryn entire to hell and leave only a little burned mark after.

Now it seemed as though this old lady they'd come to visit was also thinking how pretty George was and considering making much of him. Kathryn stood only a little away from him, with her sister Mary in between, and tried not to look around Mary—who was fifteen—to see the expression on the lady's face. If the lady said George was the most beautiful child she'd ever seen, Kathryn felt that she would likely burst, like an unseasoned log thrown onto a hot fire. Not because she wanted the grand lady's attention, but because the favorite of the family was always George, or else one of the other boys, or else yet Mary who was pretty and marriageable. For all the attention anyone ever paid her, Kathryn might as well have been as clear as water or as immaterial as air.

"Um," the lady said. And that *um* contained quite a different consideration than the one she'd given Charles. Her stick tapped the floor, *tap, tap, tap,* but she did not move, as though she were involved in some great consideration.

For a while silence reigned, and then her voice rang out, clear and sudden, like the thunder clap from the clear sky. "Look up, boy," she said. "Look at me."

And on the heels of that, she made a sound, not quite a laugh and not full disgust, but something between. "Edmund!" she said, her voice still cracking. "What manner of coward have you bred?"

This time Kathryn dared look around Mary's skirt. She didn't fully need to, because she could smell the acrid odor of urine thick in the air, and sure enough, on the front of George's hose and down his leg, there was a wet mark and a puddle forming beside his slipper.

Again Kathryn's father tried to say something, but the lady paid no more attention to him than she did to George, left standing there in his wet hose. Kathryn heard George sniffle and guessed that shortly he would start to cry, but she was more worried about the lady who now stood close enough to Kathryn for the little Howard daughter to discern the fine lace ornamenting her expensive clothes and to smell the wondrous rich perfume of her garments.

Mary curtseyed deep, in the way she'd been taught, and the lady snorted, looking her up and down. At fifteen, Mary, like Charles, had grown. Unlike Charles, nature had seen fit to fill in her outlines to those of a woman, widening in chest and swelling in hip, but with long legs and a fine, pleasant face. She, of all the children of Edmund Howard, had black hair, with just a little bit of a curl to it, and looked, to her younger sister's eyes, like a full-grown woman and just what Kathryn wanted to be, particularly as today she wore a fine velvet kirtle and bodice, with bright peach-colored sleeves of silk, with many bright ribbons hanging from them.

Kathryn thought for certain that the lady would be impressed by Mary, as she hadn't been by any of the others, but she didn't seem so. She responded to Mary's curtsey by raising eyebrows that, this close, looked to be almost nonexistent, and by turning over her shoulder to look at Kathryn's father. "This is your get, Edmund?"

Edmund Howard mumbled. Kathryn could get from his voice nothing but the words "not sure" and the words "believe so" as well as "Leigh." Leigh was the name of her older brothers and sisters, the children of Kathryn's mother's first marriage, before she'd married Father.

The lady snorted. "Just like a fool," she said. "To buy the house without first making sure it was untenanted." And she walked past Mary and stood now in front of Kathryn.

Kathryn stood straight, determined not to cringe and not to slouch and not to wet herself, like George. That morning, when she'd seen the little girl attired in her new clothes—a fine bonnet of satin and a gown of sarcenet, better and newer than anything Kathryn had worn since her mother died—Dame Margaret, Father's new wife, had told Kathryn to be good and behave like a grown maiden and not a child while they visited with the duchess and that if she did not disgrace herself, Dame Margaret would give her strawberries. She would not disgrace herself.

Instead, she kept her eyes on the floor, which was a yellow mosaic, and felt the blaze from the great fireplace to her right. Though outside it was warm spring, a sort of damp chill clung to the room so that, with the proximity of the fire, her right side baked while her left froze. She looked at the floor and expected the stick to start tapping again at any moment, as the lady gave some opinion of Kathryn and moved on.

Instead, a hand like a great claw came to take hold of Kathryn's small, pointy chin and pull it up. The hand felt dry as paper and as tough against the little girl's skin, but its grasp was like iron. It tilted Kathryn's face up to look into the face of the old lady. Her nose was just a little hooked, just like the nose of Father's new wife, and her eyes were dark grey and keen, giving the impression of seeing right through people. "What is your name, chit?" she asked.

"Kathryn, madam," Kathryn said, her voice coming out all shy and piping, sounding much younger than she was, much younger than she liked to sound. And then because she remembered her remarks about Mary, "Kathryn Howard, madam."

A dry chuckle answered. "Aye, Kathryn Howard, indeed," she said. And then turning to her father, "How old is she, Edmund?"

"Ten," her father said, in a tone of great assurance. Then cleared his throat and hesitated. "Or maybe eleven." There was a short pause. "She might be twelve at that. You see, I was away from my family so much, because of debtors laying wait for me at the home of my wife and children that I—"

"That you have no idea how old your children are," the lady said. And snorted. "Ten is full young to go in service, Edmund."

"I am sure she's not that young," he said. "And she is sharp, is Kathryn. Anything whatsoever that you teach her she can learn and in no time at all. Bright and capable is Kathryn and—"

"A grace she must get from her mother," the lady said, cutting whatever else Kathryn's father might have wished to say in the girl's favor.

Kathryn's mind was turning on the words *into service*, very much at doubt as to what they meant. The Howards had servants, of course. More when her mother was alive or when her father's last wife, Dame Dorothy had been alive, because their money sustained—her father said—more people to attend them. But even on Father's money before he married Dame Margaret, they had attendants. People who cooked and tended to their clothes and emptied the slops. Was Kathryn, then, to be one of these? Every sense revolted.

The servants at the Howard home were village boys and girls, whose fathers were farmers or servants themselves. And if there was a thing she knew, and knew well from her childhood—many times repeated to her by her late mother—it was that her name was Howard, and she was the granddaughter of a duke.

The lady stepped back once, twice, regarding Kathryn from beneath her almost-not-there eyebrows, and Edmund Howard cleared his throat. "Only one of them you must take, madam, if you please, because though Anne has got me the post of comptroller at Calais, it is not enough for a man of my birth to keep himself and all my children, and I—"

"And you have not been granted full access to your new wife's fortune, she being no fool," the lady said and snorted. "Very well. I will take one of your sorry brood."

She looked away from Kathryn and toward the beginning of the line and Charles again, and Kathryn could hear her stick go *tap-tap-tap-tap-tap* on the floor as she considered each of the Howard siblings in turn. Charles—*tap*—Henry—*tap*—George—*taptap* in annoyance, followed by a loud sniffle from the despised boy—and Mary, whose renewed curtsey only earned her a *taptap-tap*. And then to Kathryn. And her stick stopped.

A great sigh escaped the lady's lips, as if she'd done all to keep it still, but it would not do. "Oh, very well," she said at last. "She looks not the fool nor the wanton, and the thing about too little age is that you grow out of it. I will take Kathryn."

Kathryn almost yelped then. What could the lady mean by taking her? But then she remembered that her new stepmother, Dame Margaret, had promised her strawberries, and she stayed still. Her father had come to her side, standing between her and the great fireplace, which meant that his back must be roasting. He laid his warm hand upon her shoulder. "What an honor, Kathryn. Curtsey and thank the duchess!"

Kathryn curtseyed automatically and heard her voice pipe up, "I thank you, Your Grace, most heartily."

"Yes, yes," she said impatiently, even as she looked toward a distant side of the room and said, "Tell them to fetch me Mary Tilney, and quickly."

Kathryn's father pulled her aside and toward the fireplace, and there, a little apart from the others, and from the lady who had walked away to sit upon a chair a little way off and survey her family with renewed distaste, he whispered, "Mind your manners, Kathryn. Remember to obey God above all else, and the duchess as you would God, and all will be well."

Kathryn felt her hands clench into fists. "But the strawberries—" she said.

"Heh?" her father said.

And at that moment a girl maybe Mary's age came in and curtseyed to the old lady, who told her, "Take my granddaughter Kathryn and show her to the maids' hall and put her in the way of being useful. She may share your bed."

More quickly than Kathryn could think, the girl had her by the hand and was pulling her along.

Kathryn never saw her father again. And she never did get the promised strawberries.

Two

Down the hallway, up a flight of stairs, into a long, spacious hall floored in yellow and black tiles, Mary Tilney turned around, half dancing as she did. "Kathryn!" she said. "Thou joinest us just in time to go to London for your cousin's coronation." She giggled a little as she skipped backward, nimbly. "Is that not grand? What luck. Perhaps, being Queen Anne's cousin thou wilt be able to get nearer the pageant or even—" she looked at Kathryn, a spark of curiosity in her eyes. "Maybe be in the pageant yourself?"

Kathryn had no idea what Mary spoke of. She followed haltingly, frowning. She'd heard there was a new queen—or at least she thought that was what the adult conversation around her tended to. Not that anyone explained too clearly, but everyone spoke of Queen Anne and the old Queen Catherine. Kathryn had always felt a little sad for Queen Catherine, because they shared a name. But everyone around her seemed pleased by Queen Anne's rise, and Kathryn assumed they knew best.

But the truth was that none of this had mattered much to Kathryn. Kings and queens and the court had seemed a very distant thing. More important was moving with Father from lodging to less expensive lodging, until Father had married Dame Margaret and they had moved to her house. Shortly after that—perhaps at the same time—Father had been named comptroller of the king's port of Calais and then Dame Margaret had got them clothes and sent them to see the duchess, and told Kathryn she was to behave and she would have strawberries.

In Kathryn's mind, it all muddled: The new queen and the change in her family circumstances; her father's new job, and this seemingly disastrous being left behind among strangers. Her hands closed on the stuff of her skirt, which felt much too fine and unaccustomed, and made her let go in one startled movement. "My . . . cousin?"

"Lor!" Mary Tilney had turned away, but now turned back laughing, as they climbed stairs and entered yet another corridor, the beams overhead painted in blue and gold. "You mean you don't know!"

"Queen Catherine?" Kathryn asked.

Mary laughed. "Fancy you not knowing." She had a beauty mark on the corner of her mouth that waggled up and down with suppressed laughter, before she covered her mouth with her dainty hand. "Why! Queen Anne, of course! Her mother was a Howard, who married Thomas Boleyn."

This idea so overwhelmed Kathryn that she kept quiet as they ran past open doors showing rooms decorated in a style that Kathryn had never seen, nor even dreamed of. There had been so many different houses in her life, starting with her mother's comfortable but strictly regulated house, with the nursemaids and the servants and every child—Leigh and Howard alike—set in a proper schedule and constrained to do the proper things. Then there had been various houses and rooming houses, after her mother's death, then the house of Dame Dorothy, till she died, then rooming houses again and now, just for a few weeks, there had been the home of her new stepmother, which was opulent but perhaps not as comfortable as Kathryn's mother's.

But this home was as different from that, as . . . as the tavern where they'd stopped for a bite of food on the way was from any home. This home, so far, had more rooms than any other home she'd ever been in, and each lavishly, invitingly furnished with cushions and painted furniture and . . .

Kathryn stopped at the open door to a large room, forgetting to follow Mary. She was conscious, though she did not devote much thought to it, that Mary had gone ahead, her steps retreating—then come back, steps approaching again. "Fie, what holds you?" Mary asked.

Kathryn was looking at a bright room with a broad window in whose embrasure a spacious window seat nestled, covered in many-colored silk cushions. Disposed around the seats were a harpsichord and lutes, polished and shining. In a corner of the room stood a harp, with a carved wood frame. Against the other wall, stood the pianoforte in polished walnut.

"Aye, come, Kathryn, what look you on so lost?"

"Is it . . ." Kathryn asked. "Is this where musicians come to play?" She couldn't imagine where the duchess would sit, much less anyone else. But in Kathryn's short life, one enjoyment stood out—even more than her love of strawberries—and that was her love of music. When she'd been fortunate enough to listen to a good choir at church, she'd felt as if she could stay there forever. One of her maids had told her this was all heaven was—that there was a great choir, singing God's glory forever. It made heaven a very-desired thing.

Mary laughed, amusement and indulgence in her laugh. "Ah, no, Kathryn. Sometimes we have musicians who play for Her Grace, but this is where the musicians come to teach us to play."

"You learn to play?" Kathryn asked with amazement. Her whole life, though her brothers were given masters, there never seemed to be quite enough money to pay for little Kathryn's lessons.

"We all do. And you will, too," Mary said. "We are, after all, young ladies of quality, and playing well is part of the graces that will find us a husband or see us through in court." With a sudden gasp, Mary added, "You'll probably go to court, Kathryn, soon enough, to serve your cousin the queen."

But the court and all its wonders were too distant a thought to Kathryn. Instead, she thought of learning music, and her heart sped in her chest, till it would seem as though it would break through. Her house—even when she lived with her mother—had never contained any of these musical instruments, not even a lute. She didn't remember ever hearing her mother sing, so perhaps Mother didn't like music. Or perhaps there was more to it. Perhaps Mother hadn't been able to afford a master for so many girls.

But Kathryn knew her voice was sweet. When she sang about the house, not even Dame Margaret bid her stop. And the idea of knowing how to accompany herself, how to make sweet sounds upon all those interesting instruments, buoyed her along on light feet, as Mary opened a tall oak door onto a vast room.

The room contained six beds, disposed about its walls, and it had mullioned windows, set with little squares and leaden strips. Through the windows, cold white light poured, lighting a scene of utter confusion.

There were dresses and caps tossed about everywhere, and what seemed like just colorful lengths of fabric thrown over the beds all around. Most of all, there were girls—more than ten of them, though Kathryn stopped counting at ten—all of them much older than Kathryn, talking and laughing and, some of them, sitting upon a bench by the fireplace sewing.

In one corner of the room, a girl stood, and a woman who looked much older than them was engaged in . . . doing something with fabric around her. Kathryn thought that the woman was a seamstress trying a dress on the girl, but only perhaps because she herself had a new dress made for her so recently.

As all the girls turned to look at her and Mary, silence fell in the room. The girl standing with the fabric around her turned also, to a sharp reproof from the older woman, "Now, Mistress Jane!"

This confirmed that the girl was having a dress fitted. Mistress Jane was a thin, pinched-face creature, and the velvet wrapped around her was burgundy and so rich that it made Kathryn stare in admiration. It seemed sad to waste it on Jane, who would more likely look even smaller and sourer within it.

Kathryn was thinking this as Mary giggled and said, "I give you her grace's granddaughter, Mistress Kathryn Howard."

Without thinking, without conscious effort, Kathryn curtseyed.

Like that, the noise resumed, and from the noise, many words emerged. "So little!" "Granddaughter? But I thought Her Grace had only—" "Well, step-granddaughter, then." "To live with us!" "Well, then, be nice to her." "Oh, I will. Cousin to the queen and many favors in her giving."

All of these brought peals of laughter, and the older girls approached, surrounding Kathryn, circling her about, pulling her chin up to look at her face.

Mary stood aside through all of this, looking exactly—Kathryn thought—like a puppeteer, who had once come to their house when her mother was still living. The man had made many dolls dance and fight upon the stage, and, afterward, while the room applauded, he'd stayed aside with a satisfied smile upon his face.

Now there was a like smile on Mary's face. That is, until the older woman came from the corner of the room and stood there, looking at them all with her hands on her hips. "Well," she said, and the way she said it, it was a judgment on all of them and perhaps on Kathryn most of all. "Is she to go to London with us then, on the morrow?"

Mary's smile disappeared. She frowned, the sort of frown people gave when they were thinking deeply. "Well, I vow," she said. "I did not ask, but I don't see how not, for no one of quality is staying here, and surely the duchess wouldn't leave her granddaughter to the cleaning servants and the stable hands."

The seamstress made a sound that signified as clearly as if she'd said the words that the duchess might well do anything and that this one servant had no high opinion of her mistress. She primmed her small lips. "I don't suppose, Mistress Tilney, that Mistress Howard has brought a trousseau with her or that you've been put in charge of her gowns."

"Well, no," Mary said. "I've not—"

"Did you bring gowns, Mistress Howard?" the woman asked.

And because she sounded exactly like Dame Margaret, Kathryn heard a quiver in her voice as she said, "No, an' it please you. This is the only good gown I have, and Dame Margaret had it made, because she said everything else I have is rags and tatters, not fit for a beggar."

"Well, an' it not please me," the seamstress said, setting off a round of giggles amid the girls. "And I warrant Her Grace will never give it a thought, but a Howard and the cousin of the queen cannot go to the festivities in that way. You, Mistress Bulmer, and you, Mistress Tilney, and any other of you who have outgrown gowns recently, bring them to me. I see I shall not sleep tonight."

Before Kathryn quite knew what was forward, she was set in the corner of the room where the light from the windows fell stronger, and the woman was draping her in much too large gowns and marking alterations with chalk and needle and thread. The other girls gathered around and watched and made suggestions, even while the seamstress muttered under her breath about the horrors of such a noble girl being dressed in hand-me-downs and seemed to justify herself to someone invisible by saying that it was impossible for her to do but as she did.

"Oh, don't fuss," one of the girls finally told the seamstress. "No one will know they're hand-me-downs, you do the thing so cleverly." She looked Kathryn over with bright blue eyes that sparkled with amusement. "And she looks so well in your confections. She's a very pretty child."

While Kathryn blushed with pleasure, another girl gave her a sweet. "Here, Kathryn," she said. And stepped back and said, with laughing voice, "You're very beautiful, Mistress Howard. I vow you'll get yourself a great and brilliant match as soon as you're grown, and make us all insane with jealousy."

This caused all the girls to laugh.

Kathryn chewed her sweet in confusion, wondering if they were making fun of her or simply very happy girls. But when Mary Tilney put a hand on Kathryn's shoulder and said, "You'll be fine with us, Kathryn, we'll look after you." She had no reason doubt them.

Three

KATHRYN felt as though she were living in a tale like gypsies sometimes told on the street corner for a coin or two. Or like players enacted in inns or even at church at Christmas, with angels and maidens dressed all in shimmery fabric, all speaking lines very prettily.

Kathryn had been to London before, but it had never been like this or looked like this, and she had to think it must be a dream. This idea seemed all the more likely because of the travel in the carriage from Horsham, with all the girls laughing and singing and eating many good things. The carriage was soft and inside the seats were comfortable, quite a change from traveling to Horsham with her father, on horseback. Not that she'd complained of being held in front of him in the saddle, but this was so much better. She'd slept and wakened and slept again. And then she'd entered a magical land.

First there was Her Grace's palace at Lambeth, across the river from Greenwich Palace. The palace of the king himself.

Her Grace's home at Lambeth made Horsham look pedestrian and tiny. And then there was London itself. Kathryn had seen London before—had been in London before, between cheap house and dilapidated hostelry, but she had never seen London like this. The city, entire, was transformed as though by the hand of a magical power.

That first trip was well before the coronation of her cousin Anne, whom she'd never seen but to whom she'd become very attached all the same. *A queen. My cousin, the queen.*

In her mind, Anne wore gold and jewels, a pretty crown sparkling upon her head, ermine and furs and all the things Kathryn had heard about but had rarely seen and certainly never owned. Kathryn wanted Anne to be everything that Kathryn had ever dreamed a queen might be. By now, she'd heard so much about Anne, whom the king had loved, unavailing, for years on end, that she felt as if she knew her cousin, as if her cousin's coronation was the attainment of Kathryn's own dreams. And the excitement in the city was scarcely less than her own.

Her Grace's Lambeth residence sat across the River Thames from Greenwich Palace. The river itself did not thrill Kathryn, who had seen it before and knew that the water could stink, particularly on a hot summer day, and that the noblemen on barges often held a hollowed-out orange filled with spices and other scents to protect themselves from the ill humors of the river.

But even the river seemed milder now. Every day, from the time Kathryn arrived, new barges appeared on the Thames, all splendidly decorated, all illuminated at night with luminaries. From these barges, as the darkness fell, came the sounds of songs and drinking, though Mary Tilney and her other new friends told Kathryn that wasn't part of the coronation pageant, yet. "Just the common folks, who guard the barges," they said, "amusing themselves. Look, you, if you think this is grand, you shall be all astounded when the pageants start."

They said it and giggled, and their eyes sparkled. The excitement within the house matched the excitement outside. All the girls were deciding which clothes they should wear for the coronation, dreaming of all the esquires, the knights, even the great lords who would be coming to town for the festivities. And now they blushed, and now they sighed, and they paraded about in their clothes and praised each other's looks or suggested perhaps a little change. They braided each other's hair, and tried coifs and bonnets.

Absent from all this was the duchess, which seemed to Kathryn passing strange. "Why come she not?" she asked Mary Tilney while Mary carefully braided Kathryn's hair two days after they arrived to town. "Care she not how I do? If she's my grandmother—"

"Hush, girl," Mary Tilney said. "And do not move, or your hair shall be all askew." She tugged gently on Kathryn's auburn hair, not enough to truly hurt but enough to make her mind. "Her Grace is busy with her own preparations, for you must know that she was called to hold up Queen Anne's train during her coronation. You can see how important that is, and how she must make sure she disgraces neither her name nor her family, neither her dignity nor the queen's."

Kathryn nodded, impressed, and earned another light hair pull for it. "Be still, or I cannot make you look pretty for the coronation. Do you not wish to look pretty for the coronation?"

The girl so very much wished it that she lost herself in a reverie, where it was herself holding the royal train, freighted with jewels and hemmed with ermine. In her little dream everyone, from the highest in the land to the lowest, bowed not just to Queen Anne—a shadowy figure who, in Kathryn's imagination, looked just like a grown-up Kathryn—but to Kathryn herself, the queen's most beloved cousin.

She was awakened from this when one of the girls—a Dorothy Barwick, who was somewhat older than the rest—came running into their chamber, "Why are you here?" she asked, and before either of the girls could answer. "Oh, mind that not. Make haste, make haste, there's the queen's barge coming up the river to the Tower, and what a sight that is to see."

"To the Tower?" Kathryn asked, unable to move, even as Mary Tilney let go of her hair and got up in a rush. Mary, already three steps away, turned, even while Kathryn looked up at her. Kathryn knew she must look pale, for she had felt the blood leave her face, as she stood there, staring. "But—" Even such as she—and she knew she was a provincial with little knowledge of the world—knew that the Tower was where traitors went and people who had conspired against the king's majesty.

She remembered her father and mother talking about someone who had gone to the Tower and then, shortly thereafter, *as was expected*, had been beheaded. She looked at Mary, while the pretty tower of dreams she'd built in her head came tumbling to the ground. "What has the queen done, to go to the Tower? How did she lose the king's love?"

For a moment, Mary stared at Kathryn looking quite blank, and then a grin spread across her oval face. "Oh, Kathryn, you goose. No, it is not that the king no longer loves the queen. On the contrary, it is of his great and reverent love for her that she goes to the Tower. For she must spend the night there, before her own coronation. Why, he's even making sixty knights of the bath, which is only done when a king or queen is crowned."

"Oh," Kathryn said, and her resistance melting, she allowed herself to be pulled out of the door of their sleeping chambers—which were much like the ones at Horsham, only with more gilding on the ceiling and more vibrantly painted walls, and down the hallway, to a room on the opposite side, facing the river.

The mullioned windows had been thrown open, allowing the mild May air to flow in, full of the smells of the city—smoke and animals and people—but also of the scents of wine and roasting meat, of flowers and perfume.

The river on that night was even more of a fairyland than before. Instead of the disordered, merry singing, there was more organized music that sounded much like what Kathryn was used to hearing in church, only perhaps merrier.

She watched, her eyes growing wider, her mind wondering at how many people were down there, so many—and all to honor one woman. Well, truth be told, a queen. But queen or not, surely she was flesh mortal, and one day—however long ago, and Kathryn, who was less than clear on ages, would not dare hazard—she'd been just a girl like Kathryn.

Her mouth falling open, she listened to the praise of the queen sung by many choirs on the river and watched the torches and lanterns reflecting upon the water as though another realm of light were down there. She said, "I did not even know that I was cousin to kings and queens."

This got her an odd look from Mary Tilney who had, unaccountably, got bored with watching the aquatic procession and was fidgeting with the strings of a lute, picked up who knew where—perhaps trying to duplicate one of the tunes being sung down below. "What mean you, Kathryn? Doubt you that you're related to Queen Anne? Her mother was a Howard and so, Mistress Howard, are you!"

"Oh," Kathryn said, feeling as though there were a reproof behind the words. "An' I didn't mean that. I meant Queen Anne's parents. Force, her mother might be a Howard, but her father must have been some great personage, the ruler of some kingdom."

This made Mary titter, and her titter was echoed by one or two of the ladies who stood by. "Hear you that?" Mary Tilney said. "Thomas Boleyn a king . . ."

"King of the merchants of London," another girl said.

"But . . ." Kathryn had never learned much of history—or indeed of anything formal that people might be taught. She was not a slow girl, but she had realized, from living as she did with these other ladies, that other women got an education quite different from hers. Why, even her Leigh sisters had masters hired for them and were sent away, when much younger than Kathryn, to learn deportment and other accomplishments from some great house. But there never had been any money for masters for Kathryn.

She had learned her letters from her mother and was easier reading than writing. Writing and the forming of letters had never been enforced, so she wrote in the sprawling childish hand that she'd first tried upon the paper. And, too, she found when she tried to write, every word deserted her, so that her language came out ill-formed and twisted, more concerned with how she'd form the letters than with what she was trying to say.

As such she had not learned much, but she had read the few books available at her mother's house, and then at her first stepmother's house. Most of them were lists of peerage or else long stories of someone or other who had gone to war.

However, with all that, of one thing Kathryn was sure. Kings married queens, not just anyone that they found wandering about their palace, save only, mayhap—and she was not sure on this but thought it only happened in fantastical stories—as her nurse had told her about a king who had found a naked maiden sitting on a branch in the forest and married her. But this was not in the peerage books, and Kathryn thought it might be a lie. So kings married women who were already princesses, themselves, the daughters of kings. In fact, she remembered when people spoke of Queen Catherine that they said she was the daughter of the Spanish king.

So how was it possible that Queen Anne should be her cousin on her mother's side, and yet her father not a king?

"She was just a maid of honor to the queen," Mary Tilney said. "The daughter of a gentleman, like the rest of us, perhaps lower born than you, Kathryn Howard, for her father does have merchant blood."

"But how did she then become the queen?" Kathryn asked.

"Ah, that, little one, is because she captured the king's mind and heart that nothing would do for him but to marry her. Remember we told you how she caused him to love her and write her poems! Why, he even said that she has a soul worthy of a crown."

One of the girls said something that sounded to Kathryn's ears like "Faith, it's not her soul—" but quieted as Mary rounded on her.

Kathryn didn't mind. She had become used to the sometimes coarse jests of these girls who, like her, had come from their homes to serve the Dowager Duchess of Norfolk in the hopes, if Kathryn well understood, that they would either learn graces, which would enable them to aspire to a higher post, or that they would meet someone who would marry them and . . .

Kathryn's mind stopped on that. Surely they couldn't all become queen. No. Despite the confusion there seemed to be in the land, with the now divorced Queen Catherine and the newly married Queen Anne, and those that said Queen Catherine was not divorced and that Queen Anne was but the king's concubine, yet she knew well enough that only one person could be queen at once.

But that did not mean that all these ladies could not aspire to very grand marriages. Dukes and earls, perhaps. And Kathryn, who was now the cousin of the queen herself, might even aspire to marry some foreign prince.

She stayed up late, watching from the window as the sparkling lights shone and blinked on the river. The others promised her many delights tomorrow.

Unlike the duchess, none of them would get near enough to watch the coronation itself, nor the royal supper or other festivities, but there were better things for them. "Faith," they said. "Wine will flow from fountains, so that it runs down the gutters and every guild in the town will stage a pageant or a tableau for the queen. Ah, such things you'll see!"

And Kathryn, nodding dutifully along with it, fell asleep. She did not remember being taken to her bed or lying down to sleep. But the night long she dreamed—and that she remembered—of pageants and tableaus, of fairies and angels.

And amid all of them there was a grown-up Kathryn—herself, not Queen Anne—who had found a prince who would take her away and make her queen of her own land.

In the dream, Kathryn could not see the boy's face, save for knowing he was tall and fair, with auburn hair running toward red, and that he treated her as though she were the most important thing in all creation.

For a moment she woke up to a great noise, like thunder, and through her sleepiness was conscious of Mary Tilney telling her not to be a goose, "for it is only the thousand guns being fired in salute at the Tower."

Kathryn had fallen again into her dream-prince's arms. As he twirled her in a delightful dance, she could see herself as Queen Kathryn, on a throne, receiving her vassals, and she sighed, impatient at her youth, longing to be grown up. After all, Kathryn had never been the center of anyone's love—not her father's, not her mother's, certainly not either stepmothers'.

How excellent it must be, how wonderful, to be the center of everyone's love and have a whole kingdom worship her beauty and excellence. Faith, she would not even mind if they were foreigners and spoke an odd language.

In her dream, she felt the crown upon her head, and it seemed as though it belonged there by right.

Four

KATHRYN was lost. She thought it was her own fault, but that didn't seem to matter. What mattered was that she was lost, and she must find her way back to the group with the other ladies-in-waiting to the duchess.

They'd been on a barge. She'd been awakened early to be dressed in her best, and to have her hair dressed and adorned all over with flowers. All of which took much too long because the duchess kept calling to her ladies to come bring her now this and now that, and to make sure she had everything ready for her own appearance that night.

By the time—after a late dinner—that they'd set out upon the barge reserved for them, Kathryn was already sleepy. The barge glided smoothly on the Thames, as though the river were a sheet of glass and the barge a toy with its bottom lined with fabric. The air was mild, the river lighted by so many candles as to make the evening look like mid-afternoon. The barge of the attendants of the Dowager Duchess of Norfolk displayed flowers in banks and beds, leaving the young women barely enough space to sit or stand in, amid the fragrant, colorful blooms.

Kathryn sat on a long bench, amid the flowers, leaning right against Mary Tilney's velvety sleeve. She felt a curious mixture of excitement and tiredness that reminded her of when her brother Charles had exchanged the very small ale drunk by the children with a pitcher of father's best ale. She remembered then—as now—her heart had beat very fast, but her mind had been clouded as if already half in a dream.

She remembered only vaguely, as if in a dream, asking Mary, "Where is the queen?"

Mary had shaken her a little, as if to wake her, and said, "The queen is going out on the road, goose." Which confused Kathryn as to why they were in a barge and why so many barges all around were so lavishly decorated, if the queen were not among them and not to see them. But then she half slept, and when she roused again to seeing her surroundings, they were at a dock and gentlemen were surrounding them, helping them out.

Out through a throng of common people—the ladies escorted by gentlemen in the livery of the duchess. Though she'd never seen the gentlemen before, she noticed that they seemed too well behaved to be mere servants—in fact they were the gentlemen equivalent of the ladies among whom Kathryn had been included. They spoke fair, and they treated the women most gently, and it seemed to Kathryn that the ladies did not dislike it, either. In truth, from the smiles on some of their faces, Kathryn judged that they had known the gentlemen all along and were greeting them as old friends.

Her own hand was grasped by a gentleman with a leonine mane of blond hair and bold, smiling green eyes. "Hello, there, milady," he said, with just that little hint of amusement to their voices that quite grown-up gentlemen felt toward girls who weren't quite ladies enough, but thought they hid. "Who might you be?"

Mary Tilney, laughing, leaned forward. "How, now, Manox. Her name is Kathryn Howard. Mistress Kathryn Howard, daughter of Edmund Howard, the hero of Flodden Field, and don't you be getting fancy dreams now, because for sure if you attempted anything, her family would be the end of you."

Kathryn only understood half of that, but she understood the replying smile in Manox's eyes. "Very well, then I shall not attempt to ingratiate myself with the lady, though, faith, the temptation is great."

Everyone around them laughed, and Kathryn frowned, certain she was being laughed at but not quite sure how or why. What she disliked most about her new position was that no one was willing to tell her anything that would make the world around her less bewildering. It was almost as though they liked that she be kept ignorant and the power this gave them over her. She misliked it much and let her little frowning face glare at Manox, even as he bent a melting look on her. "Oh, I've displeased you, Mistress Howard. And when I particularly wished you to love me well, too. I'm such a clumsy brute, then. What am I to do?"

His expression of woebegone confusion was such that Kathryn couldn't help but smile back. "And there you go, Mistress Howard," he said. "Keep that smile on your lips. An' pretty lips they are." He patted her hand, resting wholly in his, which was much larger than hers. "They will be your fortune. And now let us go, for the queen approaches."

Where they went, through the throngs that jostled and pushed at them, was to the side of a road. In the distance, Kathryn could hear music being played and a great voice declaiming something in the tone of a priest making a sermon. And then along the road, slowly, came a cortege which resolved itself. There was Queen

Anne—Manox pointed her out to Kathryn—under a rich canopy of gold cloth, in a robe of purple velvet decorated with ermine over that, and a rich coronet with a cap of pearls and precious stones on her head.

Behind her, the duchess carried her train. The duchess wore a robe of scarlet with a coronet of gold on her cap and looked, oddly, as though she'd wakened and donned her clothes while she was young and had grown old in them without noticing. The coronet of gold on her cap spoke of her high station, and though Kathryn knew it was a great honor to carry the queen's train, she wondered if the duchess could have carried it—as great and heavy with pearls as it was—if there were not a gentleman also supporting it in the middle. She wondered if he was a duke.

As the queen passed, the ladies and gentlemen around Anne sang out "Long Live Queen Anne," but it seemed to Kathryn that around them some of the ruder people had shouted insults and said the queen was a whore, which made no sense at all.

After the queen came ten ladies in robes of scarlet trimmed with ermine and round coronets of gold on their head. Next came the queen's maids in gowns of scarlet edged in fur, too many of them, it seemed, to count.

Kathryn's mouth dropped open as she stared, and she did not know if she'd have been able to imagine such grandeur had she not seen it. She'd just realized the importance of being the cousin of the queen of England—she, little Kathryn Howard, to whom no one had ever paid much attention. Even her dreams of how the queen would look had fallen short. Queen Anne looked just short of the angels in glory. If the queen could command such finery! Well . . . what could she not do for her little cousin?

In Kathryn's mind there was the story from the Bible, in which someone tells the Lord that the slightest word would suffice to heal him. Kathryn felt like that, too. Like a glance from the queen or the slightest notice of Kathryn would make the girl from the most wretched creatures into that great lady of her dreams, the one who had foreign princes at her beck and call.

And just as she thought this, a troop of men coming after the queen started flinging coins about at the crowd, as calls of "Long Live Queen Anne" redoubled and the other calls that said ugly, had-to-be-false things were all but silenced.

Kathryn noticed Manox catching coins in the air and pocketing them, as did the other ladies and gentlemen.

Kathryn was small, even for her age. The coins flew over her head, and she could not reach them. In frustration, she leapt about, trying to pick a glittering coin out of the evening air, but someone taller always got it.

She ran toward the front of the crowd, and ahead, along with the procession, to stay with the throwers of coins, and she leapt, her hand extended.

A gold coin hit her palm, and she closed her fingers about it and turned to show Mary her coin. But there was no Mary nearby, or none of the familiar faces.

A coarse man pushed at Kathryn as he grabbed a coin from next to her face—quite accidentally backhanding her.

Kathryn put her hand to her cheek and fell to sitting on the muddy ground. She cried out but no one came. She was quite lost.

Five

SHE traced her steps back, but could not find the rest of her party. She imagined them concerned, worried about what the duchess would say if they lost Kathryn.

Holding her pretty new skirt up from the muck on the streets, she traced her route all backward but couldn't find the docks where their barge had landed. She couldn't even find the river, though she knew that it could not be that far from the road.

The streets, filled with people who pushed her this way and that, were like a landscape one sees in dreams, which shifts and moves if you try to focus upon it. There was nothing but people everywhere she looked. Some very well dressed, some beggars in rags, all of them intent on going about their own business and paying no attention at all to her—or so it seemed to Kathryn.

None of them was familiar, and to none of them did Kathryn feel she could entrust herself. Her nurse's and her mother's dark muttering about people who did great evil to young girls, or else who held them for ransom, had not made much sense. They still didn't. But the warnings did come back to haunt her mind like remnants of a half-forgotten lore. All the strangers around her seemed menacing and strange.

She walked past a fountain that seemed to be running with red wine and from which many men jostled to fill cups and flagons and jugs, each man carrying at least two vessels, one in each hand, and one man—making his tottering way across the road—seeming to carry three jugs in each hand through some great feat of balance.

Hurrying past the throng around the fountain, she found herself grabbed, her hands held by some very dirty, ragged man, who smiled at her from an almost-toothless face and led her in a mad reel, faster and faster and faster, while someone she could not see played upon a flute.

Faster and faster, till he let go of her, and she went reeling against a wall, which felt greasy against her palms. Someone else tried to grab her, but she shied away and covered her face with her arms and ran headlong down a street.

With her arms wrapped over her head, she could not see which way she was going, and presently, she felt a hand stay her about her middle, and a voice say harshly, "Halt, mistress, else you be trampled."

She looked up just in time to see a horse go by, passing so close that the hand at her middle had to press her hard against the wall.

The hand, she saw, looking down because it was more pleasant than looking up at the steaming body of the animal who'd almost trod her down, was a well-made one, and encased in a suede glove of pearly grey. The hand of a gentleman. The gloves disappeared into a sleeve edged all around with lace. Her gaze continued up to a sleeve of dark burgundy velvet slashed through to display a vivid blue silk, which was attached to a doublet at a broad shoulder, which in turn led to a manly neck, and hence to the face of a young man, just a little older than Kathryn, who might have been the foreign prince of her dreams save that his fair-skinned face split in a smile and the voice that emerged from his lips came in a good English accent. "Faith," he said. "You are but a little girl. What are you doing alone here? Are you lost?"

She wanted to tell him she was lost and also that she must find the duchess's retinue, but the way he said she was but a little girl stung, and instead, she stomped her foot—to little effect for there was only mud underneath—and tilted her face up, her chin sticking out proud and defiant, and said, "I am not but a little girl. I am Mistress Kathryn Howard, the daughter of Edmund the hero of Flodden field."

The merry blue grey eyes looked like they would like to laugh, but something of recognition flitted across the man's gaze. Caught between laughter and something that might very well be admiration, he bowed low, and said, "Well, I beg your pardon, then, *Mistress* Kathryn Howard. All the more so as we are in the way of being cousins on your mother's side. My name is Thomas Culpepper." He frowned a little. "But if you're Edmund's daughter, what are you doing in London? Is he not the comptroller of Calais?"

"Yes, or at least—" Or at least Kathryn had heard of his new post in Calais, though in that as in all else, no one told her exactly what it all meant. "But I'm not living with my father and his wife. I am a maid of honor to the Dowager Duchess of Norfolk."

"Oh," Thomas Culpepper said, and pursed his lips. "And Her Grace being busy today, I suppose her maids . . ." He frowned again. "Well! It is not done and it is not right."

His voice sounded so put out that Kathryn shied away. But he laughed a little. "Oh, fear not, fair Kathryn. You're with me now, and you are safe. We'll find those who should have kept you close."

He took Kathryn's hand in his and led her trippingly through the streets. And Kathryn found all was different. The drunks and revelers who before would skirt too close to her, close enough to scare her, now took one look at Thomas and gave them a wide berth, so that they walked, as it were, in a safe aisle of their own amid the pageantry and revelry of the night.

And the revelry itself, which had seemed such a disorganized dance, now resolved itself into tableaus in honor of the queen—here four nymphs held up tablets praising her and the son she would bear the king; there another tableau compared her to Saint Anne, Mother of the Virgin Mary; still farther ahead, a group of musicians played music in her honor.

Thomas, Kathryn's hand on his arm, explained all this to her, seeming very amused at her naïve curiosity. And then at long last said, "Aye, but the maidens of Norfolk are hard to find, are they not?"

Kathryn nodded, obligingly, but she cared not at all, now, if they ever found them. Or at least, she thought they would have to find them, and sooner rather than later, for Kathryn surely couldn't stay the rest of her life with Thomas Culpepper, no matter how handsome he might be or even that they indeed might be cousins.

Still, she didn't want to find them very quickly. Oh, no. She'd feign stay with Thomas as long as she could.

Ahead there were royal servants dispensing meat and bread, and Thomas procured food for them both, then wine from one of the running fountains, in cups that he procured Kathryn knew not where. He led her to a little space where stairs ran up to the fifth floor of a house, and they sat on the steps side by side eating, while he asked Kathryn where she was staying and where she'd lost her companions.

He listened, also, with just the slightest smile of amusement, to

Kathryn chirruping about her new clothes, the greatness of the palace at Lambeth and even of Horsham, the strictness of Dame Margaret and the great injustice of her never having got strawberries.

Kathryn knew other boys his age. Charles, her brother, must be close to it, if not the same. But Charles and her friends were always impatient of Kathryn. They'd never listened. Thomas Culpepper listened and didn't call her a goose or ask her if her wits had gone wandering or inform her, in a stern voice, that well-brought-up maids did not talk to young men. No, Thomas listened and asked questions, and if his blue grey eyes sparkled with amusement, it was always an amusement mingled with delight, as though he found her amusing beyond all other entertainments.

"And now," he told her, when they finished their meal. "I shall take you back to the palace at Lambeth myself, and deliver you to the duchess's household. If those maids be not at home, they're in amusements no young lady should partake."

He led her, through the streets, but not in any great hurry, showing her many more tableaus on the way and delighting her with explanations, particularly when she presented to him the notion that nymphs or not, ladies should not be dressed only in transparent fabric. "For it just isn't decent."

"Is it not, Fair Kathryn?" Thomas asked.

She shook her head, and he laughed. "But that is what they wore, you know, in antiquity, when they roamed the world."

"What?" she asked. "Like the lady my nurse told me about who went all naked through the forest till a king found her and chose to marry her?"

"Likely," Thomas said, with a whoop of delight, though Kathryn could not think where the delight came from. "Likely she was a nymph."

"Well, if she were so," Kathryn said, thoughtfully. "It was ill done of him to marry her, for she was not used to clothes, and what will people think of a queen going naked about the palace? And you know," she added, "likely they made her uncomfortable, like when people are used to going about barefoot and are forced to wear shoes. They don't like it, and no more would she." She stopped because Thomas had pressed his free hand to his mouth and looked like he was about to burst into loud laughter.

"Likely," he said, from behind his hand. "Likely you are right. The king ought to have remembered that Caesar's wife must be beyond reproach." With this cryptic remark, as though it had helped him control his humor, he uncovered his mouth, and said, "I see you are wise as well as beautiful. I trow, if you're not spoken for when I come of age, I'll speak for you myself. Would you like to marry me when you grow up, Kathryn?"

And Kathryn, who till then had thought that nothing but a prince would do for her, looked up into the impish eyes and smiled. "Likely," she said. "Likely I might."

He laughed loudly and picked her up and carried her the rest of the way, which turned out to be very little, till he delivered her to the palace at Lambeth where one of the housekeepers opened the door and made many exclamations of surprise at seeing Kathryn alone with a gentleman.

Kathryn was so tired by then that she could not follow everything Thomas Culpepper said. But words emerged from his haranguing of the servant. "Too young," he said. "Too fair." And "Too innocent." And then a lot about how someone of her station shouldn't go about unattended.

The housekeeper bobbed so many curtseys she looked like one of those mechanical contrivances that move up and down as a handle turns—or perhaps as though she were trying to learn some difficult dance. "I'm sure, sir," she said, a lot, and twisted the corner of her overdress, as though to punish it for her shortcomings. "I'll tell the young ladies, sir," she said. And "It was very badly done, sir."

None of her words seemed to stop his lecture of her, which took a long time to come to its proper conclusion, which was "She is a Howard, and she should be watched and cared for as such. Remember, woman, that your house has the cousin of the queen herself in its charge. If the king should hear!"

This caused at least three bobbing-up-and-down curtseys, and finally Thomas bent to speak to Kathryn herself. "Thank you for the pleasure of your company, Mistress Kathryn Howard. You have made what would have been a night of revelry something quite other—and I don't think I am displeased." He bowed to her. "When I next see you, I shall bring you strawberries."

Kathryn, led to the maidens' dormitory by the apologizing housekeeper, thought of Thomas Culpepper's tall, straight back disappearing into the London streets and thought that though she was not at all sure what he meant, she was sure of two things: One, that he would indeed one day bring her strawberries. And the other, that she wasn't sure she cared at all, as long as he brought himself.

Opening Rose

Six

"THE queen," the duchess said, and let her hand, and with it the letter she was holding, fall. "Has delivered herself of a princess."

For a moment silence reigned in the room in which all the maids of honor had gathered around Her Grace. Outside the mullioned window of the chamber, the wind blew bitter and harsh, denuding the last leaves from forlorn trees. Drops of rain clung to the windows, diminishing the light received from the slate grey skies above.

The duchess sighed, and as if this were the signal, Mary Tilney piped up. "But, sure . . ." She cleared her throat. "Didn't the astrologers say she was carrying a son?"

Kathryn looked down on the embroidery she was doing—with twisted, uneven stitches. Mary had insisted she must learn this—one of the graces of womanhood—but Kathryn felt about it much the same way she felt about forming letters. It was a skill requiring much application and, at the end of it all, not seeming to produce enough satisfaction. Mary had drawn the figure for Kathryn to embroider, Kathryn's initials in a design of thistles, and said it would make a right handsome cap, but Kathryn looked doubtfully at it. Perhaps it would. When seen from a distance in ill light.

"Don't be a fool, girl," the duchess stormed. "Astrologers are, like all learned men, capable of going wrong. Anne has produced a daughter . . ." She chewed on her lip. "The king will never forgive her for this. She's done no better than the old queen."

"How can the king hold her guilty for it," Kathryn asked, so suddenly that it surprised even herself, and it took her a moment to realize that the words had issued from her own mouth. "How could she control it?"

She got a chilling look from the duchess. "There are things," she said, "that a smart woman can do, thoughts she must think and prayers that would allow her to give her husband a son, if she only took care."

Kathryn looked at the duchess's awful eyes, intent and far to keen and fixed on her, and knew that she was meant to just accept the words as the gospel truth. Or else, she thought, I'm supposed to lose control of my bladder, like my brother. Instead, she smiled back, "But then," she said, "if it were so easy, would it not be something that Queen Catherine, herself, would have done and thereby avoided being set aside?"

The duchess rose. She walked over to Kathryn and stood by her, looking down with that glare. "You have a tongue in your head, girl. And if you want to keep both head and tongue, you'll learn to control it." She looked around the room, with its rich hangings, and the fifteen girls crammed into it. Kathryn and Mary sharing the window seat, others in benches, and a half dozen on the floor, all working some form of sewing, or at least doing so in appearance—in truth they'd been keeping Her Grace amused with gossip about the court and the various rumors crisscrossing London, until the matter of the queen's labor was resolved.

But the duchess who'd been smiling and nodding to their chatter had gone, all at once becoming grim and brooding. The walking stick, which she'd rarely used lately and not used at all during Queen Anne's coronation, was sought for with the questing hand. One of the girls ran out and returned almost immediately carrying it. The duchess took it in her hand and leaned her weight into it. "We are," she said, "going back to Horsham. I have had enough of the court for the nonce."

She left the room, and the frenzy started. Mary jumped up immediately and said, "Come, Kathryn, we have trunks to pack. And to be traveling in this weather, too. How dreary it will be. If only you'd kept your mouth shut!"

"Why should I?" Kathryn asked. "And how could I, when the duchess is saying that the king will now love Queen Anne less for not having given him an heir? Surely . . . I have many siblings, and I have heard talk in the kitchen, too." Various kitchens, including some of the rooming houses where they'd lodged between her father's marriages. She wasn't about to tell Mary that whole story. "And forsooth, if there were, indeed, something a woman could do to determine she has a boy, all women would know it."

Mary sighed. "Perhaps you're right," she said. "And yet you had no business speaking to the duchess on it, for you must know that everyone will blame the queen for not giving the king an heir. It is just the way of the world."

"Well," Kathryn said, as they entered their dormitory and Mary started gathering arms full of dresses that had been scattered all about. "Well, then the world is wrong."

This brought a peal of laughter from Mary, laughter of the kind that Kathryn had often brought to her when she'd first come to live in the duchess's household. The beauty mark on the side of Mary's mouth wiggled up and down. "Indeed, Kathryn. Wouldst though change the world? Most of us," she continued, the mirth subsiding, "would be glad enough to change our station. Particularly now as we must go to Horsham, and Horsham is so deadly dull in winter. There's nothing to do and nothing to see, it's all mud and fields all around, and more . . ." She sighed. "There isn't even a good New Year celebration. I'd hoped we'd stay at court . . ."

"We're not at court," Kathryn said sensibly. "We are only some miles from London proper, close enough, I trow, to visit, but no one has asked us to visit." In fact, since the events of the coronation night, Kathryn had not been out of the house, though Mary Tilney and her sister Katherine, Alice Restwold, and Dorothy Baskerville had often been out together and often spoke to each other when they returned from the city as though they had shared some great secret or some wonder they could not communicate to the rest of the household.

"Do you perhaps leave friends behind?" Kathryn asked, and looking up, was surprised to see that Mary Tilney was blushing dark and looking around, as if to see if anyone was close enough to hear them.

"Have I said ought—?" Kathryn started, but Mary, having asserted there was no one nearby, shook her head, and nearing Kathryn, spoke into her ear in a fierce whisper, "Speak not of friends, Kathryn, for those are such as we are not allowed to have."

"Oh, but . . . are we not friends?" Kathryn asked back curiously.

Mary sighed as though she were speaking with the feebleminded, and shook her head hard, then hissed again, her breath hot against

Kathryn's ear, "Kathryn Howard, no maiden is supposed to be friends with men."

"Men!" Kathryn said, thinking of the night of the coronation and the way the maids of honor of the duchess had met the men at the dock when they came forth to the coronation. She remembered the smiles, the easy looks, and the way she'd been foisted off with Henry Manox, as though all the other ones were spoken for. She felt her own cheeks heat, both at the thought of what might have gone on the rest of the night—while she was wandering lost about London and being squired by Thomas Culpepper. Not that she resented being escorted by Thomas, even if he had not yet visited or brought her the desired strawberries.

However, she thought what her friends had been about had, force, been far more interesting than her own adventures. "Men," she said again lower, and as Mary moved to step away and resume her task, Kathryn reached over and held on to her sleeve, pulling her close. "But Mary," she said, whispering back. "You're the one who told me that the woman is to blame if she displeases her husband and that . . ."

Mary shrugged her shoulders and threw her head back. "Listen to me, Kathryn Howard, for if you're going to get any joy out of life, you must know this. There is but one thing certain—after marriage a woman is her husband's and his every whim is to her like God's upon the Earth. Which is why she must do what she can to have a life and enjoy it before marriage. Understand you this, Kathryn?"

Kathryn nodded but was not sure at all she understood. After all, what life could she have—she who was all but a prisoner of the temperamental duchess's household, taken here and there as suited that noble lady's mood, and never her own woman? How could she have her own life, then? Oh, perhaps Mary and Alice and Catherine had managed it, but faith, they weren't Howards and they weren't the cousin of the queen—whom, though she'd seen her only once, Kathryn inexplicably felt herself linked to.

It was as though a thread united their fortunes, and one must rise and fall as the other did.

Seven

If her fortunes were tied to Queen Anne's, they looked bleak indeed. Oh, no one told Kathryn everything, but even after they retreated to Horsham, where the countryside was a sea of mud, news filtered to them.

There were rumors that all was not well at court. The king avoided the queen. He showed impatience at her. There were rumors about various young ladies who had captured his fickle majesty's interest. There was no more talk among the maids or even among the staff, who were ever more apt to talk of romance and intrigue than the household, of a romance such as would be immortal to history. And no songs filtered down from the court when the rare visitor came—or at least no songs that were said to have been composed by the king for the queen.

Songs became very important to Kathryn that winter. The masters at Horsham were shared by all the ladies, and—she thought—not all that knowledgeable. At least, she had some vague idea her Leigh sisters had Italian masters for the spinet and virginal, for the lute and harpsichord.

Kathryn was one of many under the tutelage of these masters, who seemed to have gotten their learning of music from their church choirs—or else perhaps from itinerant jugglers.

But they did well enough to teach her the basics: how to pluck the lute in a fashion pleasing enough to accompany her still-piping little girl's voice to the tune of the current songs from court. And while she sometimes noticed that Alice or Mary spent a goodly amount of time waiting for a particular rider from the court or another, she herself cared only to know what songs were sung at court now.

It was her amusement, picking up a lute from the practice room and finding a solitary place in which to sing all her newly learned songs, while accompanying herself with the lute.

And when spring took too long to turn warm much less acknowledge the nearness of summer, on a dank, dark day when the rain wept against the mullioned windows and all outside was an indifferent sodden mingle of grey sky, brown mud, and trees caught halfway between the two, with their branches raised up to the sky like penitents imploring in vain for mercy, Kathryn had taken the lute and walked to the corner of a far-off hallway.

Gone were all her dreams of ever marrying a prince. It would be lucky enough, she thought, if Queen Anne didn't get divorced and end up put away in some forgotten castle, as old Queen Katherine had. Kathryn had heard in one of the recent bits of gossip from court that one of the foreign ambassadors had called the queen "that old, thin woman."

Kathryn recalled the radiant face surrounded by rich fabrics on that coronation procession and could not reconcile it to such a description, but perhaps that was how things worked, and everyone now would say bad things about Queen Anne who had once praised her. If that were true and the queen were to be divorced, then what would become of her young and penniless cousin?

Alice, who now shared Kathryn's bed, had teased her by saying that if all else failed, the Howards would at least arrange Kathryn's marriage to some wealthy country squire. Kathryn wished she could be sure of this. Her childhood, now that she knew a little more of the world, had come as though into sharp relief. She could see in her mind's eye how abandoned by the whole family—how forsaken—her father had been.

She knew, had heard often enough, that when he was young, he had been heroic enough at Flodden Field to have a poem written about him and to still be talked about in admiring fashion. But much good that had done him. He had married none but widows, and though they be wealthy widows, none had been wealthy enough to support him in the lifestyle other Howards took for granted. Even when royal favor had descended upon the family, nothing had happened to make Edmund Howard's life better but the post of comptroller at Calais, which had by itself been unable to provide for his numerous family, so that he'd had to ask the duchess to take one of his many superfluous children.

For that matter, it was quite possible he had managed to dispose of most of his other children to other relatives. Kathryn did not know. None in the family were inclined to write, and none saw it fit to send her letters. She might as well be forgotten as living with the duchess.

When it came to a marriage for her, who would make it? The duchess? This was most unlikely, as her main preoccupation seemed to be the running of her vast estate. Tenants and lands and various responsibilities consumed her wholly when she was not taken up with the affairs of her step-granddaughter the queen or with her own advancement in courtly favor. Those of her maids who married did so through the arrangements of their family. And Kathryn, when it came to arrangements, had no family. If her father or brothers were still living—and as much as she'd heard of them, they might be dead—they had forgotten her. She was probably thirteen. Her confusion came from being none too sure, because her father hadn't been sure. Her mother had been sure, but her mother had died before Kathryn had a good idea how old she was. She'd grown up hearing her father give her age as "Six, perhaps seven, or yet she might be eight." And on through the years. She was now thirteen by the highest of those estimations, which was how old she felt when comparing herself to the other girls about her. Alice would be the same age or a little bit more. It wasn't Kathryn's fault that she was by nature small and of little stature so that she would, perforce, seem younger than her mates.

If she were thirteen . . . Well, then she was more than a year older than her mother had been when she'd married her first husband. And she would be one year short of what was called "the full fire of fourteen," a woman's most desirable age.

And she was—she paused by a window and tapped the glass pane with her cold finger tips—immured here, in a house in the middle of nowhere, trapped in the heart of a winter that refused to depart, though it already be late May.

In this mood, forlorn, feeling like the last person in the whole world and all but forgotten by man and fate, too, she walked a long time, taking random turns into little used parts of the house, along the yellow-mosaic floors of the hallway.

She came, quite without knowing how, to a place where the hallway ended in a sort of rounded alcove where a window seat stood by a large mullioned window. It was a handsome window seat, carved in oak, and a handsome window through which a lot of light came, despite the driving wind that was tapping upon the window like a living thing. Like the fingers, Kathryn thought, of all those who had died out in a storm and had come back seeking the warmth of humanity.

There was a layer of dust on the seat and it was quite devoid of coverings, so Kathryn thought it hadn't been used in very long. Gingerly, she brushed the dust off with her hand, then sat with one of her legs bent and folded under her body, and her skirts disposed in a wide fan about her. Thus disposed, she turned her attention to the lute.

She started with the ballad of the king who had found the naked nymph—Melusine—in the forest and had taken her home to be his own. From Margaret Bennet she'd heard the rest of that story, which, as she had predicted, did not end well. The lady, like many of a supernatural nature, seemed to partake in demon kind and, upon being discovered in her bath—though Kathryn never understood what was shocking about that—had taken her two younger children and flown out a castle window, leaving behind the fiery marks of her feet upon the stone.

Of this the ballad spoke, and this Kathryn sang with all her heart, even though she tried not to think about what Catherine Tilney said, that the child that Melusine had left behind was an ancestor of the kings of England. It seemed very unlikely, for the king didn't seem at all to be in the nature of a nymph. What would half-demon kind have to do in the world, much less on the throne.

She played, satisfying herself with the chilly notes of the ballad and its chillier conclusion. And then she wound into the next one, almost without thinking—a ballad the king had written for Queen Anne when he was still courting her, called "Greensleeves."

Though it was a courting song and it could be merry, there was something about it that spoke of haunting sadness, of unattainable dreams—like Kathryn's erstwhile fancy of marrying a prince and being loved by all.

She was closing on that song, doubtfully, with much hesitation, when she heard a tap upon the floor. The tap was almost imperceptible, just a touch of a walking stick, but it was recognizable enough that Kathryn jumped up and was making a curtsey before she was fully aware what she was about. "Your Grace," she said. "I'm sorry. I didn't mean—" She stopped because she wasn't fully aware what she might be apologizing for.

While the maids of honor had assigned duties and things they must do—at least in theory—they were light enough that the young ladies often had much time on their hands. And though the duchess's decree was that when they found themselves with time on their hands, the girls were to improve either their skills or their souls, by sewing or praying or learning some other art that would be useful to them as married matrons, she never checked to make sure they were thus occupied. Of course, it was the policy of the maidens to stay away from Her Grace if not required to be near and to never give her a chance to wonder what they were about.

In Kathryn's mind was some vague notion that she shouldn't be here, she shouldn't be doing this. But, to her surprise, the duchess's hand came down quite softly upon her inclined head, and she said, yet more softly, "Stand up, girl, I want to look at you."

Kathryn rose and stood, uncomfortably, while the duchess's sharp eyes looked her up and down, then concentrated on her face for what seemed like an eternity. "There's something in you," she said at last. "Of your cousin Anne. Though I'll be cursed if I can say what. Your hair is auburn while her black hair is her greatest glory. And your eyes are not quite the same shape. You have the Howard nose, straight and fine, as does she, but your mouth and chin and the whole of it are quite different, and yet, when I saw you sitting there, playing, I vow for a moment I thought it was Anne herself when she was young . . ." She sat down beside Kathryn and rested her hands on her walking stick and her chin on her juxtaposed hands. "For a moment, I thought it was her—her soul . . . her spirit."

The duchess's words were so chilly, so distant, that Kathryn crossed herself hastily. "Your Grace!" she said. "The queen has not died."

The duchess lifted her head enough to shake it. "Not that I know, no. Though word is that she's with child once more, and you know . . . It is the destiny of women to suffer the danger of the childbed. I only had one son, and that easy, but . . ." She rested her chin again and said, "How old are you, Kathryn?"

"An' it please your Grace, I think I am thirteen."

"Ah, yes . . ." the duchess said. "Your father seemed none too sure of the ages of his children or even which children were his. He was odd that way. Between that and the gaming tables . . . No wonder he could never capture royal favor. Do you game, Kathryn?"

"I never have," Kathryn said, wondering at the odd conversation and considering in her mind whether the duchess's wits had gone wondering. For how could Kathryn gamble when she'd never had any money or anything worth gambling? Even her clothes were hand-me-downs, now supplemented at the hem with yet another panel of fabric, since she was growing once more.

"Good. Don't you. It consumes the soul." A silence fell and for just a moment Kathryn wondered if the duchess had fallen asleep till the words came, "Only there's perhaps another kind of gambling. Stand again, girl."

Kathryn stood.

"Turn around," the duchess said, and Kathryn obeyed, and obeyed once more when the duchess said, "Again."

The duchess sighed. "Of course, Thomas Boleyn made sure his daughter had teaching and preparation, which you came to me without, and you must have got very little since you came to me as well . . ." She sighed. "I confess that I took you only because Edmund would have me take one of his brats, and I had no high hopes of you. Why should I? None of your sisters . . . Not even your Leigh sisters, displays any promise. Your mother was a worthy woman, but . . . not what anyone would call a beauty and certainly not one to shine by her looks or demeanor." She tapped her walking stick slowly, and Kathryn, looking at the floor, didn't dare look up to see what was in duchess's face. "Do you speak French, Kathryn?"

"No, Your Grace."

"German?"

"No, Your Grace."

"Um . . ." *Tap-tap-tap.* "But you play. What instruments do you play?"

"The lute, only, your Grace."

"Um . . ."

"And only because you've been so generous as to provide me with masters that—"

"Don't be foolish, I provide all of my maids of honor with masters. Not very good ones, but in most cases suiting the interests and inclinations of the young wretches. But you have something special in the way of voice, and your handling of the lute quite reminds me of Anne." She was silent a moment, then said, "Do you ride?"

"I beg your pardon?"

"Do you ride horses, hunt . . . those pursuits."

"I had a horse when my mother was alive," Kathryn said. "It wasn't . . . It was old and very gentle, but I quite enjoyed riding. I've never hunted."

"No. Well, the fashion of the court is for women who can do both, so we shall have a riding teacher for you and as for hunting . . . we'll see what offers when there's a chance. Do you dance?"

"A . . . a very little. My sisters used to teach me, you know, and my brothers." She felt animation come into her voice. She had not realized how happy she'd been in those dance sessions with her family or how much she missed them. "Just a little dance, you know, in the family."

"Of course. So. We shall get you dance masters, too. You have a good lithe body, and should your cousin . . . That is, after the queen delivers herself of a prince, and when you're a little older and more knowledgeable of the ways of the world and the ways of the court, we'll get your cousin to find you a place among her ladies. With your figure and your manner and that voice of yours, I vow you'll marry very creditably."

"But I speak no French," Kathryn protested, remembering how the conversation had started. "And no German. And I don't much like writing."

The duchess smiled. "Ah! All those . . . are vanities of the present age. Women who speak Latin and Greek, who can speak foreign tongues and who are versed in the way of male minds. All foolishness I vow, and that's why they have such addled wombs that can't bring forth proper issue. We'll have none of that with you, Kathryn. If you need to write, I'll find you a secretary among my other maids. I trow, as you are, you already know more than most maids at court when it comes to the arts of the pen. Leave well alone. Anne, with her poems . . ." She sighed. "Well, it might all turn well, yet, if she brings this one to term, and if it is a boy, and why should she not. Princess Elizabeth is a lusty wench, and there's no reason at all that her brothers should not be the same and numerous, too."

The duchess sat awhile in silence, as though seeing something in her mind that Kathryn was not privy to, but when she spoke, it was as though she'd been talking to Kathryn all along. "Yes, it will do very well. We'll do that then," she said. "And you'll make a marriage that will quite outshine all the other girls. Howard girls always do. They have a fire in them that is hard for any other family to imitate. You'll do very well. Now sit, girl. And play me something merry," she cast a glance out of the window. "The wind and the rain and the chill are playing havoc with my old body, and I'd fain remember what it was to be young."

Eight

"It is a Henry, Kathryn, and bless my soul," Alice said, as she peered at the bit of red lace upon the dusty oak floor. "It is a Henry our Kathryn will marry."

It was July, and the heat, long delayed, had arrived with unusual force. The open windows allowed in no more breeze than an oven, and like the exhalation from an oven, the little current of air was tinged with even more warmth than in the penned up dormitory.

Unable to sleep or even to think of sleeping—at any rate it was just after supper and too early to sleep—the girls had gathered in the center of the room, with two candles purloined from the kitchen. Catherine's friend—who was understood to be male, though his identity was never revealed—had given her a parcel of sweetmeats, which she generously shared with her fellows.

Kathryn would never remember how it started, but the idea had come that they could throw remnants of lace upon the floor and that when the strips fell, they would form letters that would show whom each of them would marry. It was a harmless enough game and had been going on for a while.

Alice had claimed the ability to read the confused twines of lace as being words, and a ritual had developed. The maiden for whom the divination was being done kissed the bit of lace and then the scrap was thrown in a spot of the floor that had been cleared of the customary rushes. Alice squatted next to it, with her candle, peering at the turns and whorls as though she were privy to ancient secrets that could tell her meanings others could not perceive. She'd announced names for each of them. Edward for Catherine, who had blushed prettily; Charles for Mary who had said she would rather die, bringing peals of laughter from all the other girls who clearly had a particular Charles in mind; and other names that Kathryn didn't remember.

Then it had been Kathryn's turn, and she'd kissed the lace, somewhat hesitantly because it was by then quite dusty from its use. Alice had flung it, and Alice was squatting next to it, peering. "It is a Henry, Kathryn! You shall marry a Henry!"

Kathryn tried to remember any Henry that she would be in the least interested in marrying, and said, in a voice that came out more sour than she'd meant it to. "The only Henry I know is my brother, if he still lives. The duchess said he was too fat and ruddy to live."

The girls laughed at this, and Joan said, "There are many Henrys, Kathryn, and perhaps you haven't met the right one, yet. Now you'll be on the alert for one, and know just how to bring him about by your arts and allurements." She gave a little flick of the hip as she spoke, and the other girls laughed.

"No, I vow," Dorothy said. "It is no one important, but only the scullery boy, for only yesterday I heard him called Harry. It is fair Harry who will sweep our Kathryn off her feet."

"I vow he does enough sweeping," Kathryn said. When she had first come to the duchess's household, this sort of teasing would have reduced her to tears, and she still was not very good at doing it to others, but she knew how to take it when aimed at her.

"Oh, yes, and they'll run away with his broom and—" Joan said.

"Sweep our way to the coasts of Ireland, where we shall become pirates," Kathryn said.

"Just so!" Dorothy said, and all the girls broke into peals of laughter.

Their laughter was interrupted by a throat clearing, by the door. "Her Grace," the old retainer said. "Has asked Mistress Kathryn Howard to come to her."

"Kathryn?" Mary asked, at the same time Kathryn said, "Myself?"

"Just so," the servant said.

"Aye, perhaps she's had a marriage application from a Henry and wants to tell Kathryn about it," Joan said. It brought no laughter, all of them being too curious to laugh now. It was too early to help the duchess get ready for bed, and at any rate, the people who normally helped the duchess into bed were her undressers, not her maids of honor. When she called one of them, it was usually to read or write something or else to play to her after she'd gone to bed. She'd never called Kathryn, who at any rate could neither write nor read very well. So it must be for some other purpose she was summoned, and that purpose was usually bad news.

Or at least, Kathryn thought it must be bad news as she walked behind the servant's upright back and grizzled head down the corridors to the duchess's sitting room. That it was to this particular room she'd been summoned worried her yet more, because this was the place where the duchess transacted household business and other official matters relating to her estates and her retainers. When a maid was summoned to it, it was usually to let her know that someone had—indeed—put in an application for her hand;

that the family had summoned the maid back for some purpose, usually marriage; or that someone in the maid's family had died.

As she passed through the door the servant held open and curtseyed low in the direction of the duchess's chair, Kathryn wasn't sure which of these would be worst. "You summoned me, Your Grace?" she asked.

"Indeed, Kathryn. This is Henry Manox, the son of my neighbor, George Manox, and cousin to my attending gentleman, Edward Waldgrave."

Kathryn, confused by the introduction and the name Henry, raised her head to see the same leonine head devilish green eyes she had seen on coronation night, just before the gentleman in question bent in a low bow and extended his hand, clearly waiting for her to give him her hand to kiss.

But Kathryn, shocked, after the events in the dormitory, could only think that George Manox was not titled and surely her stepgrandmother wouldn't do this to her, throwing her away on one such as him.

Not that she had anything against Manox. He was still—as he had been more than a year ago—slim and shapely, with broad shoulders and a small waist delineated by his well-cut doublet. The hose-clad legs beneath that were shapely enough and muscular, and the face, of course, with its shock of fair hair and impish expression could not fail to please. But, by the mass, if Kathryn was going to be bound to a man for life and have to serve him and obey him her lifelong, she hoped he would be more than the son of a country esquire. And probably not, she thought, the firstborn, or the duchess would have mentioned that he was the heir to George Manox.

She looked from the smiling young man to the duchess who was looking very contented and satisfied and rather like a dog that has just performed a very clever trick. She looked back at Kathryn and smiled. "Well, girl, what say you?"

Kathryn had no idea at all how one replied to an unwanted marriage. She'd heard stories—which girl of her generation hadn't?—of girls wholly cut off by their families, or else turned out onto the street because they refused to marry someone. But it couldn't be possible that they were marrying her off like this, without even asking her opinion—even if they despised it. And the duchess had asked what she said.

She licked her lips and cleared her throat. "Well, Your Grace, that is . . ." She looked at the gentleman out of the corner of her eye and remembered his quite forgetting he was chaperoning her as he ran about catching coins at the coronation. "Well . . . Master Manox seems well appointed enough, and he is, of course, of respectable parentage."

The duchess made a sound at the back of her throat that sounded as if she were getting ready to spit. "Responsible parentage, girl? What nonsense is this? What does his parentage have to say in the matter."

Kathryn was so surprised, she was momentarily speechless, but she managed to shut her mouth with an audible snap, then open it again, to say in a voice that sounded thin and squeaky. "Why, why . . . parentage is everything in a marriage, is it not?"

"What?" the duchess asked, sounding shocked. Had the old lady gone mad? For certain many of the older people liked to complain in a forlorn manner about how all marriages nowadays were about a union of lands or of families, but they were the first to plan them, and Kathryn had never heard anyone claim that family or parentage didn't matter.

"I'm not saying that Master George Manox isn't all that is honorable and . . . and good . . . but I vow, Your Grace, you said I am after all a Howard girl and that my name alone, even if I have scant accomplishments, would be worth more as a wife than . . . than Master Manox, begging no offense." She felt her cheeks flame as she came to an end, and it wasn't at all improved by the old lady's staring at her, with eyes and mouth wide open.

The duchess looked like nothing so much as a landed fish, her mouth moving soundlessly, open and closed and then open again, as if she'd quite lost the power of speech. Kathryn imagined herself about to be turned away from the house in disgrace, and where would she go? She didn't imagine her stepmother would love her any better now than she did when Kathryn was younger. She expected the duchess's stick to hit the floor at any time, while she rose and pronounced a devastating judgment on Kathryn.

Instead, the duchess's thin, reedy laughter started first, and then her stick punctuated it, hitting the floor in rhythm with her cackling. "Well," the duchess said, as she paused to draw breath and then resumed laughing again.

She ran out of air from laughing and wiped tears with the sleeves of her gown. Through all this, Manox retained the same blush that had climbed to his cheeks during Kathryn's speech. He looked slightly offended, Kathryn thought, and she didn't look his way again.

"Bless my soul," the duchess said, at long last, and coughed, to clear her voice from the last hoarseness from so much laughing. "I forgot how dizzy wenches are. It is all marriage with you, is it not? What gave you the idea I'd got you a groom?" she asked.

Kathryn, confused, thought maybe there was a chance that's not what the duchess meant to do by introducing her to Manox, but all the same she grabbed a bit of her skirt and twisted, wondering if what they'd done in the dormitory would be counted impious and earn them all a thrashing. "You see," she said. "You see, Your Grace . . . we were playing in the dormitory. Yes, playing and . . . and . . . throwing lace and reading the name it formed."

"Ah, that game," the duchess said. "The name it forms, most times is Llllll, but silly maids read all sorts of things in it. And your bit of ribbon was read as Manox?" she sounded quite disbelieving.

"No, milady. Henry."

"Ah, Henry. Well, a good enough name, though the game be silly. I remember when I was your age I got three names in the same summer . . ." Her grin became something reminiscent, and her eyes misted again but not with laughter. "Well, Kathryn, we can say that Henry is not this Henry. This Henry was summoned here for the purpose of teaching you the more advanced playing of the lute as well as to teach you the virginal."

Henry Manox bowed again and, this time, Kathryn curtseyed. "Begging your pardon, Master Manox. Only I thought . . ."

"There is nothing to beg my pardon for. It is quite understandable," he sounded only slightly amused. "I believe we've met before, the night of Queen Anne's coronation, though you've grown quite a lot since and become such a beautiful young lady."

Unsure what to say, Kathryn bowed again, and the duchess's stick tapped the floor impatiently. "You're not here to make love to my granddaughter, Manox. As she herself said, the name Howard can hope to catch better fish. Bring forth the lute, then, and let the girl show you what she can do."

Manox got a lute from a shadowy corner of the room and handed it to Kathryn, and Kathryn, sitting down upon a chair, plucked the sleeves experimentally.

"'Greensleeves,' girl," the old lady said, and Kathryn obediently struck up the well-known melody and let her voice rise to accompany the music.

When she was done, the duchess called out, "Now play 'Alone, Alone, Alone,'" the duchess said.

Kathryn launched carefully into the more difficult traditional ballad. She wasn't certain of her fingering in certain parts, though she did her best to fudge through them and to cover her errors with her pure, high voice.

When she was done, there was silence. At long last, the duchess tapped her stick once. "Well?" she asked.

"I am glad Your Grace called me and thought of me for this employment," Manox said.

"But?" the duchess said. "You don't find her well enough?"

"Oh, she is well enough. Indeed, I thought me that an angel from heaven had flown down and landed in the room to grace us with melodies so sweet that even the Almighty in his throne would be jealous of our enjoyment. I am honored and hope only that my poor teaching skills can do justice to such an exceptional pupil."

"I said," the old lady's voice rose, acerbic, "that you were not called here to make love to my granddaughter. Lessons will start tomorrow after dinner. You may use my small study and my virginal." But she sounded pleased, Kathryn thought.

And when she looked at Manox, she was surprised to find that his gaze on her had changed. He was no longer smug and vaguely amused, but there was real admiration in his green eyes.

She went to bed with a smile upon her lips, dreaming of the lesson on the morrow.

Nine

"REPEAT that last line, Mistress Howard, please," Manox said. He sat next to her in the small study. They'd been working upon the virginal for more than a year now, and Kathryn felt herself quite confident upon the instrument.

She'd stopped marveling at the instrument itself, a beautiful creation of many-colored woods inlaid with mother-of-pearl, the whole forming a landscape of woods and lakes upon which stags and does disported in an eternal spring. That it was a great honor for the duchess to allow her to play upon it, she understood, and also, she'd come to know that all the other girls were jealous of her private music lessons upon such a good instrument.

Kathryn enjoyed knowing that the duchess thought well enough of her to let her use this instrument. And she enjoyed, even, the envy of her fellow maids of honor. For it was a thing she'd never had: the chance to be envied for something she got to see or do that was not quite what the rest of her fellows could see or do. This was something different, something important, something that set Kathryn apart.

She might be the youngest of the maids, and she might be silly at times. She might not have heard as much of court life as some of the other girls, and she might know nothing of what went on between men and women. But this she knew: her voice could rise upon a pure note and fill the room and all the listeners with wonder; her fingers were nimble on the lute; and she was fast becoming a very good virginal player. If the others wanted to envy her for that and the notice it brought her, they might as well do it, and she would warm her soul upon their envy as one warming one's hands before a fire on a cold day.

She repeated the phrasing that Manox had asked her to do and then waited while he corrected some of her mistakes in positioning. This required him to embrace her from behind and place his hands upon her hands.

There was nothing exceptionable about this. The door to the small sitting room stood wide open. Kathryn didn't think that Manox was about to try to violate her right here, and he was only doing what he had done many times before.

Why then, did her heart start beating such a frantic cavalcade, and why did her blood seem to rush past her ears with a whistling sound? Manox smelled good—of some strong perfume like pine or camphor, but more pleasant—and his blond mane tickled the edge of her face as he leaned forward next to her. "Now, put your hand thus, Mistress Howard. You see how much easier this makes it to perform the transition to the next movement? Like this. Turn and turn, and your small finger does this . . ."

She repeated the movements, with his hands still resting atop of hers, his face pressed next to hers. She could smell him, and feel his warmth and the hardness of his muscular chest behind her. He'd never seemed like such a big man when he stood next to her or in front of her, but when he embraced her like this, she was conscious of how small she was and how much bigger he was, how easy it would be for him to overpower her—to take her wholly in his arms and capture her and have her at his mercy.

For some reason, this feeling small and helpless made her pulse quicken and created a warmth within her that she was quite at a loss to explain. Overcome by it, she rushed through the movement and got it wrong.

"No, this way," he said, correcting her.

She attempted it again, this time managing it successfully, the notes rising, then turning for a smooth descent. Relieved and pleased, she leaned back into him.

He exhaled then drew a deep, deep breath, like someone who is wounded or who thinks he might drown and draws breath in big gulps, as though it might be his last chance at life. And then his lips touched her neck, right behind her ear.

She couldn't move. She was shocked by the sensation, by the sudden daring, by his warm lips tracing the soft, sensitive space behind her ear to her neck, and all the way down her neck to her neckline. "Kathryn," he said, more exhaling than speaking. "Kathryn. How I long . . . ?" He kissed along her neckline. Seizing hold of her with his strong arms, he turned her around and kissed her hard, once, upon her lips, mashing their lips together as though he wished to hurt her.

Kathryn felt quite bewildered, both by his violence and by what he was doing. She was not so naïve about the doings between men and women that she did not know that men and women kissed. She had been in the kitchen and seen the servants do it. And she'd lived at enough cheap rooming houses to have seen people kiss. It was that he was kissing her, and like this, too, as though something hurt him and he wished he could hurt her in return.

He kissed her again, this time more softly, his tongue pushing between her lips. She pulled back. "Master Manox," she said. "The door is open."

Like that he straightened himself up and away from her. He took a step toward the window, his hands flying up to his head and clasping it on both sides, as though he were horrified, and then falling again. He stared out the window. He turned toward her, his arms now limp by his side. "Master Manox, Master Manox," he said, mimicking her tones. "Is that all you can say?"

"What else do you wish me to say?" she asked, confused.

Like that he flung himself on the ground at her feet, landing on his knees with an audible crack against the floor. He didn't even wince, but his hands sought for hers, grabbed them in his. His hands felt hot, as if he were feverish, and Kathryn recoiled a little, wondering if perhaps he had contracted some terrible sweating sickness that he would give her, and then they would both die of it.

But she couldn't pull her hands away, because he only grabbed them more firmly and bent his head over them and kissed the back of her hands madly, first one, then the other, and then turned them over and kissed the palms, as though he wished he could devour her.

She felt as if he were hungry and she were his meat, and she couldn't quite understand how he could be so desperate, save that she was sure he was not pretending nor playacting, but truly, maddeningly desperate for her touch, her taste, for everything that came from her.

"The door is—"

"Aye," he said, rising from his knees. "And well I know, the door is open. Cursed be the door. Cursed be all the doors in the world, Kathryn Howard. For a year now, I've sat here with you and I've taught you, the best I know, how to play the virginals and watched your hands caress that keyboard and listened to your heavenly voice and longed, longed for something . . . some token, some show of your affection."

"What token can I give you?" she asked, feeling chilled and small.

Kathryn did not like to see anyone or anything suffer. Once, when they were in London, Alice and Mary had convinced her to go with them to see the whipping of the blind bear. They were not, of course, coarse or abandoned and therefore couldn't go to watch bearbaiting or other blood sports. But the whipping of the blind bear was only a flogging given to a bear so old that he fought it not, even as the blood ran down his hoary sides. It was accounted suitable entertainment for delicate young ladies and children, and indeed, everyone around Kathryn seemed to enjoy it marvelous much, but she had found herself thinking of how the poor animal must feel, being whipped without having done anything to deserve it, except being a bear and old and blind.

For days afterward, she had prayed that she would come by some money so she could pay the men who whipped the bear and they'd stop doing it. Her horror at the show had struck Alice and Mary as quite funny for after all, the show amused even very young boys. But Kathryn didn't like to see anything suffer.

And so, she now watched Manox suffer and didn't know how to stop it, and her voice came out small and afflicted. "I don't understand," she said. "I don't know what you want or what ails you."

"What ails me!" He gave a small cackle of laughter. "What ails me, Mistress Howard, is that I am quite immoderately in love with you."

"I've done nothing to bring this about," she said, clasping her hands together, to avoid his seizing hold of them again.

"I did not say you did," he said. "Save existing and having a face and a smile and a voice that the angels themselves would envy." He fell to his knees again, next to her, and she clasped her hands together tight, but that didn't prevent him from clasping his hands, in turn, on top of hers and holding them there very tight. "But you see how I suffer, and you're too kind, too just, not to wish to alleviate my suffering."

"How . . . how can I?"

"Only give me some token of your love for me."

"But I love you not," she pointed out, reasonably. It sounded cold said like that so she tried to explain, "I like you, of course, and you have taught me so much about the virginal, and I'm ever so thankful."

"Oh, thankful be damned," he said. "Only let me hold you against me, let me feel your body against mine, let me kiss your lips, for otherwise I shall perish, like a man in the desert, denied the water of life."

She looked back at him, worried, hoping he was lying or perhaps having her own—but she could not see any signs that he was pretending what he didn't feel in order to get her to do what he wished, and he did indeed seem to be in great distress. "I would . . ." she said, "relieve your distress if I knew how . . ."

"Just kiss me. Hold me," he said.

"Not here!" she said, in a hurry, looking toward the door, afraid one of her fellow maids or the duchess herself would come by.

He prized her hands apart from each other and held them in his, looking into her eyes, "But you will do this for me," he said. "You'll let me hold you."

She inclined her head. "If there was a way."

"There is always a way," he said. "If you . . . if you'd be so kind as to come . . . to meet me . . ."

"To meet you where?" she asked.

It seemed to her he thought but for a minute, and then he rose, swift, in one motion. "Put your hands back on the keyboard," he said, and as she obeyed, he came up behind her, and held her, his hands over hers, as though he were correcting her position. "Go you to church," he said, "after our lesson."

"To church!" she said, shocked. The church on the duchess's estate was a small chapel where mass was said each morning and evening. But it was still a consecrated place.

"In the middle of the afternoon," he said. "There shall be no one there. There is no chance of anyone interrupting us."

Kathryn squirmed uncomfortably, aware that her every movement brought her in closer contact with him. "But . . . It is the chapel. It is consecrated, and there is the sacrament there. No, I couldn't."

"What a goose you are," he said lightly, and kissed just the edge of her ear. She could see that she would have to go with him, indeed, to a private place, else he would be doing this all through the lessons, and it was only a matter of time till they were caught. "Do you think the sacrament can see us, then?"

"Yes."

He sighed. "Very well, then, at the entrance to the chapel, there are the stairs that lead to the upper level, where the vestments are kept. Between the chapel and the stairs, there is a dark space. If we step in there, faith, no one can see us—as dark as it is."

Kathryn thought of it and nodded. "Very well."

"You will meet me, then? Oh, angel." He pressed closer against her from behind, his body warm and strong and seemingly capable of overpowering her.

"Not here," she said urgently.

"No," he said, and stepped back enough that though he still leaned over her, holding her hands in his, she could no longer feel his body pressing up against her. "After our lesson," he whispered. "Meet me there."

She nodded once, as steps approached from the hallway toward the door.

"This is how you move your fingers, then," Manox said. "Now, let's try the last movement through again."

Katherine did, her hands trembling, feeling Manox's hot hands upon hers. Despite her tremors, it was perfect.

Manox removed his hands from atop hers as the movement concluded, and she could feel him stepping back and straightening up, and she let her body go limp, allowing the tension to leave her.

From behind came the tap of a walking stick and then the duchess's voice, "Very well done, Kathryn. You are to be congratulated, Manox!"

Ten

SHE did not dare avoid the rendezvous. Oh, the temptation was there, as Manox, having bowed to the duchess and thanked her for her kind words, collected his music and left, looking very proper, as though nothing more had happened between them than the most ordinary of music lessons.

"You're improving greatly," the duchess told Kathryn. "And I can tell you love playing."

Kathryn, turning around and standing, awkwardly, asked Her Grace how she could tell.

"It's the way you're flushed and happy," the duchess said. "As though you'd come from a lover's embrace. Your cousin Anne always looked like that when she'd been playing or composing as well."

"Was she one of your maids, madam?" Kathryn asked, because she would rather think of anything else than how close the duchess had hit near the mark. Because though she was not Manox's lover, that was undoubtedly what Manox wanted.

"Anne? Oh, no. Not she. Too fine for my commanding. Her father wished that she and her sister Mary would be great ladies, you know, and his having merchant's blood, he knew that would require as good an education as any ever seen in this kingdom to carry off. So as soon as they were old enough, he sent them to France to be educated at the French court. They went as part of the retinue of our king's sister, Lady Brandon that is, when she married her first husband, the French king. I think Anne was all of eight when they went." The duchess shook her head as she reminisced. "But Anne still visited often enough when she was in country, and of course, I visited once or twice myself. And she was like you about the music."

"Oh. How . . . how learned and . . . and wonderful she must be," Kathryn said. In her mind's eye she could see Manox would already have reached the space behind the chapel's stairs, and she wondered what he'd do if she didn't hasten to join him. In the disturbance of mind that seemed to possess him, it was all too possible that he would stalk back here and demand she embrace him in front of the duchess.

"Indeed," the duchess said. "She was always, in a way, too grand to be just a gentleman's daughter. We should have known she would end with the crown." She sat down on the chair by the virginal and, looking up at Kathryn, seemed to realize for the first time the girl's discomfort. "What is wrong with you, girl, need you visit the room of easement?"

"Yes, madam," Kathryn said, seizing upon the excuse with relief. "An' it please, Your Grace."

"Well, go then," the duchess said. "I would think you'd have seen to it before coming to your lesson, but hasten you hence."

Kathryn hastened. Only instead of rushing toward the bottom of the garden where the privy to which the duchess had alluded so delicately was located, she took a sharp turn at the back door, and keeping close to the house and hoping none of her fellows would cross her path, she rushed in the semishadow of the building toward the chapel.

Should anyone ask, she thought she could tell them that she was going to pray. The truth was that she was praying hard enough. Praying that Manox had changed his mind about wanting to hold her and kiss her. Praying that he wouldn't have lost all patience and decided to proclaim their rendezvous in front of the entire household, praying that if he were there and he truly wanted to hold her and kiss her, it wouldn't be unpleasant.

She didn't think it would be that bad. She remembered the heat in her body in response to the heat from his and half feared she would like it much too much, even though she was sure she didn't like Manox himself, not that way. Oh, he was well enough as a music master, but she was sure she didn't wish to marry him or be attached to him and compelled to obey him the rest of her life.

But when she reached the space beside the entrance of the chapel, there was no one else about. The deep recess between the stone wall and the climbing stone steps was so dark that she was not sure whether Manox was there or not till she heard as if a sigh from the space and then his voice, more breath than whisper, "Kathryn!"

Steeling herself against the horror of entering such impenetrable darkness, she stepped into the space. There was a moment of disorientation for, though her eyes were open, she could see nothing, and then she felt his hands on her, tentative, on either side of her waist, pulling her to him.

Like this, in the dark, unseen, he seemed bigger, overpowering, his arms surrounding her, his body pressing against her, his hair tickling her face, his lips kissing her, first her forehead, then moving down slowly, down one side of her face and then the other, kissing down her graceful, long neck to the hollow of her throat. "Ah,

Kathryn, you came," he said, and resumed kissing her yet again. She could feel him press against her, and against her stomach she felt a hardness that she judged to be his male part.

It felt full large, full hard, and very hot, hotter than even his heated hands or his hot breath touching her. Her heart swelled with pride because, though it might be wrong, it meant she had a sort of power over him—the power to make his body react, whether he wanted it or not.

In her pride, she allowed him to hold her close, her face pressed against his velvet doublet, his lips now kissing at the top of her head. "You are the kindest girl that ever lived," he told her. "As well as the most beautiful, possessing the voice of an angel."

He lifted her off her feet and held her up, his powerful arms around her waist, his lips meeting hers. For a moment of confusion she wasn't sure what he wished, and then his tongue was in her mouth, caressing her tongue.

Her eyes used to the darkness, she could now see him, though dimly. As their faces parted, she could see his filled with something much like an ecstatic joy, his green eyes shining in delight. "Ah Kathryn, if only I were a lord and had a title and could make you mine only. I'd own the prettiest songbird that ever was."

She didn't want to be owned but neither did she think they should be talking, for someone walking by the dark space next to the chapel and hearing voices come from it would immediately know someone was there. If the person who heard them happened to be a moralist or otherwise inclined to interfere in the lives of others, they would be dragged out in disgrace, and then all would be lost.

Instead, Kathryn submitted to more kisses and more embraces and, when he seemed calmer, escaped into the daylight, tugging at her disarrayed garments and combing her disheveled hair back under her bonnet.

At least, she thought to herself, that was done and it hadn't been unpleasant and no one had caught them. Now she need not worry about Manox again.

Eleven

"PLEASE meet me at the customary place," Manox whispered as he leaned over her to pick up the books from atop the virginal.

Kathryn looked up, confused. "Why? Why?"

He looked at her, then leaned again, to pick up a book he let fall onto the keyboard, "I must touch you again. I must. It's a craving that has me in great suffering . . . The madness of it . . ."

"But I let you!" she said. "I let you once."

As she hissed her response, she sharpened her ears for the duchess's footstep. Lately, the old lady had taken to dropping in on them, and she might do so at any minute.

"Ah," he said, and his hand, seeming to fumble for a book, managed to drag up the front of her dress, slowly, caressingly. "Ah, but once is not enough, Kathryn. You must come meet me. You must let me . . . touch you again. I shall go mad otherwise," he said.

She sighed. "Very well."

After the lesson she hurried to the space, but this time he did not call her. Instead, he reached out for her, and before she could recover her breath, he'd dragged her back into the narrow space and was on her. This time his hands were on her everywhere, over the dress, feeling every turn and nook of her body, from her swelling breasts to her nascent hips, to the legs beneath.

Quite before she could tell what he was doing, he had her skirts in his hand, and he was lifting them.

"Master Manox!" she said, though she normally avoided saying anything.

"Please," he said. "Please, only let me touch you . . . beneath your clothes. Let me feel your secret, madam."

She opened her mouth to protest but at that moment, half in horror, half in incredulity, she heard the *tap-tap-tap* of the duchess's walking stick on the path next to the space, accompanied by the sound of her footsteps and the sound of another, heavier set of steps.

"We will have three masses tomorrow then," the duchess said. "Since it's the anniversary of my late husband's death."

The other voice, recognizably the priest's, answered something that seemed like a long oration on some subject—perhaps even in Latin, Kathryn thought, since the man was quite capable of answering in Latin a question as to whether it was raining.

Manox had her skirts in one hand and his other hand was questing beneath, feeling her things and then dipping beneath her underwear, to feel at the cleft between her legs.

To Kathryn the feel of a hand there—other than her own, and that only when hygiene necessitated it—was so strange, that she squirmed and would have called out, only she was mindful of the voices in the path. The duchess was saying, "No, I would not use the white roses. You remember how my lord felt about—"

Manox was now using both hands to untie Kathryn's undergarments and to pull them down, till they were around her ankles, effectively entrapping her, making it impossible for her to take more than a very-hobbled step. She wondered what he meant to do, as he let her skirt fall, and it seemed to her that he had fallen to his knees, though it was hard to see in the deep darkness.

And then she felt his head beneath her skirts, his beard tickling her knees, her thighs, up and up. She felt his lips reverently kissing her where she scarce dared touch. This time, a sigh escaped her, but the duchess didn't seem to notice, as she was saying, "We shall have some greenery in vases," and the priest was mumbling something in return.

And then Kathryn felt Manox's tongue licking along the length of her cleft, and she had to bite her lips together not to moan.

He licked and he sucked, and he seemed to know things about her body that she did not herself know.

She was torn between horrible embarrassment at what he was doing, this strange kind of kiss that, perforce, could not be natural nor normal, and excitement mounting from her body at the ministrations of his tongue and lips.

He found some part of her that seemed to be a trigger of some sort. The more he licked, the more his tongue played on that spot, Kathryn felt as though pressure were building within her being—a pleasurable, warm, insistent pressure but pressure nonetheless.

She put her hands on either side toward the rough, cold, damp stone walls, afraid she would otherwise utterly lose consciousness and fall, as the pressure built and built till there was nothing else in the world but a desire for a release that she wasn't sure could come or would come.

If she'd not been conscious of the *tap-tap* of the walking stick upon the path outside, she would have let go and screamed her need and her desire for release.

But she dared not and followed the sound in her mind, as the walking stick seemed to distance itself. She wondered if she was dreaming, if it was her desire building up that had caused her to dream this, but at long last, she couldn't but risk it.

As her pleasure reached some sort of apex and mingled waves of release and joy washed over her, making her legs weak and her body tremble, she let out a long moan and then a long sigh.

She would have fallen then, save that Manox caught her. "You taste," he whispered sweetly, "as beautiful as you look and almost as beautiful as you sound."

Twelve

KATHRYN never quite knew how it came to happen, except that Manox's suffering seemed to grow with her yielding and every time she met with him and allowed him to touch her in intimate ways, he wished for more. For a year they met at their music lesson and were proper and right, but she sat through the lessons stiffly and trembling, because she knew what would come after.

Part of it was fear—fear of being discovered and shamed, fear of what the duchess might do if she found what was happening under the chapel stairs. But there was also another type of worry for, though the encounters were pleasurable—or at least often brought her to gasping pleasure—they also were in a way against her will. She enjoyed Manox's hands on her, not because they were Manox's hands, but because they were hands. She enjoyed attention and praise—she'd had so little of it in her life.

But she didn't like Manox, or not outside the common way. He had taught her music, and for this she was grateful, but she did not imagine a future with him. Even her dim memories of her night on the street squired by Thomas Culpepper were more exciting and romantic than all she did with Henry Manox. And a superstitious fear gnawed at her mind that she might have to marry him—that this would be the end conclusion of all her escapades—because the lace thrown onto the dormitory floor had said Henry, and behold, Manox was Henry.

If Kathryn was going to have to spend most of her life obeying a man as though he were God on Earth, then she would surely want it to be a man of some worth and situation. Not Henry Manox, second son, music master, bound to work for what he could get. She knew where the end of that journey lay—she'd been born into it, in the family of a younger son, her impoverished father.

What she did for Manox, she did because she thought it would relieve his suffering. And what she did was never enough.

As he leaned over her during the lesson, to correct the positioning of her fingers—an endeavor that after two years of learning the virginal was quite needless, as her positioning was perfect or as perfect as Henry Manox could teach—and readied to whisper in her ear, she whispered fiercely back, "It is no use, Mr. Manox. Be content with what you have got so far. Be satisfied."

She could see his expression reflected in a bit of silver leaf on the virginal's figured back, and she saw that he had a certain and sure expression when leaning over her, but now the look in his eyes faltered to something like momentary panic, then disbelief. "You can't mean that," he said.

"Be sure I mean it, Master Manox."

"But . . . But we haven't . . ." He let go of her and started pacing, toward the window, then back again, his eyes wild, his hands clasped on either side of his head, as if he were a man ready for Bedlam. "But can you not see my suffering?"

Kathryn played on, hoping the duchess wouldn't hear a long silence in the playing and come to see what was about. "I can see your suffering, yes, but I do not know what I can do to relieve it. What you have asked me to do I've done, but what I've done never seems to relieve your pain, only to bring on a more pronounced bout."

He paced some more. On the keyboard, her fingers flew, heedless, from a traditional ballad to something that more closely resembled a march. She wondered if this was what the priest meant when he talked about a lady's citadel of virtue being under siege. It didn't feel like siege, not unless the conquering armies lay on the floor and writhed about moaning and screaming and telling the resisters to relieve their suffering.

"How can you say you've done all I want?" he asked, as he came behind her and, once more, put his hands over hers, stilling them. "How can you claim my suffering should be quite relieved? Don't you know what the sight of you does to me, the scent of your body, the memories . . . ?"

She shook her hands, trying to dislodge his. "What I do not understand, Master Manox, is what you mean by this. What can you expect me to give you that will quell such intemperate urges?"

"Some token of your affection for me!" he said.

"What token should I show you? I will never be aught with you, and you are not able to marry me."

His hands convulsed upon hers, as though weathering a blow, and they trembled a little, but then he clasped her hands with renewed fervor. His eyes, reflected in the reflective bit of silver designed to figure the summer sun above the pasturing deer and the forest lakes, were wild and desperate. "Only, only, Mistress

Howard, this one token give me. Let me do no more than I've done before, but only touch you the same way in the light and see your body. Only this token I crave, and then I'll let you be."

"In the full light?" she asked. "It cannot be done."

"It can," he whispered, his mouth close by her ear and his words passionate. "Only hark to me, it can. If we go into the church at our customary time, we can get behind the altar, and there no one will see us if they only casually glance into the church."

"But what if my grandmother or the vicar should . . ."

"Ah, Mistress Howard. For a year we've been meeting beneath the stairs, and we've seen signs of life there but once. Surely our luck won't desert us now. And it's just the one time, and then on my honor I will let you be."

"On your honor?" she asked, to verify.

"On my honor I will, Kathryn Howard. I shall teach you the virginal and nothing more."

Kathryn took a deep breath. Her fear of carrying on such illicit relations in the church, where the holy sacrament would be exposed, was as strong as ever, but so was her wish to be rid of these demands of Manox's, these impetuous sighs and sad, imposing moods. She shook her hands to rid them of his, and she said, "If you will promise me, then, on your honor as a gentleman," she said. "That this be your intention and no more, and that once this is done you won't any further importune me, I'll let you. But the once only."

She felt, even as she said it, that there was some certain lack of force to her position, for before to, she had acquiesced to the one time, which now extended to hundreds of times, in the dark space beneath the stairs.

He inclined his head. "On my honor as a gentleman," he said, "I so promise."

"What promise you?" the duchess's sharp voice asked from the door.

They both jumped, in confusion, both probably reddening to their hair roots, and both quite disoriented. Kathryn's mind raced madly. How long had the duchess been there and why had they not heard her approach. What had she heard, and more important, what would she make of it.

Kathryn took a deep breath and then another, and between one breath and the next, she realized the duchess could not have heard anything incriminating, or at the very least nothing fatally so. Had she heard such, then she would surely have been laying about with her walking stick and probably sending Manox off on the spot. Instead she sounded merely curious.

"Why, nothing, Your Grace," she said, without getting up from the virginal and fumbling with the music on its stand. "Only what a start you gave us, coming in cat foot like that."

"I did not cat foot, wench, only you and this fine gentleman here were all involved in some hot dispute. I would know about what."

"Only this, madam," Kathryn said, hearing Manox's breathing still irregular and knowing that if left to himself he would make quite an incoherent protest. "That Master Manox believes I cannot play this quite difficult piece of music without error. He says if I do, then he will be done with me as a pupil, and I need no more attend his lessons and he will no further importune me with his corrections."

The duchess gave a low cackle, and said, "Oh, but you are a

wench with sauce. Your cousin Anne . . ." She hesitated. "Well, it might have brought her low, her sharp tongue and her demanding ways, but then even now, I wouldn't put it past her to bring the king around her finger again, even from the Tower as she is. This whey-faced wench they say that the king is all taken with is no stop for my granddaughter Anne."

Kathryn inclined her head. She had heard about the trial and that her cousin was in the Tower, accused of bewitching the king and of many other foul deeds that no one would speak of directly in front of Kathryn. The duchess said it was all falsehood and lies, but Kathryn wondered if it were true. Not the foul deeds, of which, at any rate, she knew nothing, but the witchcraft. For, as she got older and more advanced in love lore, Kathryn learned that if one bewitched a man and attached him to her by those foul means, he would likely turn on her as the devil collects his due. Surely that described the mad desire and the oh-so-fast fall in the affair between the king and Kathryn's cousin.

"Well, girl," the duchess said. "Are you going to play, then? You have Master Manox's word for it that if you do and do it well, he will no more importune you. Isn't it so, Master Manox?"

"Indeed," Manox answered, his voice trembling only slightly. "Indeed, Your Grace, it is."

"Of course," the duchess said, sitting herself down in her customary chair by the virginal, which she occupied whenever she came to hear Kathryn play. "Mind you that to take the word of the grandson of a yeoman for that of a gentleman might very well lead you astray yet, but for the nonce we'll pretend Master Manox's word is good, and we'll try his forbearance."

Kathryn lowered her head and took a deep breath and played,

her fingers flying on the keyboard as though self-willed and habit guided, though she'd done this piece no more than twice before.

When she finished, there was silence for a moment, and then the duchess cackled. "Well, I trow, Master Manox, that she has bested, and she is done with your lessons now. What say you?"

"I'd say she's performed admirably," he said. "And that from this day forth, I'll importune her no more."

Thirteen

It was cold and dim in the church, though neither so cold nor so dark as it had been in their customary space. When Kathryn got there, Manox was already waiting, sitting behind the altar, so that he would be wholly obscured from the door.

When he saw her arrive, his eyes quickened, reflections striking deep in the green eyes, like light seen through murky water. "You came," he said.

"Aye, and I keep my word," she said. "And so keep you yours."

"Oh, indeed," he said. "Indeed, I will."

"It was not easy," she said, "to leave, for I had to entertain the duchess with many a madrigal and air, and only that her chamberer Mary Lassells came to call to her for some duty or another did she agree to go and leave me alone long enough to come here."

He smiled at her. "But you did come."

She saw in the complacent smile the beginning of his belief that she would come here again and again at his command, just as she had come to the space beneath the stairs, and she thought it best to nip the thought in the bud. "Only the once, Master Manox, and then, remember you, your promise to importune me no further—for this is the way that fools behave when nothing may come of it."

"If only I had a name," he said softly. "Or a fortune."

"But you have neither," she said, cruelly, nipping such dreams in the bud. "And therefore enough now. I promised to give you this one token, to put your suffering to an end. If you claim that I only inflamed you further, nothing can be done, but I'll have to tell the duchess you've been importuning me for favors beyond your station."

He looked as though he were about to reply to her, but instead he shook his head and said, gently, "Only this once. Now sit you, fair Kathryn."

Kathryn sat. The stone floor behind the altar was so cold that she could feel the chill even through her heavy brocaded skirts. And it was not just the normal flagstones back there but one long, unbroken stone, with faded names and dates on it. Some ancestor of the Norfolk clan lay buried there, Kathryn thought, and in thinking so shivered, imagining what that worthy person, probably old and humorless, would think of his descendant Kathryn disporting herself upon the grave stone.

She crossed herself reflexively and kissed the back of her hand to ward off any evil that might come to her from this act. And found Manox's eyes on her. "Do you always cross yourself, then, before these amusements?"

Kathryn couldn't answer but only fix him with her unvarying glare until he chuckled, as if to convince her he meant nothing by his comment, and reached over, pulling her to him, kissing her lips tenderly, once, twice.

To Kathryn it seemed very strange. These caresses she'd enjoyed before, in the dark space beneath the stairs, and they had seemed well enough, or at least none too bad. But now that she could see Manox, she found herself paying less attention to the sensation of his lips on her and the way his tongue quested into her mouth. Instead, she marked how he closed his eyes when he kissed her and how the eyelids that descended over his eyes were so pale and fine that you could see the tracery of veins upon them, like a purple spiderweb.

For some reason the sight put her off and made her feel quite distant and unmoved by those hands that were running up and down her bodice, stopping to cup her small breasts, by those lips that were kissing her fervently from brow to neck and then back up again.

Like this, in the light, it all seemed very contrived. Henry Manox's look of exquisite delight at such a small pleasure seemed to her to be as much playacting as genuine. He looked to her like nothing so much as like her mother's cat when Kathryn had been very small.

Her mother's cat was a small tom, scarred by a hundred street battles. Kathryn had seen the miscreant often beating up the smaller cats around the house to steal their food, cowing the females into accepting his amorous advances, and ruling the whole house with an inflexible will barely contained in the small, scarred grey tabby body.

But only let the creature go near Kathryn's mother, and gone was the overlord and warrior that everyone else in the house knew, the small demon with the sharp claws. Around Kathryn's mother, the tom was all meek and mild, rubbing on her ankles, and bleating a thousand different complaints about his condition and the harshness of the world.

And regardless of how much Kathryn or her siblings told their mother, she would not believe them. Instead, she would give the cat milk and fish and the best of her plate, for which he would show great and extravagant gratitude and pleasure, until her mother defended the cat to Kathryn, saying, "You see, he is such a small animal and so mild. I am sure all the other cats brawl with him, and that he goes unfed and uncared for unless I am here to feed him. Mark how he relishes his food, and how much gratitude and pleasure he shows. The poor creature."

Now, it seemed to Kathryn, that Manox showed gratitude and pleasure in exactly the same way, save only that he didn't purr, and as she watched him—while he kissed the small space exposed between her neck and her dress—she found herself thinking he looked more and more like tom, until a giggle escaped her.

He looked up, surprised.

"I beg your pardon," she said. "It is only you look so much like Tom."

"Tom?" he asked, and there was a sudden stab of something dangerous in the liquid green eyes, as he pulled his head away from her. "Tom Culpepper?"

She could only giggle again and say, "No. An' bless your soul. Tom, my mother's cat."

He looked confused for a moment, then frowned at her. "And in what way am I like a cat, Mistress Howard?" he said. "Is it only that you think you run me tame?"

"Oh, no," she said. And her courage failing her to explain that he looked like a cat feigning ill-treatment, she could only say, "No, only you look like Tom when he got a tasty morsel of fish."

"Oh is that so?" Manox asked, and arched an eyebrow and smiled, impishly. "But that is only, madam, because you are my tasty morsel, and I would fain devour you."

With that, he pulled up her skirts and tugged roughly at her linen underwear. "Oh, no, Master Manox," she said, as she endeavored to cross her legs. "For you shall not do that here, not in the full light of day."

"It is not full light," he said. "But rather dim. Besides which, you yourself promised me that I would be allowed to do what I have done before, only this time seeing what I do. Can you deny we've often done this before?"

She could not deny it. In fact it was one of the few things she truly enjoyed about their encounters—Manox's skilled mouth upon her most secret parts, the way his tongue caressed her, while the fire and the pressure mounted within her till they exploded in blinding pleasure.

She let him pull the skirt fully up, till it covered almost to her chest, leaving her legs uncovered and cold, lying against the frigid stone behind the altar.

He removed her underwear and cast it aside. She let herself fall back against the stone, willing herself not to think and certainly not to look at what he was doing. If she closed her eyes, she thought perhaps it would be easier to pretend they were still in the safe haven under the stairs and to banish from her mind the image of the tracery of veins on the back of Manox's eyelids and the ridiculous look of exaggerated pleasure upon his face.

She felt his breath on her thighs, and then his lips, their touch velvety soft. She responded to the pressure of his hands against her skin, by opening her legs wider by degrees. She felt his breath touch her open crevice, and then his fingers run its length wonderingly.

"An' I wish," he said, softly, "that I could have your maidenhead."

"For sure you may not, Master Manox, for that is for my husband, and besides, I am sure that it would hurt."

"Oh, but I would treat you so well afterward, that would make you quite forget your hurt."

She started to close her knees. "Master Manox!" she said. "You promised, and on your word as gentleman, yet, that you—"

"Easy, easy," he said, and his fingers caressed the inside of her thighs again, in a coaxing manner, teasing her legs into opening once more. "Only you let me do this thing . . ."

She let her knees fall open and presently Manox's skilled lips returned to their work, and she sighed out a full exhalation of pleasure, as she felt the familiar pressure and heat build within her, demanding release.

"Ah, you slut! Have you no shame, then!" A hand grabbed at her hair, pulling her up. She opened her eyes halfway between being brought off her back and to her knees and then by force of having her hair smartly pulled to her feet.

Her open eyes revealed a ruddy hand on her hair, attached to a ruddy arm, which was a woman's but muscular enough to belong to a working man. And beyond the hand and the arm was the red, screaming face of Mary Lassells, Her Grace's chamberer, who was hurling abuse upon Kathryn's head, shaking her, calling her the worst of sluts and the most abandoned of whores.

Even this, Kathryn thought, dazed, as her undergarments were shaken in front of her eyes and she was enjoined to put them on, even as a slap cut through the air, to sting against her cheek, was far less terrible than what was befalling Manox.

Manox had got Her Grace's attention. And Kathryn, through her own distress, as ready tears sprang into her eyes and rolled down her face, could see that he was by far getting the worst of it.

The duchess had taken the walking stick and forgotten quite that it was necessary to her walk—or that she pretended it to be so. Instead, she was using it as a weapon, raining blows upon Manox's head and face. "Knave," she said. "Seducer. Think you that my granddaughter is for the likes of you. How far has this gone? Answer me! How far?"

As she spoke, she chased the gentleman who tried to escape, and who, Kathryn realized, had his codpiece quite undone, his member bouncing and bogging through the opening, like some self-animated thing as he jumped and cringed, trying to evade the duchess's stick.

Pulling her underwear up and fastening it, crying, Kathryn thought that now the duchess would send her back to . . . Her mind boggled at the thought as to where she'd be sent. Though it hadn't been said to her as such, she could tell from the way people spoke of him, that her father must be dead, and she didn't know where her oldest brother was or what authority he could have over her.

Wherever Charles was, she would warrant he was of no estate to support a sister. Or indeed, anyone, save maybe himself and even that doubtful. So, where would the duchess send her? She could not think and wasn't sure of anything save only that this would not end well.

Sniffling, she saw that the duchess had brought Manox to bay underneath a niche of the Virgin. He was flat against the wall beneath the niche, and unable to stretch to his full height, for if he tried, his head would strike the pedestal on which the statue stood.

"Tell me how far this has gone, Manox," the duchess said. "Have you had carnal knowledge of my granddaughter?"

"I swear . . ." he said. "I swear by the Virgin an' I have not."

"Meant you to?" the duchess asked, terrible, her walking stick raised.

"I was hoping . . . that is . . ." He sniffled, in turn, and the walking stick came at him from the side and caught him a blow that sounded like a hollow knock, and caused him to half stand and hit his head against the stone pedestal with an even louder hollow sound.

"Ah, you knave, you fiend. You were hoping that while she was otherwise distracted by your caresses you could slip the weapon in and her unknowing."

"I—" he said. "I never thought."

"For certain you never thought, you ill-gotten fiend, for if you had you would know that had you achieved your end there would be nothing for us but to put an end to your existence. For shame on you." She caught him a blow with the stick to the other temple, and again he tried to rise in reflex and hit his head.

And then she was raining blows on him, while he screamed, and then he whimpered. Kathryn, staring, openmouthed, thought only that he seemed very little brave now, and very little manly. Those powerful arms that had seemed so capable of holding her place, that broad chest, well developed with muscles, all of it seemed insufficient to ward off blows from an old woman's stick, and all he could do was snivel and beg that she would stop, and that he would not, in the name of the Virgin and the angels and the whole heavenly host do such a thing again.

"You are right, you will not," the duchess said, her voice full of grim satisfaction as she continued to belabor him with her stick. "For from this day forward you are not to be left alone with my granddaughter at any time. And what is more, my fine cockerel, you are not to darken my threshold nor come sauntering your fine ways over my household. You are a serpent in the garden, young man, and you will not be allowed to tempt the innocents in my house."

At last the duchess stopped, either because her arm had grown tired or because the sight of Manox, beaten and sniveling, tears dripping from his nose and chin, a big scrape on his forehead and both eyes blackened, filled her with a sense of satiated revenge and, perhaps, with just a little bit of pity. "Do yourself up, you wretch, and get out of my sight."

Kathryn, whom Mary Lassells had stopped beating, at least after that first, halfhearted attempt to slap her, had only the chamberer's hand still grasping her hair to remind her that she was not well out of this.

She watched, with half pity and half apprehension as Manox limped from the chapel, his hands fumbling at his crotch. He failed even to throw her a single look as he left.

For a moment the only loud sound in the chapel was the duchess's labored, fast breathing. As that calmed down, she turned to Kathryn and said, waspish, "As for you, my fine lady, you will come to my chambers, so I may speak with you."

Fourteen

THE duchess stormed into her rooms ahead of Kathryn and disposed herself in the largest chair, staring at her errant granddaughter with a frown that indicated she was considering a line of sufficiently horrible punishments and finding them all insufficient.

Kathryn, facing the all-seeing eyes dared not move, till the duchess said, "Sit you down, girl."

Kathryn skittered sideways to fall upon a tambour which happened to be just lower than the chair, making her feel even smaller than her natural short stature, as she looked up at her grandmother. And was surprised. She'd been so shocked in the—at any rate dim—chapel, that she'd not paid any attention to how her grandmother looked. Now she realized there were dark marks under the duchess's eyes, and a look as though she had been crying or were deeply perturbed. Had Kathryn put those marks there?

The duchess stared at her a good long time, dispassionately. "Are you still a maiden, Kathryn?" she asked at last. She might as well have been asking if Kathryn had made a good dinner the night before.

"Yes, Your Grace," Kathryn said, and ducked her head. "I know what it might seem like to you, milady, but . . ."

The duchess snorted. "What it seems like is like a young girl too full of her own affairs and a silly infatuation for a virginal player. Is that what it is, Kathryn?"

Kathryn sighed, then shook her head. "It was him who wanted to touch me," she said. She looked up at the duchess. "He said it hurt him to love me so much and to be gratified, not to have . . . not to have a token of my esteem."

The duchess frowned. "Do you esteem him then?"

"Only as a teacher," Kathryn said. "And . . . and as a friend. But it was, you see, that he seemed to suffer so much, and I didn't want him to suffer, and he said if I met him under the stairs of the chapel, where it's full dark and where he could kiss me and hold me, he would be well."

The duchess covered her face with her hand. Kathryn did not know what this meant, but she watched the gnarled, old, but still slim fingers clench tight, then let go, then clench again, as though behind the protective screen of her hand the duchess were rationalizing some violent passion. "Mea culpa," she murmured at last and, lowering her hand, looked up at Kathryn. "I should have taught you better. I should have realized how tenderhearted you are. Your mother . . ." She inclined her head and paused, as though considering what best to say next. "Your mother was tenderhearted, too. Soft. I didn't know her well, but what I heard of her led me to believe so. Beware, Kathryn. Better a hard-hearted wench than a soft one. Your mother's soft heart saw her married to your father, who spent her money and wore her out in bearing child after child."

"But he was never made happier, not when I let him hold me,

not when I let him feel my privy place beneath my clothes, not even when I let him kiss it."

"And that is as far as it goes?" the duchess asked. "It went no further than that?"

Kathryn shook her head. She told the duchess what had passed in the music room that day. The duchess made a face. "Well, I know, for I heard most of it from outside the room," she said. "And it both appalled me and filled me with pride for you, since it didn't seem to be your desire, and sure it was not you begging. Kathryn, your liaison with Manox is the talk of the kitchen maids, Lassells tells me. They have often seen you and Manox secreting around to your hiding place, and they wondered what was toward. The talk was that you had pledged your troth to him, and indeed that was my fear. That and that things had gone too far."

"No, madam, I know that removing my maidenhead would hurt, and I was not about to let someone like Manox, for whom I don't care much, do it."

Again the duchess's hand went to cover her face, and again it clenched over her eyes, as though she were trying to control thoughts she didn't wish to admit to. "Where do you get your morality, girl? From what you hear in the kitchen?"

"No, madam, only Mary said that it is our duty to get our happiness and our love before we are consigned to our husbands, who will then be to us as God to the Earth, and whom we'll never be able to escape or disobey. And so I thought . . ."

"You know what the Church says. Surely, Kathryn, before you came to me, were you not given religious instruction?"

"The Church . . ." Kathryn said, but then, her mind reviving. "But the Church says so many things that we do anyway. That we should not kill, and yet, how many prisoners go from the Tower to the block?" It seemed to her the duchess flinched. "And it says we should not covet, but don't all of us covet something? And it says—"

"Enough," the duchess said, with a tone of finality. "If piety doesn't move you, then we shall try practical matters." She was quiet a moment, then spoke in a harsh tone, seeming to move her mouth only the minimum to get the words out. "Yesterday your cousin went to the block."

It was like a bucket of freezing water thrown over Kathryn. Like icy water, the words stopped all her thoughts, and caused her to shiver and blink in confusion, as though she'd been asleep or walking in some dream up till then and had only now been brought fully awake. "My cousin . . . The queen?"

She had known, of course, that the king had stopped loving Anne. That much was obvious even a year ago. And for the last few months there had been talk that she was accused of treason, of witchcraft, and of other foul but never explained things. There were rumors too that the king's affections had turned to another woman—whom the duchess called only a whey-faced wench—and even that this woman was already pregnant.

But all along the duchess had also been getting letters and reports from her friends in the capital, and there had been indications that the queen would perhaps be offered a way out of the country, perhaps to a foreign convent. And there had been stories that she would be spared, and even other stories that were the king but to see her, he would love her again.

Kathryn hadn't wanted to believe that the beautiful cousin she'd seen but once, the glittering queen on whom all of Kathryn's hopes for elevation rested, now lay dead. She realized that her eyes had filled with tears when she felt one tear drop down her chin. "How . . . how . . . ?"

The duchess shrugged. "The how is simple enough, if you mean the physical means of her death. Her head was cut by a sword, wielded by a headsman sent for from France, for she feared that the ax would not take it off swiftly enough and that she should suffer. The king loved her enough to grant her that mercy still . . ."

It didn't seem like a great mercy to her. "But she was so beautiful," Kathryn said. "And her daughter is the princess . . ."

"Who knows for how long?" the duchess said. "For I doubt me not as soon as the whey-faced wench should give the king a son—and capable of it, too, she is, coming from a family that breeds like hares in the fields—Elizabeth shall be declared a bastard, just like Mary, Catherine's daughter." She looked up. "But perhaps you should understand more about this. Your cousin Anne fell not of adultery—" She glared at Kathryn, as though daring her to disagree with this assessment. "No matter how many swear to it or how many confessions were extracted under torture, I shall never believe that Anne Boleyn was stupid enough to play false on the king of England. Even if she didn't love him. Even if she didn't care for him at all."

"No. Your cousin Anne fell from treating the king as just a man." She grimaced, the grimace resembling a smile. "Which might be well, since she rose also by those means. She rose to the heights of a crown because the king knew she loved in him as a man and not merely as the king of England or for the king's power. But then, once she'd ascended, she continued treating the king as a man, and there was her grave error.

"A husband, no matter whether he's king of mucksman in the nearest pigsty, should believe he is the king of his wife's affections. This is why it is said that the woman should obey her husband as the Earth obeys God. While Anne might not have been adulterous, she gave the king to understand that her heart didn't rest, entire, in his command, and by doing that she made him insecure. And by making him insecure, alas, she made him suspect her of having other loves and other lovers. And because her husband was in fact the king, he could get those suspicions confirmed no matter how outrageous. Now, my dear, what does that tell you about how you should behave yourself and why it is important to me that you haven't lost your maidenhead?"

Kathryn blinked. The tears were still falling down her face, leaving cold trails. It seemed to her that she must have fallen asleep in the chapel, over the grave of that long-dead Howard, and be dreaming all of this. The duchess could not have come upon her and Manox and interrupted them thus. And having come upon them, the duchess wouldn't show the worst of her wrath to Manox. And if she did so, she wouldn't afterward take Kathryn to her room and there spend time instructing her on the value of a maidenhead. "I don't know," she said miserably.

The walking stick rose, and Kathryn cringed, but it only came down in front of her feet and tapped out, insistently, as if to call her attention. "Don't be more stupid than you can help," the duchess said. "And listen to me. It matters because your husband will want to believe, even if you have never met him before your wedding day, that he is the king of your heart from the moment you take vows. And believing that is easier if he thinks the fortress of your body has not been broached."

"Oh," Kathryn said. She did not know what else to say or do, save that she had never thought of it that way.

"As a girl and—" The duchess reached over, her hand touched Kathryn under the chin and forced her to put it up, to show her face. "A not uncomely girl, you belong more than to yourself. You belong to your family. And to God, of course," she added, as though not so much acknowledging the Almighty's claim as dismissing it by stating it. "Your beauty will serve to attract a husband—one who can make a strong alliance with our family and help all the Howards grow strong. And your affection, given to your husband, your careful treatment of him so that he believes himself a god in your eyes, will convince him to give every advantage to our family." She nodded. "And you will give him lusty children that will augment the family. Do you understand?"

Seen like that, it seemed to Kathryn that her entire future was already decided from this moment until she should rest quietly under a stone. "Yes," she said softly, not sure that she felt very happy about this idea. When she was little, she and her brothers—and sometimes her sisters, too—had played at being pirates and robbers, at fighting in the highways or in wild cavalcades in the moonlight.

Now she thought that all she'd ever get to see, all she'd ever get to do, would be life as she lived now, only in a house that would be her own, a house where she would be kept and have children—lusty children, at that—to enrich her husband's and her family's network of connections.

"Oh, don't be so sad," the duchess said. "It is not a bad lot . . ."

Kathryn thought that the duchess could say that for she had been widowed any number of years and did exactly as she pleased with her household and with all those around her. "And . . . a marriage for me, Your Grace?" she said at last. "What are . . . How are the chances that there shall be one?"

The duchess sighed. "Lower now, of course. With your cousin dead and that wench in her place, all the benefices and all the gifts will be going to the Seymours. But there's nothing so sure in the world but that things will turn. In a year or so, we'll look and find you a match. You're what? Between thirteen and fifteen, we thought? Well, you can wait yet, young Kathryn. But until then, remember the best gift you can give your husband is the gift of your maidenhead and, with it, the certainty that he's the first and most important person in your life. Guard it well, until you find the one you're going to marry."

The Open Rose

Fifteen

"THERE is no reason that you shouldn't have riding lessons," the duchess had said. She'd said it after the house had been shuttered to mourn Anne's death—a convenient way, the duchess said, of avoiding the visits of locals bearing more venom than sympathy for the family—then unshuttered again, and after a mild spring had given way to a mild summer. "There are several gentlemen as came from the court to join my household, and one of them ought to be good enough to teach you to ride. As for hunting . . . well, we'll see to that afterward, for surely you must know how to hunt as well, even if the best husband we can procure you in the future is a country squire."

She'd looked Kathryn over. Kathryn had just come back from a walk in the orchard, and was flushed with the exertion and feeling rather happy. "Though it seems a waste," the duchess said. "If we can reach no higher for you, but there it is. We shall hope for the best. And meanwhile, we shall teach you to dance and to ride, to hunt and to behave like a lady should." Her gaze fell to Kathryn's ankles, and she frowned. "Why are your ankles showing, girl?"

"If Your Grace pardon, but I grew . . ."

The duchess sighed. "I shall give orders," she said, "to have two new gowns made for you. None too expensive, as we're not likely to leave the country soon. Perhaps ever. But decent enough to cover you and allow you to look like you belong to your station. Do you believe you'll grow more this season?"

"An' it please, Your Grace, I do not know."

"No, you wouldn't," the duchess said making it sound as though the ignorance were a perverse quirk on Kathryn's part. "Very well, I shall arrange for you—and I suppose the other maids are in need of it as well—to have dancing and riding lessons."

And so the lessons started. They didn't seem to Kathryn to tend to very much and, truth be told, they weren't much more exciting than the riding lessons that she'd had as a little girl. While the duchess kept a goodly stable—it was said that in her youth, which Kathryn believed had been at the time of the Wars of the Roses, the duchess had been a good horsewoman—the two men who had recently joined the duchess's household and been deputized to help the maids at their riding lessons were clearly fearful that they might damage such delicate pupils.

The horse chosen for the lessons was at least as old and as docile as the one she'd ridden in her mother's house, and though the other girls delighted in pinching it and slapping it in a vain effort at making it go faster, Kathryn couldn't bear to make a creature suffer for her present amusement, and so she endured with good grace, or at least not too bad, the glacial pace and the hesitant ways of the old horse. Sometimes she was conscious that around her, the other girls were flirting with the gentlemen supposed to teach them, and that they all made fun of her for going so slow and not minding.

But Kathryn was suffering under the twin dampening blows of her affair with Manox being found out and of Anne's execution. She dreamed sometimes that she was Anne, walking from the Tower, shadowy in the background, to a barren square, where she laid her head upon a block. She dreamed of the ax whistling down. And she wished she could forget, but she could never. Instead, awake or asleep, she remembered how her hopes had been blighted by Anne's death. Who now would want to allay themselves to a family in disgrace?

She knew that the duchess still got news from the court, but she did not talk about it. And Kathryn, mindful that they'd hope for the best but knew she might have to be wasted on a country squire, took her turns around the riding paths in the garden upon a horse so old that he might be dead on his feet and no one have noticed yet.

A week or so later, dance lessons were started, this with a proper dancing master and no gentlemen at all in sight, but only the girls, partnering each other, as they were led with strict formality through the exacting dances.

Kathryn found she rather liked to dance, and her mood improved. It stayed higher, though not high, till a few days later when she approached the yard for her riding lesson and found two different and much younger gentlemen waiting with three horses. Their horses were something very beautiful in horseflesh, nervous, long legged, looking spirited and attired in the best dressings a horse could wear, all with inlaid silver. The horse waiting Kathryn looked not at all like the old, moribund creature she had importuned with her riding for the last several days. Instead, it was lower in the saddle than the boys', but—from what Kathryn could tell from the horses she'd seen in the past—well furnished of bone and flesh, and with glossy smooth skin.

It was white, with a dark mark upon its head, and it had eyes as deep and velvety soft as a young child's. More important than that, though, it seemed smart and alert. And it was outfitted with a side-saddle, so there could be no doubt at all that it was intended for Kathryn.

She'd come out of the house tying her bonnet and now paused, having made only a simple knot in the ribbons, and stared at the horse and then one gentleman or another. "Did the old horse die?" she asked. "Or did they just finally perceive that it was dead when it fell over?"

The young man nearest her, whom she was sure she'd never before seen, graced her with an impish smile. He had dark hair and dark, dark eyes, the color of midnight, the same lack of color as the space beneath the stairs outside the chapel.

Kathryn remembered being caught, and looked away from the young man and toward the other, whom she remembered, though she'd never exchanged words with him. He was one of the duchess's retinue, Edward Waldgrave. She remembered that he was also cousin to Henry Manox—even if better furnished with both rank and money—and just as fair and wild-haired as his cousin, though his eyes were a dark blue to Manox's impish green ones. She inclined her head to him, soberly.

"Ah, Mistress Howard," he said, with equal sobriety, as though he were aware of what must be on her mind. "No, indeed. The other horse still thrives and is well enough. But the gentlemen teaching you thought you were good enough on horseback that perhaps you were ready for a beast with more blood . . ." He smiled. "Still perfectly well behaved, of course."

"Of course," she said, and looked at the dark-haired man, waiting for him to introduce himself.

It was Waldgrave who introduced him, though. "And that is my friend, Francis Dereham," he said. "Who has but joined the household, needing to leave his surroundings behind for a bit."

"Pleased to make your acquaintance, Master Dereham," she said.

"As pleased as I am to make yours, Mistress Howard," he said, in a perfectly proper way. But something lay behind the property, and Kathryn was not sure what. All she knew is that light and shadow played in his dark eyes, and seemed to give them unsought for depths.

It was the leaves of the trees overhead, Kathryn told herself. The leaves and the sun, playing in his eyes, and nothing more. But, as he dismounted, and he and Waldgrave, very properly, helped her climb her horse, it was as though—it seemed to her—something shifted in Dereham's expression. He'd seen her ankle, she thought, and looked at him, disturbed, wondering if such a thing should give him some great thrill.

His gaze met hers with neither shame nor openness, and a slow smile slid upon his lips to disappear as quickly as it had formed.

She could not read his thoughts. Now and then, she would look toward him, during their ride, and it seemed to her he was immersed in some secret and strange plotting, so intent was his look, so dark his expression.

He was the one who corrected her, too, while Waldgrave rode by placidly, not seeming to care whether she was hurrying the horse or not. But Dereham was very careful, watching her always and with an attention that might have denoted ulterior motives or, there again, might simply have been directed at the way she rode and what she did with the reins.

His comments to her were the most prosaic. "Pull yourself up, Mistress Howard, and make sure to rest your feet on the footrest, else, once we teach you to ride faster, you'll slide out of the saddle entire."

And then later. "Do not pull the reins so, Mistress Howard. You're going to hurt his mouth."

And then again, "You may now spur him a little. He can give better than this."

They rode for an hour, never deviating from the paths of the orchard, and he never told her anything that was less than proper, but Kathryn sensed something from him—something both dangerous and thrilling, both intense and well controlled.

She watched how his heavy dark hair fell over his forehead and how he pushed it back, and she found herself imagining that he held her in her arms and kissed her.

Then she shivered as she remembered the duchess's sermon on the all-important maidenhead and how Kathryn should preserve it at all costs.

But surely, she thought, as they returned to the stable, kissing had never broken anyone's maidenhead, else hers would already be well lost. And surely, she thought, as much as she had despised Manox's touch for being Manox's, she had enjoyed being touched all the same.

She realized, of a sudden and unlooked for, that she missed being held and caressed, as though her body—once having known it—had now a craving for a man's touch, as though it were a food that she would like to enjoy again.

A sigh escaped her, and she realized that Dereham was looking at her as she sighed and that he smiled a little just at the corner of her mouth.

She felt her color come up in waves, and looked down at the saddle just as they came to the stables and Waldgrave dismounted and tied the horses. He then walked toward Kathryn, to help her dismount. Somehow, though, Dereham was already there.

"Don't trouble, Waldgrave," he said. "For I am here, and no more is needed." He reached up, his hands on either side of Kathryn's waist.

It could have been an embrace, or he could have pulled her close to him, but he did not do either. Instead, he lifted her, at arms' length from the saddle and, effortlessly, set her on the ground, next to the horse.

"Such a small lady," he said, and grinned at her.

She curtseyed to him but dared not answer. She was thinking of the feel of his hands—so powerful and strong on either side of her waist. She remembered how large and powerful Manox had felt when he bent over her, but then later she had realized he was not so very big and that it was only her own small stature that made him seem so strong.

But now she had grown and gained weight, and even so, Dereham could lift her from the saddle with no effort at all, as though she were a small child or a feather.

She walked toward the house, her face warm, her body tired from the more arduous ride than she'd grown used to. She had supper with her fellow maids of honor, and she tried not to consider or think of Dereham and who Dereham might be and what he might be thinking.

But though she put him entirely out of her mind while awake, at night she found that he came back to it in dreams, his lips smiling enigmatically upon his unreadable face, while his dark eyes looked at her with a strange sort of hunger—a hunger that mirrored her own.

And then he pulled her to him, his body next to hers, and their embrace went on and on.

Sixteen

"HE's well born, and he is a gentleman of substance," Alice Restwold said, when Kathryn Howard, late the next night, her knees wrapped in the sheet and thin blanket she shared with Alice, asked about Dereham. She had had one more disturbing lesson with the dark gentleman with his unreadable gaze. And though she'd enjoyed riding the horse more than at any time in the past, his company discomfited her. She wondered what he thought of her when he looked at her so steadily during the rides. And she wondered what he meant to do about it.

Alice's answer was casual in response to what Kathryn hoped was her own casual tone.

"He's normally in the Duke of Norfolk's household," she said. "One of his gentlemen. Only he came to us just now, as I understand there was some misunderstanding or some problem," she said, "at the household."

"What kind of misunderstanding or problem?" Kathryn asked. She braided the end of her hair as she spoke.

"How am I to know?" Alice asked irritably. "No doubt one of the stupid things that men do. A duel or an unsuitable woman or words said that the duke misliked." She shrugged, consigning all those offenses to the same level of unimportance.

"And why comes he to us?" Kathryn asked.

"Ah, that—" Alice smiled. "First, the duchess likes a well-turned man around her, and force, you must agree that he's as well turned a man as ever any eye has seen."

Kathryn made only a noncommittal noise, and shrugged. She was remembering two strong hands lifting her from the horse, as though she were of no consequence at all, her weight less than a child's.

Alice gave a gurgle of laughter. "And besides, he's very much in love with Joan Bulmer."

This statement, so casually uttered, startled Kathryn very much, but she thought she had suppressed the tremor of surprise, because Alice did not remark on it. "Is he now? But how can it be, when he's only now arrived?"

"Oh, we've known him for years and years," Alice said. "Remember the night of the coronation? He was one of the gentlemen who received us—waiting for Joan already he was. And then, you know, when we lived in London we were so close to the household of the Duke of Norfolk that he and Joan could make sure to meet often."

"Are they going to marry, then?"

Alice shrugged. "I don't believe so. For you see, I've heard that Joan's parents are preparing a marriage for her."

"Ah," Kathryn said. "Lucky Joan."

"Think you so, indeed?" Alice asked. "Don't you think that while we live here we may do as we please, but once we're married and consigned to the work of our lives, we'll live only for the pleasure of our husbands and the birth of our children?"

Kathryn sighed. "I know not," she said. "I know only that I would fain be married and know there was someone out there willing to marry me than to live here in this uncertainty."

Alice laughed at her, throwing her head back. "You don't have to worry about that, Kathryn, sure, for even if you buried yourself in the country in a high tower, men would beat a path to your door and climb the tallest height for your favors."

"Perhaps," Kathryn said. She'd heard this before. How beautiful she was, and how attractive to all men. If it were true, she saw none of its effects. The only man who had asked for her favors so far had been Henry Manox, and he'd done it in such a way as to make it not at all flattering to her. She sighed as she remembered that Thomas Culpepper had never even bothered to visit, much less to bring her the promised strawberries.

Oh, she was willing to admit that when they'd met she'd been much more the child than she was now—her breasts just nascent, her mind still provincial and small and looking to the girls around her as guides that would take her through the bewilderment of adult life, more than as equals and companions and—in the case of Alice who merely came from a well-to-do rural family—somewhat inferior. She hadn't learned to value herself then, and she didn't think about herself as a woman, yet, so how cold she blame Thomas for not thinking so.

"Remember when we did the divining in the dormitory, that summer?" she asked Alice.

Alice started to shake her head, and Kathryn cut in, impatiently, "With the lace."

"Oh," Alice said. "Oh, yes, I remember. Great fun, was it not?" she said leaning back onto the smooth round log that served them as pillow.

"Remember then you said that I would marry a Henry?" Kathryn asked.

"Did I now?" Alice asked. She frowned, as though trying to reach back through the clouds of memory to remember such a small and unimportant fact. "And did you like that prediction?" she asked.

"No," Kathryn said. She shook the blanket out and lay herself down fully under it. "Not at all, for I know of no Henry whom I might marry."

"Save only Henry Manox," Alice said, and the way she said it made Kathryn realize that the talk in the household had gone further than the kitchen maids.

She considered ignoring Alice's comment, but then thought that it would be best if such talk were put to rest and properly, and her ignoring it would not do such. "I was a very young girl," she said in tones that sounded, to her own ears, like the duchess's for all that the duchess was not her blood relation. "And it is all past."

"Yes," Alice said. "I heard he got a position teaching music to the children of Lord Bayment."

"Has he now?" Kathryn said, and felt a small prickle of conscience, because all this time she knew that Manox had not the substance to live on his own without a patron and yet she had never enquired how he lived or how well he did. "I am glad. He is a good music teacher. But I am sure he is not the Henry you saw on the lace that night."

Alice cast her a curious glance and frowned slightly.

"Are you sure you read the lace carefully that night?" Kathryn asked.

Alice giggled. "Oh, Kathryn, I was only fooling, and I don't even recall what I saw or what prompted me to say it was the name

Henry. You see, I . . . I was very careful not to tell two ladies the same name, and all I knew about you was that you had no lover."

Kathryn felt angry and was not sure why, but she thought it was that she couldn't depend on anything that Alice said. Had she lied then, or was she lying now? Had she read Henry in the lace, or had she made it up, whole cloth, for a game?

Kathryn turned away from Alice and tried to go to sleep, but it took her a good long time. And when she finally slept, it was to dream of lace falling on the floor of the dormitory, again and again, slithering like a serpent and willfully forming itself into the name Henry.

Seventeen

THE rides continued, faster and faster, more and more daring. A few weeks later, Kathryn was riding through the paths of the forest with Dereham and Waldgrave.

She'd grown confident enough in her mount, and Waldgrave told her she would make a fine horsewoman. This surprised and pleased Kathryn, though she thought that perhaps it shouldn't have been so unexpected. After all, she'd played all kinds of physical games with her brothers—chasing and running, climbing and throwing—and at none of them did they excel more than her, though she be the smallest.

Kathryn enjoyed the rides and, if she were to admit it, she enjoyed the company of Francis Dereham. She looked in vain for signs of his present attachment to Joan Bulmer, but she saw none, save once, as she approached the stables, ready for her ride, she saw Dereham and Bulmer speaking to each other by a little flowering edge. Only they didn't seem to be loverly. In fact, Dereham was shaking his head and Joan looked as though she were ready to spit. As Kathryn walked past, Joan gave her a long, evaluating look and said in a spiteful tone, "Well, I care not, Francis Dereham, only be sure that your blood is good enough before you take that step."

Kathryn didn't know if Joan meant his blood to be his ancestors or if she simply meant that force of the blood, the strength of will, that was often referred to by the same name. It was none of her care, and she walked on.

Francis Dereham was in a black mood throughout the ride that day, and after he had pulled her from the horse in a customary way and set her down on the ground in front of the stables, he'd kept his hands on her waist.

Kathryn's heart sped up, and she thought—madly—that he was going to kiss her. She could almost feel those generous, sensuous lips against hers, and she felt her body go limp in response, ready to swoon into his arms.

But then Waldgrave slapped at Francis's arm and said, "Not here, man. Don't play the fool."

Francis shook, as though waking up, removed his hands from her waist, and made her a deep bow, and Kathryn left, feeling strangely unsatisfied.

Though she normally paid little attention to the moods and humors of her fellow maids, save only those of her closest fellows, she noted now that Joan Bulmer looked as if she were in deep melancholy and also that she, for no reason that Kathryn could imagine, kept giving Kathryn the blackest of looks.

The whole event made Kathryn feel uncomfortable and, the next day, it was with some trepidation that she approached the stables for her riding lesson. Only she found Francis Dereham in an expansive mood and Waldgrave seemingly morose.

Nothing in particular happened during that lesson, except that

Dereham offered to race Kathryn, and Kathryn raced by his side, well ahead of Waldgrave, and as fast as the wind among the paths of the forest. Faster and faster, and Dereham could not lose her, though they left Waldgrave behind.

After a long while Dereham slowed the pace of his horse, and Kathryn matched it, and because the animals looked sweaty, they walked the horses back to the stable. During that time they said almost nothing, which for Kathryn was very strange as she dearly loved to talk and tease. She didn't know if it was strange for Francis Dereham, but the occasional stare from his dark, dark eyes was all she could handle.

As she was leaving the stable, Waldgrave came in, riding his horse apace. He looked at Dereham and some intelligence seemed to pass between the men, then Dereham shrugged as if to say he didn't care. Kathryn, in turn, unable to understand what was happening, decided it was nothing to do with her and walked out. But Waldgrave cut her path at the door. "Mistress Howard," he said.

The way he pitched his voice low seemed to Kathryn as though he could want nothing proper with her. It reminded her of Manox and his ways. She took a step back, afraid of what might follow, and he said, "Mistress Howard, hold. I would . . . that is, I have a letter for you."

Kathryn looked at him in astonishment. "A letter," she said. "But we've barely spoken three words together."

"Oh, not from me," he said. "From my cousin, Henry. Henry Manox."

"What does Manox have to do with me that he should be writing to me?" Kathryn asked.

"Only he's working for a lord's household, teaching music to children, and always he says that he'll never forget you and that he's always thought himself bound together to you by promise."

Kathryn frowned. "There was no promise between us, no, and nothing to bind us either."

"But he said," Waldgrave started.

"Well, then he was mistaken."

Waldgrave proffered a much scuffed, folded piece of paper, sealed with wax. "If you'd but read his letter. He said that whatever you did, you should be sure to read his letter, for he is pining with loneliness for you."

Kathryn shook her head. "He has nothing to say to me, nor I to him," she said, and walked away so blindly that she almost ran straight into Francis Dereham. He had the oddest smile on his face, and she wondered what he meant by it. Perhaps he had heard her discussion with Waldgrave, and perhaps he truly thought she had pledged her troth to Manox. She didn't know why this idea vexed her so, but it did, and she slapped her bonnet against her thigh as she left the stables area to go to her room.

That night she was called to play for the duchess and her company—the Duke of Norfolk, who was visiting. As always, her playing was much admired and complimented, causing her to smile broadly and show two little dimples on either side of her face.

They asked her to play everything, from airs to madrigals, on the lute and on the virginal and finally the duke told his stepmother, "Well, you are right. There is something of Anne to her, and sure her playing is enchanting. Quite the best musician I've ever met. I'll see what can be done. I'll make enquiries."

After the duke had left, the duchess asked Kathryn to stay

behind, while her chamberer undressed the old lady with hands made deft by practice. "Do you wonder, Kathryn," the duchess asked, "what the duke wants?"

"Indeed," she said, "I don't, for I vow it won't be anything to do with me."

But the duchess laughed and said, "Forsooth, so modest, child. It is indeed to do with you. We're arranging to forward a great marriage for you. But there, I won't say more for fear of casting ill luck on the endeavor. Know only that your grandmother and your loving uncle are thinking about you."

Kathryn curtseyed and said thank you and left the room wandering what marriage they could possibly be forwarding for her while the pall of Queen Anne's execution still hung over the family. But she desisted from trying to understand it; for sure, if it were someone she knew, then the duchess would have told her who it was. And if it were not someone she knew, at least she was fairly sure it would not be a mere country squire; if it were, then the duchess would not say that it was a great marriage.

In this knowledge, she went through a curtain into a passage that led out of the duchess's chamber proper. At that moment, she heard footsteps behind her, and turned, in time to see Mary Lassells with pursed lips and an expression of great disapproval, standing right behind her. Since the last time the woman had been that near had been while she'd grabbed at Kathryn's hair and slapped Kathryn's face after catching her in the church with Manox, Kathryn was discomfited enough to step aside.

Noticing that the woman was holding a large basin full of steaming water—probably the remnants from helping the duchess's night grooming—in her hands, Kathryn leaned forward, to open the door, but for the second time that day, she was accosted with very odd words, "If you please, Mistress Kathryn Howard, I would have words with you."

"I beg your pardon?" Kathryn asked. "What can you have to say to me?"

"Only this. That on a recent errand for my lady into Horsham proper, I came across that Henry Manox with whom you used to be so pleased."

"It was a long time ago, and I knew nothing. I only tried to make him stop besieging me," Kathryn said. "I have told my grandmother everything."

"Yes, milady, and so you say." Mary made no move to put down the massive basin but stood there holding it, as though it were no encumbrance at all and she could not feel the weight of it. "And you might be telling the truth at that, but I'll have you know I accosted Manox and asked him why he's playing the fool." She frowned. "For you must know that more than once in the past months I've heard rumors that he was talking about you and saying that he intended to marry you, and I told him he couldn't be that foolish, for if he tried to do any such thing, your relatives would very quickly end his life. And then he told me that perhaps it was so, but it did not matter as his intentions toward you were strictly dishonorable. That he meant to have you, without ever marrying you, and that you'd promised him that he could have your maidenhood, though it hurt you, for you knew he'd be good to you afterward."

Kathryn felt as though the air escaped her lungs. She put her hand in front of her mouth to stifle a scream that was more than half frustration and rage. "What means he by this?" she said at last. "Has he run mad? For in the church that . . . that day you found us, he told me this, and I told him that I did not wish him to have my maidenhead and that—"

"Yes, milady," Lassells said, and it was of a sudden clear to Kathryn that the woman wasn't angry at her, but rather angry at Manox and afraid for Kathryn and Kathryn's reputation. "I know, I heard. My Lady and I went there almost as soon as you did, only delayed because she got the letter about . . . about Queen Anne, and we went in through the back, but I heard you say that to him clear as day, and it was clear to me, too, that he had been practicing the grossest deception on you, and that you had been doing nothing but trying to get him to stop importuning you, only you did not know how to do it." She sighed. "But I thought you should know what he's been saying. It is my opinion that he's mad with rage at failing to engage your affections and distraught that you didn't, indeed, pledge your troth to him. And when a man is like that, he can do or say anything. And now that my lady is trying to arrange a marriage for you . . . and such a marriage, too . . . Well, then, I think that you should meet with Manox one final time, and arrange it so that he knows if he continues speaking, you have friends as will avenge your honor. For I'm sure," Lassells went on, earnestly, "that any one of Her Grace's gentlemen will do that."

"I . . . yes, I will meet him," Kathryn said. "If you think it will help. Only not in the chapel and not under the stairs."

"Oh, no, madam," Mary said. "I will send word that you will meet him in the orchard tomorrow after supper, and if you be willing, I'll stay in the shadows a little far off, not close enough to eavesdrop, but close enough to rescue you should you need my assistance."

Eighteen

THE riding lesson was after breakfast, a breakfast of bread and cheese and ale of which Kathryn hardly partook, because she was thinking of the interview with Manox. She tried to put it out of her mind, for what use was there to thinking about it all day? And she was not supposed to see the man till the evening.

But worry lingered. She could tell herself that she was not worrying, but she could not actually banish worry as such. She could simply make it hide under a blanket of normalcy.

"So sad, Milady?" Francis Dereham asked her, as he helped her onto her horse. "It seems to me what you need is a good run through the paths in the preserve."

It seemed to Kathryn that, on the other side of her, Waldgrave sighed deeply, but she smiled at Dereham, showing her dimples. A wild ride through the forest was exactly what she needed, and she was glad he had realized it and made her realize it, too. "Indeed, sir," she said.

Once the horses had warmed to their paces, Dereham spurred his horse, and Kathryn too spurred the horse she was riding, and they hurried along faster and faster till Dereham slowed, as he had the day before. Only this time, as they came to a stop deep in the forest, he jumped from his horse and tied the animal to a nearby branch, then led Kathryn's horse, with Kathryn still on it, to the same point, and likewise tied it to a tree.

Then, without warning, he reached up, his hands around her waist, as he had done dozens of times before, and pulled her down from horse. Only this time, unlike the times before, instead of setting her on the ground, he pulled her close to him before setting her down, so that she was standing as close to him as a woman could be to a man when her feet touched the mossy floor of the forest.

"Master Dereham," she said, only her voice came out all breathy and odd, as if pronouncing her name made her dizzy. As though the thought of him were claret poured directly into her mind. "Master Dereham," she said again, and lest it be taken for a reproof, stretched her little hand and grabbed hold of his doublet and made as if to pull him closer, were that possible.

He smiled at her and put both arms around her, his dark, dark eyes seemed to shine with an interior light, as his eyelids descended halfway upon them. "Ah, Mistress Howard, you don't know how long I have wished to do this."

"Do what?" she asked, and then squeaked as he brought his lips down upon hers and kissed her hard, his tongue pushing its way between her unresisting lips and teeth, and playing with her tongue as though it were a snake disporting itself in its den.

She'd never felt anything like it. Oh, she'd done this, or very much the same, with Manox. But the feelings that went with it were all different. Kissing Manox had been fun, in the way that being touched was fun, and because she was the absolute center of Manox's attention.

Kissing Dereham was something wholly different. She wanted him as much as he wanted her—she could feel it in their kiss and in the little moan that escaped her and caused him to hold her yet tighter and kiss her yet more passionately. He moaned back into her lips, and his arms pulled her hard against him.

She could feel his manhood, hard and hot against her stomach, but she did not wish to pull back nor ask him what he was about. Instead, she threw back her head and willed herself to enjoy this kiss. Dereham's mouth tasted of the best ale, and like the best ale it felt as though it would turn her head. And his mouth and hers felt as though they should be linked, as though only then would they feel complete.

When his tongue withdrew, her tongue followed his, into his mouth, and he made a sound of surprise at it and let her kiss him, taking the lead in the game in which, until so recently, she'd been the prey.

"Mistress Howard, I didn't know you could kiss," he said.

"Master Dereham, neither did I. It only . . . it only feels natural."

He raised his eyebrows at her, forming two perfect dark semicircles against his broad forehead. "Indeed, it does, Kathryn Howard. I think I fell in love with you the moment I saw you, and that I was born to kiss you and to be kissed by you."

"They told me," she said, panting a little, with lack of breath and with her own daring, "that you were courting Joan Bulmer."

"Oh, that was so long ago," Dereham said, and smiled disarmingly. "And I was but a fool who knew no better. I didn't know you, Kathryn." He paused. "And they told me you were betrothed to Henry Manox."

"Oh, no, sir, I never was. Only he cried so much for my love and told me he would die without it and in common charity, I let him kiss me, but"—she hastened to add—"it was not, you know, the same as kissing you. For I had no joy in it."

He narrowed his eyes at her but smiled at the same time, giving the impression that he was tempting her to some exquisite pleasure. "But you have joy of my kissing, have you not?"

"Oh, so much," she said, and with that, rose on her tiptoes to kiss him again.

She didn't know how many times they kissed or how hard, because like time in paradise, time spent kissing Francis Dereham was perfect and without form or struggle. At last, it seemed to her she heard, very distantly, the sounds of hooves, and Francis pulled back from her.

"Hark," he said. "It is Waldgrave that approaches. Not that he'll tell on us, but all the same, this might not be the best of places to kiss you, for you see anyone might spy us at our pleasure."

As they pulled apart, Waldgrave had indeed arrived next to them and was sitting on his horse, patiently, waiting while Francis Dereham helped Kathryn up on her horse and then, after unfastening the animals from the branch to which they were tethered, mounted his own horse. "No, this is not the best place, Mistress Howard," he said, and grinned at his friend. "I shall have to ask Waldgrave to teach me his way."

Waldgrave scowled. "An' the trellis is sturdy enough," he said, and spurred his horse on and out of the way. It wasn't till they'd got to the stable and after making sure no stable hands were near that Kathryn, as Francis helped her down from the horse, dared to lean closer and ask, "Pray tell . . . the trellis?"

"Indeed. My fellow Waldgrave is mad in love with your bedmate, Alice. Nightly he climbs the trellis so that he may enjoy, as it were, paradise at the top."

"But . . ." Kathryn said. "She is my bedmate. They can't be meeting upon my bed. I do not sleep that soundly."

Francis laughed. "No, no. It is not like that. As I understand, there is another room or closet to which your room leads, and which was quite empty before Waldgrave and Alice managed to pull a mattress in there—one of the straw mattresses that was supposed to be discarded last year when the new ones were stuffed. The only thing you missed, Mistress Howard, was that your bedmate is not always there the entire night."

Kathryn remembered times of waking up in the middle of the night with Alice slipping back into the bed, her cold feet sliding in alongside Kathryn's body, and of sleepily asking Alice what she'd been about and being told that Alice had only been using the chamber pot. Now she knew better and felt an utter fool to have been thus led astray.

"Oh, I shouldn't feel bad to be taken in by Alice," Francis said, as though reading her mind. "For I am to understand she's the most accomplished little liar and thief. Edward Waldgrave brags that every other night at least she gets hold of the key from the duchess's own room, so she can let him in through the dormitory door all right and proper, and spare him the trouble and danger of climbing the trellis."

"How odd," Kathryn said. "And I never suspected any of this. It is as though I never knew Alice at all."

"Aye," Francis said, and there in the stables, it was clear that he didn't dare kiss her, but it was equally certain, from his gaze, that he longed to. "Aye, but you see, by learning all the contrivances we may use, they have paved the way for us. And now we shall enjoy the fruits of their labors. I can't promise, Mistress Howard, that I'll make it up the trellis tonight, but I will do it as soon as it is possible."

Nineteen

"MASTER Manox," Kathryn said, as soon as her former music teacher met her in the orchard.

It was obvious he had dressed in his best—a doublet that looked brand-new and was made of brocade, slashed through to show silk at sleeves and body. And he had a brand-new cap upon his hair, and he approached her with a smile on his face.

The face itself looked deeper, and the eyes more deeply carved than when she'd last seen him. It seemed to Kathryn that Master Manox must have slept badly since he'd last seen her or, perhaps, slept not at all.

The way he looked at her was hungrier than ever, and for just a moment, she was afraid he'd embrace her or kiss her or take hold of her hands. After the bliss she'd known in Dereham's arms, she wasn't sure at all that she could take the more common and coarser touch of Manox's hands.

"Kathryn," he said, and extended his hands to her, then, noting that she clasped her hands behind her back, let his own fall. But his eyes still burned with feverish hunger, and his voice shook with passion as he said, "Oh, I have missed you."

She didn't know what to answer to that, so she looked at

her feet, and she said, "I have heard you've been telling lies about me."

"Lies!" he said. "What lies have I told? And who told you so? I sent you a letter through Waldgrave, but he said that you wouldn't even accept it."

"I don't like reading," she said. "Or at least I don't like reading letters where the handwriting is formed whichever way, and besides, Master Manox, we have nothing to say to each other."

He put his hands forward again, as though he would hold her by the shoulders, and she stepped back hastily and said, "Do not touch me, or I shall scream."

"But, Kathryn! You met me under the stairs to the upper level of the chapel. And you met me in the chapel itself, behind the altar. How can you now pretend we never knew each other? And what could make you scream at my touch?"

"I never wanted to meet you," she said, hearing a faint note of hysteria in her voice. "You know I didn't. I only did it because you told me you were suffering and that my allowing you to touch me would relieve you. But it never did, and you just demanded more, and my grandmother said it was all a ruse, of the sort that men use to get women to let them into their beds."

"How can you say that?" Manox asked, his eyes blazing. "How can you say that, Kathryn, when you know what we were to each other."

"What we were, Master Manox? Have your wits gone begging? Didn't I tell you often that you were nothing to me nor could you be? That you could never marry me?"

He shook his head, as though by shaking it, he could deny the words she said. "But it is not like that," he said. "You enjoyed our kisses and embraces. I remember. I remember the sighs that escaped your lips and the moans—" Again he took a step forward, as though determined, once more to show her she could enjoy it.

And once more, Kathryn stepped backward, trying to avoid his hands. "We are not here for that, Master Manox, nor do I wish you to touch me or kiss me or hold me ever again. I've been brought to the grave conscience of my error, and all I want now is to keep myself pure and honest for my husband."

"Pure and honest!" he said, as though the words rankled. "My cousin tells me that Dereham is mad over you and that you encourage him."

"I don't know what your cousin tells you, nor is it any of your business whom I may be mad over. My aunt's chamberer, Mary Lassells, tells me that you have been telling everyone that I had pledged my troth to you, which you know well I've never done; and also that I had told you that you could have my maidenhead, even if it hurt me, because I knew you'd be good to me after; and also that your intentions were strictly dishonorable and you had no intention at all of marrying me, but only wished to see how far you could take your affair with me."

At these words, boldly spoken, Manox stopped. A wave of color came up from his neck into his cheeks, and it told Kathryn, clearer than anything else could, that Manox had indeed said those words to Mary Lassells. Whether he'd meant it or not was something else, something that Kathryn had little interest in knowing.

Manox clasped his head, the way he did when he was distressed. "Mary Lassells was so earnest and so full of herself," he said. "And I remembered the way she'd slapped you in the church, and I thought only of not getting you in further trouble, Kathryn. I swear on my soul's damnation that's all I thought of."

"I do not care for your soul or its damnation," she told him.

"Only that you stop telling these lies about me. I am only a poor girl, with no dowry and a marriage to get, and your loose tongue could damage my chances forever."

"It is only the great love I bear you that makes me say things," he said. "How am I to bear the thought that you are in another's arms? That there is someone else kissing your dear lips? That you allow a man full of coarse intent to caress your body, which should be mine only?"

He fell to his knees in front of Kathryn, and before she knew what he was about, he had taken hold of the hem of her dress. Kathryn was taken with great fear that he'd repeat his old tricks and kiss her privy parts right here, even as Mary Lassells spied from the shadows. But even as Kathryn took a step back, Manox was kissing the hem of her skirt, as though she had been a saint or a creature of great virtue. "I can't eat," he said piteously, looking up. "I can't sleep. I don't know what to do but pine for you."

"Well, then you can go on pining," she said, pulling her skirt away from his hands and mouth. "Mistress Lassells told you that if you married me, my relatives would put an end to you. I am now telling you that if your talk doesn't stop—if you insist on broadcasting lies about me from the rooftops and whichever way—I shall myself ensure that my friends destroy you utterly."

She stepped back farther. Manox hadn't got up from his knees and was staring at her with a horrified expression, when she said, "I do not want to be angry at you, Master Manox. Only keep your mouth shut, and we shall remain the greatest of friends." And on those words, she turned her back on him and marched right into the house and half ran up the stairs to the dormitory, where she hoped Dereham would join her.

Twenty

DEREHAM did not come up that night, and the next morning, while they were riding, he informed her that he had tried, but it was too likely he'd be seen climbing the trellis and, therefore, he'd felt it would be better not to risk it.

They rode into the forest well ahead of Waldgrave, who did not even make an attempt to follow, and when they were tired, they dismounted and walked their horses while talking. She told him about her meeting with Manox. It seemed natural to do so. As though she should tell him everything always, and it would only make sense that he would understand it and support her. And he seemed to, nodding as she spoke. "An' if he speak again, we'll make sure he suffers for it," he said.

He seemed to completely understand why she'd felt she had to allow Manox such liberties, and he was gentle about it when he told her the duchess was correct and that men would say the most outrageous things to women to get their love.

Then Kathryn told him about the duchess and the Duke of Norfolk, and what they had said about getting her a husband. This got a serious, worried frown from him. "I wish . . ." he said.

"Yes?"

"I wish I could offer for you, only right now I may not, as I do not quite have the means. Mind you, I will once my uncle dies. I wish . . ."

"Yes?"

"I wish you could promise me not to marry anyone for a few years, for it is bound to happen that I shall come into my inheritance, and then I will come to your grandmother and ask her for your hand."

Kathryn laughed. She hadn't meant to, but she couldn't help it, "Only, Master Dereham, I know not if I can do that. You see, I am only a girl and the daughter of a younger son. I cannot delay my marriage, nor do I have any means by which to do so."

He shook his head, and suddenly he turned, walking backward in front of her, next to his horse, holding the horse's reign. "Kathryn, pledge troth with me. Say that you will marry me, promise. Make a contract with me, for if you are married to me, then they can't make you marry anyone else. And if they do, you can tell them there is a prior contract and demand a divorce."

But Kathryn shook her head, doubtful. "I barely know you, Francis Dereham," she said.

"But do you not love me?" he asked. "I loved you from the moment I first saw you, your auburn hair, your beautiful eyes."

"Aye . . ." Kathryn hesitated. A part of her told her that, indeed, she loved Francis Dereham. But something deep within whispered that she could not trust herself to tell him so. She had known him so little. She remembered Manox who, though she'd never loved him, had seemed to be wholly devoted to her and never capable of causing her any harm. And hadn't Manox been spreading lies all over the length of the countryside. How could she trust anyone now, especially anyone she'd known such a short time.

"We will see by the by, Master Dereham," she said, and that was the only thing she would abide by, the only answer she would give him.

They returned to the stables, and if she fancied that Dereham looked a little stormy and a little angry over her refusal to pledge herself to him, she could not help but think that such roiling emotions looked good on his countenance, as he frowned and cast her smoldering looks from beneath the half-closed lids of his dark eyes.

It was exactly, she thought, like the knights in the romances of old, who were brought to grief by careless damsels and burned with an interior fire for them, despising themselves and unable to hurt the object of their desires and, yet, feeling that they had been betrayed or, perhaps, only loved insufficiently well.

He kept his silence when she curtseyed to him and left him to go back to the house.

That night she didn't expect to see him, and while Alice was combing out her brown locks, Kathryn got into bed and covered herself with her sheet and her thin blanket. She had removed her skirt, and had only, upon her body, the shirt that she'd been wearing underneath her bodice and her kirtle. It was long enough, reaching to her knees, that she would be quite decent, should she be forced to get up, and it was the clothing in which she usually slept.

She turned on her side and promptly went to sleep. In the middle of the night, she woke up a little, and it seemed to her that the bed had moved, the mattress shaking. She thought it would be Alice getting out of bed or perhaps in it.

And then she felt cold lips at the back of her neck, while cold fingertips pulled her hair aside, so that the lips may kiss her. "Kathryn, sweetheart. It is I."

She turned, still half asleep, and looked into Francis Dereham's dark eyes, barely visible by the light of the moon, which came through the window and bathed the room.

"Oh," she said, rubbing her eyes.

He smiled at her. "How prettily you sleep," he said, "like an innocent child, and so beautiful, I thought it would break my heart to wake you."

He smelled of roses, she thought, which made sense if he had climbed up the trellis that went from the ground to the window of the dormitory, since that trellis this time of year was loaded with fat, open red roses.

He now produced just one of those roses, and caressed her forehead and nose with its velvety petals. "It waylaid me on my way up the trellis," he said, and smiled. "It asked me where I was going, and I told it that I was going to see one who was far fairer than the moon up in the sky and, force, much brighter than the sun during the day, and then it begged me that I should pick it off it its stem and carry it up to you. And so I did. I had to hold it in my teeth, since both hands and feet were to be used for the climbing, but how could I refuse the wish of a flower that desired but to see true beauty before it wilted and died?"

She giggled, as he kissed the rose, then laid it upon her chest. Looking around she perceived he had opened the bed curtain a little to come in and hadn't bothered to close it after. Through that opening the moonlight came, and she liked the way it shone upon his face, making him seem very pale, and his eyes and hair darker than ever. But she dared not be like this, with him, in bed, and the curtain open. Let the curtain be closed, she thought and provided they speak in whispers, no one would know that he was not Alice.

He objected to the comparison, even as he closed the curtain.

"Fie. You cannot think I sound like Alice, even in a whisper. Surely my manly and distinguished voice sends different vibrations through you."

Kathryn blinked. "Art drunk?"

"Only from your presence," he said, and grinned disarmingly. "Your eyes have bewitched me, your smile has entranced me, the sound of your voice makes me stumble like one quite out of his senses, and your smell"—he inhaled deeply—"is far sweeter than that of any rose. If I have to die, fair Kathryn, let me die in your presence."

"I think you are drunk."

"In truth, I am not. Only happy that after so much waiting I have finally made it here. Alice, who does not treasure the joy of sharing your bed as she should, is off to her secret room with that laggard Edward Waldgrave, and I am here with you for the night, when I am all yours. What do you think we should do, Kathryn?"

Kathryn, smelling the rose, looked shyly at him. "Well," she said. "I would like to kiss you."

"Well, then kiss me you shall," he said. "Provided only that I may be allowed to kiss you also."

She started to protest that he was drunk or mad, but he didn't give her time, as he leaned in and closed her lips with a kiss.

Kathryn was afraid he would be like Manox and that after kissing her he would want to lift her shirt and look under it at her body and feel her skin and perhaps even kiss more intimate parts than Kathryn had ever thought anyone would want to kiss. But he did not do so. Instead he kissed her and let her kiss him, their lips joining, their bodies pressed against each other, until it seemed that the only breath they could draw was through each other's mouth.

After a long time, Kathryn, blissful, happy in Dereham's arms, felt her eyes closed and was kissed, face and forehead, nose and lips, very gently, until presently sleep enveloped her completely in arms as soft and loving as those of any lover. She tumbled headlong into them and woke up the next morning with Alice asleep next to her.

She would have thought it was all a dream, except that next to her on the floor was a red rose, starting to wilt for lack of water. She reached out a hand and touched the velvety petals with her fingers. She had not dreamed it. Dereham had been here and—oh—how sweet he'd been.

Twenty-one

"We must do something," Alice said. They were in their bed, once more, side by side, sitting up with their backs against the log that served them as a head rest.

"Something to make it easier for them to get into the dormitory?" Kathryn asked.

Alice inclined her head to one side, as though agreeing and thinking at the same time. "Yes," she said.

It had been many days now that Dereham had come up the trellis and that she'd fallen asleep kissing him. And now Alice said, "I can get the key from Her Grace, mind you, it's only . . ."

"It's only?" Kathryn said.

"That key or no key, even when I get it, we must hide and make sure that the rest of the room does not wake. And I think it is no way to conduct an affair, and so I've thought, and I've thought, and I've talked to the other women. All of them have beaus, you know, save only Dorothy Barwick," she said. "But her I think we can tempt with sweetmeats and other dainties."

Dorothy was the least attractive of the maidens, and her lack of attraction was due to her love of sweetmeats and other dainties, which had caused her to grow fat and so slow that she could get her wind up climbing two flights of stairs to their dormitory.

"So what do you propose to do?" Kathryn said.

"Only this," Alice said, her eyes sparkling, if with the joy of intrigue or because she genuinely loved Edward Waldgrave, Kathryn could not say. "Next time I get the key from the duchess, I shall give it to Edward, who says he can make a mold of it from wax and can get a copy made from that mold by a cunning smith he knows."

"Oh, it would be marvelous if he did that!" Kathryn said.

Alice smiled. "He is quite sure he can," she said. "And Edward says that he and Francis will be quite happy to bring in dainties—sweetmeats and oranges and all sorts of sweets and wondrous foods, only . . ."

"Only?" Kathryn said.

"Only you have to talk with Dorothy Barwick, because she likes you far better than she likes me."

"Oh, no," Kathryn said. "Dorothy doesn't like anyone."

"Not very much, no. And if you looked like her, perhaps you might not also," Alice said. "But among all the women in our dormitory that Dorothy hates, shall we say she despises you a little less than the rest."

Kathryn sighed. "I cannot imagine why."

"Oh, my dear, because you are the granddaughter of the duchess and play music very well and are very pretty. Dorothy is convinced you shall go far and, doubtless, wishes to hitch her star to yours, which, you must admit, is her only chance to get somewhere."

Kathryn was not all too sure, but after Dereham came and went, the next morning she endeavored to find some way to get close enough to Dorothy to speak to her without anyone else listening in and in such a way that Dorothy might be inclined to grant Kathryn a favor.

She found it by lingering after breakfast, having finished her ale and half of her bread, she sat taking dainty bites of the remaining bread and cheese, while everyone else left the table. Everyone but Dorothy. It was a well-known habit of Dorothy's to wait till all the others left the table, and to eat any leftover bread and cheese that they had chanced to leave behind.

This time, before she reached for the next abandoned slice of bread, Dorothy cast Kathryn a sidelong glance, and asked, "Do you wish—"

"No, no," Kathryn said, and pushed her own bread across the table at the other girl. "I only stayed because I wished to speak to you."

Dorothy took the bread, but her jaws stopped mid chew. "With me? About what?"

"Well, you know . . . some of us have . . . That is, there are gentlemen who care a great deal for some of the maids in the dormitory."

Dorothy looked at her awhile with an expression that was somewhere between confusion and disgust. At length, she spoke. "I know Alice and the others have long since allowed men to whom they are not married to break their maidenhead," she said. "Sinners all. God shall have no mercy for them."

"Not their maidenheads," Kathryn said, in an appeasing tone, vowing to pay Alice back for setting her this hopeless task. "Or not all of them. I for one am still a virgin."

Dorothy looked at her then shrugged. "Not for long. Beauty is a snare that the devil sets to catch men and women in the sin of lust. It is said," she said, in the tone of one making a deep pronouncement, "that Lilith was beautiful."

Kathryn bit her tongue. Were she being her natural self, she would tell Dorothy that food was a trap the devil set to catch men and women in the sin of gluttony. But it seemed hardly worth her while, and besides, it was likely to kill any chance she might have to get Dorothy to wink at their own transgressions. "Well," she said. "And it may be so, but it is no great sin we're after, but only . . . only a little amusement in the evening. Music and gentlemen visitors and some . . . and some food. The gentlemen are willing to bring dainties. Sweetmeats and oranges and other good things to eat."

Dorothy looked up at her a long time. For a while Kathryn was afraid she would call out or say she was going to the duchess and tell her what was afoot. But instead, Dorothy chewed in silence, eating Kathryn's slice of bread and another slice of cheese and then yet another slice of bread and cheese that one of the maids who had left had forgotten behind upon the table.

"And I would have my share of these dainties?" she asked. "Even though I have no lover."

"Oh, you'll have your share of the dainties," she said. "We will let you pick first."

As the other girl nodded, Kathryn thought that it might be easier to procure a willing man to be Dorothy's lover than to bring enough dainties to satisfy her.

Twenty-two

It turned out neither was so difficult, either finding enough sweetmeats to satisfy Dorothy Barwick or finding her a lover, for once word of the maids revelries spread, it became a point of hankering for the other gentlemen in the household to wish to join in the revelry, just to be near that many beautiful women and to partake in the dainties and the feast by candlelight.

Kathryn never knew if the rather heavy young man, the scion of a local squire family, was truly taken with Dorothy or only appeared to be so to be allowed to follow these other, more socially accomplished men, into a place where all of them hankered to be. It could be either, though the young man and Dorothy sat together and kissed a lot, and Dorothy seemed to eat less and smile more than she was used to.

Other than that, the whole thing was very easy. Easier than a dream. Now that they had a key to the maids' dormitory, the young men would arrive by twos and threes, sneaking up the stairs and getting in through the unlocked door, which was locked only after their number was fully admitted.

They brought, as they had promised, candles and sweetmeats, oranges and wine, and whatever other dainties they could acquire.

By candlelight, the dormitory became something of an enchanted realm where no desire was fully forbidden and where they could engage in revels, without fear of censure from their elders.

There weren't enough beds that each couple might have one, but people didn't mind sitting by the wall, on the floor, embracing and kissing. In fact, many was the time that Kathryn and Francis did just that, holding each other and kissing, so that Alice and Edward could have the bed that Alice and Kathryn were supposed to share.

Wine was passed back and forth in cups and flagons, sweetmeats were eaten, and jokes and jests enjoyed. Kathryn played the lute sometimes and sang, taking care not to project her voice too high, that she might not wake the maids in the other dormitories or, worse yet, the duchess herself.

They ate and they drank, they sang and they kissed.

And then one day Kathryn found herself under the covers with Dereham, the curtains around the bed closed. Dereham was in his doublet, which she unfastened, questing with her fingers, to feel his shirt and beneath it is chest and muscles. He let her feel as far as she would, and then he flipped her, so she was on her back, and gently, carefully, giving her full chance to say no, he lifted her shirt.

"Such pretty duckies," he said, as he ran his hand over her breasts. "A pair of twin duckies such as I've never seen, lifelong."

She laughed at him, but it came out shaky, for the movement of his fingers upon her skin, tracing the contour of each of her breasts and feeling along them with reverent care, seemed to send her quite out of her mind. She arched into his hands, as he caressed her, and his lips joined his hands in exploring her body. "Ah, Mistress Howard, how beautiful you are," he said. "And how much I love you."

She let him touch her and caress her, until she was all aflame with his lust for her and till she wanted him as much as he wanted her. And then she turned, and she made him lie back, and she quite undid his doublet and felt his chest, and down his flat belly, onto his codpiece, where his penis could be felt, through the velvet, erect and hot and pressing against her hands as she pressed back at it. Quite without knowing what she did, she found her fingers untying the ribbons on his codpiece and setting his penis free. It felt hot and velvety against her hands as she caressed it.

Francis arched his back and moaned, and the curtains on the bed parted, and a head poked through. "Hark to Francis Dereham, broken winded," Edward Waldgrave said, sounding much the worse for drink.

Kathryn pulled her shirt down and shrieked, and Dereham pulled a blanket over to cover himself. He laughed feebly in his friend's direction, even as Waldgrave announced, "It is time to go, now, love birds, for it is not possible to stay here and love till dawn, since the servants, and the duchess and all the rest would be bound to notice it."

Dereham made a sound that wasn't quite words, which signified that he knew this well, and when Waldgrave had retreated, he turned to Kathryn, "And now, my love, now, will you pledge to marry me? For I can't imagine myself being happy with any other woman but you, and if it requires me to work or adventure or do what I must to get enough of a fortune to aspire to your hand, I will do so. Only, fair Kathryn, say that you will marry me and be my own sweet wife."

She looked at him, and she ducked her head. She had experienced such bliss with him these last few days that she could not imagine being happy—or married—with anyone else, either. "I will marry you, Francis Dereham," she said. "And I will be yours."

"Well then," he said. "We are betrothed. And you know that once we are betrothed we are as good as married and no one, not even the church, will object to our sleeping together and taking all the joys that married couples do."

"Oh," she said. Though she wasn't sure how they were to bring this about, or how she could refuse her uncle and her grandmother should they choose to marry them to someone else, yet she was sure that she would somehow manage it and absolutely sure that it was right and meet.

"And now I go," Dereham said, fastening his clothes, and leaning over to kiss her. "Keep well, my dear wife, and I shall see you in the sunny morning for our ride."

Twenty-three

FROM then on, Dereham called her "my dear wife." He procured her a length of fabric, which she gave to the seamstress to make into a cap. The seamstress embroidered it with true lover's knots, which Francis said was just as it should be.

Every night he came, and they caressed, their caresses growing ever more daring. It seemed to Kathryn that day by day she got to know his body till it seemed like she knew it as well as she knew her own—she knew how he tasted and how he felt and what each of his reactions meant, and she knew how to please him well. But as yet, they had not done that to which he referred to as what husband and wife did together.

She was afraid that she might get with child, but Francis told her, for now, he'd pull out right quick before he spilled his seed in her. "We needn't get a child unless we list it," he said. "And we won't list it until we're married for everyone to see and in our own estate."

She'd always heard losing your maidenhead would hurt, and also that you would bleed all over the bed. But it did not hurt very much, and the only blood was but a spot on the blanket. Of course, it also didn't last very long. There was the moment of his inserting his part into hers and the sudden shock of the intimate connection, and then, it seemed like, it was done.

She enjoyed most the moment afterward when he held her tight in his arms and kissed her fervently, telling her how beautiful she was and how now they were truly married.

Kathryn fell asleep in Dereham's arms, but she woke up alone in the morning. However, she fretted not, for she knew he would be back.

Twenty-four

ONE month slid into the next, their evening parties and the lovemaking with Francis, all seeming like part of some enchanted land where only good things would happen. In September they heard that the queen had an heir, and the duchess seemed unhappy about it, but not for long, for it seemed the queen, that whey-faced wench, died shortly after giving birth to the prince.

Kathryn started noticing the duchess looking at her with a long, speculative glance, while Kathryn went about her usual tasks, or sat in the duchess's chamber, playing the virginal or the lute while the duchess read and signed papers or talked to her tenants and farmers.

And Dereham kept coming into the room. Intercourse got more interesting, too, as it didn't last just the space of a breath but longer, and it roused feelings in her that even Manox's talented tongue had not managed. She learned to pleasure him, also, with her hands and her mouth and every part of her being.

"My dear wife," he called her, and well might he have done, for she was his wife in all but that neither priest nor parent had heard their betrothal. But it was learned of, anyway, in yard and dormitory. Not that they ever told it to anyone, or not that boldly.

In spring, the duchess said they would go to Lambeth again, just a few miles from London. She made some remark about the court, and Kathryn looked at her in surprise. "The court, ma'am! But there is no queen, so there can be no place for me."

The duchess looked up from a pile of papers and stared at Kathryn in silence for a moment, then cackled. "Ah, as the sun rises in the east, Kathryn Howard, there will soon be another queen."

"But why?" Kathryn asked. "How? Surely now he has a prince an' heir and—"

"And he'll want him a queen to warm his bed, aye, and to stand behind him at ceremonies. And no throne is so secure that he will not want a younger brother for Prince Edward, either, now that he's made both princesses illegitimate."

"But . . ." Kathryn looked at the lute she'd been playing and tried to count the number of wives the king had already. Three she made it, and everyone knew he had mistresses, too, like Bessie Blount, who'd been the mother of his older son. "But how many wives can he mean to have!"

The duchess cackled, spontaneously, at Kathryn's shocked look, and laughed outright as Kathryn looked yet more shocked. "He'll have as many as he wants, and his being the king. Didn't you hear, girl, about King Solomon."

"What, with his thousand wives?" Kathryn asked. The story had always seemed to her rather scandalous.

"Indeed. And he an anointed of God. So you see, the king can have as many an' more."

"But King Solomon, madam," Kathryn said, "didn't divorce them or behead them when he wished to take a new one."

"No indeed," the duchess said. "He had them all at the same time. I've always thought to myself what it might mean and how it might work. Did he have them all in at once or a goodly number of them, or did he draw sorts? And how did he stop the squabbling that is common where many women gather together? What's more, how did he know if their children were his or not? Surely he couldn't keep an eye on each of them every minute of the day nor could there be guards enough . . ." She seemed lost in thought for a moment. "Eunuchs, I suppose." And looked up to what Kathryn felt must be her expression frozen in horror. The duchess laughed again. "Close your mouth, girl, before you catch a fly. No, our king cannot play Solomon, though it's often been said he looks on the maids of honor as his own personal seraglio. But there's been no proof of that, save only Bessie Blount, and she . . . well, no better than a common drab."

The duchess stopped talking, as Kathryn managed to close her mouth and turned her attention to her lute, plucking a desultory tune upon the strings. After a while, she became aware of the duchess's eyes on her once more. "But you know, Kathryn," the duchess said, as though she were continuing an interrupted conversation and merely adding to reasons already given. "You know that the king is getting old, and soon, whatever wife he picks will be his last—and with his son still small and both his daughters declared illegitimate, think what power his last wife will have. Why! She might as well be queen herself, in her own right."

Kathryn thought about it and sighed as, for the first time, she understood what power Queen Anne had been trying to grasp when marrying a man that much older than herself. It was well known that dowagers could have more power than anyone else, male or female, for they had the normal dispensations of a woman but could rule money and lands like a man. To be the dowager of England . . .

"Ah, I see you understand," the duchess said.

And Kathryn understood indeed. The power of it and the freedom and, she supposed, the glory and power for her family. She sighed. "Ah, well," she said, "it is not likely to be anybody we know." She'd heard rumors and repeated them, while her fingers played, heedless, with the lute. "I've heard he's sent delegations abroad to look at foreign princesses, though I didn't give it much thought, what with his wife so recently dead."

"I don't give much thought to his sending delegations, either," the duchess said. "Our king has always seemed to prefer Englishwomen."

They spoke no more of the king's marital prospects or of the wondrous power that would come to his dowager. Instead, Kathryn played her lute till she was dismissed to walk out into a household that was already preparing for its trip to Lambeth.

Rugs and blankets were out in the big yard between stable and house, getting beaten and aired, prior—Kathryn assumed—to being rolled up and packed for the trip to London.

And amid the bustling servants, the confusion of horses being picked for the trip, and of carriages and litters being cleaned, Kathryn walked right into a group of her fellow maids and the gentlemen in attendance. She registered a momentary shock at seeing Manox—a thinner and unhealthy-looking Manox—among them.

He gave her a dark, suffering glance, which she guessed was meant to stab her through the soul, but she let her eyes glance over him, remembering the duchess's injunction to not try to cheer up every sad soul or heal every harm someone told her she had caused.

Instead, she joined the group without looking between whom she was standing and was startled to feel a hand around her waist, then smiled when she saw that it was Francis standing next to her.

"Hark," Alice said. "Me thinks that Master Dereham means to have Mistress Kathryn Howard for his wife."

"You might guess twice," Francis said, laughing. "And guess worse." He grinned, "Is it not so, my dear wife?"

"Indeed," she said, smiling. "It is so, dear husband."

It seemed to her that Manox flinched at her words and went a shade paler, but she looked away.

"Is that the hat made from the fabric I gave you?" Dereham asked, taking her hand and squeezed it. "What a handsome hat it is. With true lover's knots upon it."

Kathryn nodded and looked up, and Manox was quite gone.

Twenty-five

THEY came upstairs by twos and threes in the night. Dereham was, as usual, first and got into bed with Kathryn straightway, pulling the curtains closed around them. She had on her loose shirt that she wore under her normal clothes and nothing else. He wore a doublet and hose, but got under the covers, which meant, she knew, that they'd end up, sooner or later, naked in bed.

Upon first getting in bed, he kissed her hard, holding her close. "How difficult it is," he said, "to prevent myself from kissing you every time I see you."

She smiled at him, as soon as he let her go. "You were daring enough," she said. "Holding my hand like that in the yard, and calling me your dear wife."

"Well . . . an' did you not see Manox's face? He richly deserved it, the presumptuous rooster, thinking he was ever good enough to touch the hem of your dress."

Kathryn thought of Manox, on his knees, literally kissing the hem of her dress, and she shivered. Such a form of obsession seemed to her very little short of madness. What would not a man thus infected do? She suspected he would do anything and dare anything, and she did not think she was far wrong.

"Ah, Manox is all in the past now," she said, as she leaned near Dereham for another kiss. "For I am wholly yours."

He kissed her hard, then soft, then kissed her forehead, and frowned a little. "Indeed, Kathryn, and do you not forget it."

"How could I forget it?"

"I know not," Dereham said. "But I don't want to be like poor Manox, forever parted from your heart."

"How could you be," she said, taking his hand and setting it over her heart, "and you so near it."

He smiled this time, then sighed. "A time might come . . ." he said, and frowned. Then took a deep breath, as though a man forcing himself to plunge into a frozen lake. "You see, Kathryn, I heard . . ."

"What heard you? That I would forget you?"

He chuckled. His hands caressed her shoulders and ran down her sides, as though they needed to remember her contours. "Not quite that, though I fear it. I heard that your grandmother, aye, and your uncle are even now plotting to marry you."

"Marry me!" Kathryn said. "Then you heard more than I did. To whom do they intend to give me?"

"Some knave," he said. "Thomas Culpepper by name. It seems he's very great in the king's house and his favored companion, and thus they seek royal favor by delivering you onto his hand."

"Culpepper!" she said in astonishment, remembering the russet-haired man who had so devoutly squired what seemed to her now a very little girl through the perils of a London gone mad for the coronation. "Thomas Culpepper!" She realized it had been only four years ago that she had met him, but what a time it seemed. He had treated her—aye, and she had felt—like a very young girl and utterly lost. And he had failed to visit her as he'd said he would.

She'd never even seen him again. And he'd certainly never fulfilled his promises to her. "He promised me strawberries," she said, and was surprised to see a jealous look inflame Dereham's dark eyes.

"Kathryn!" he said. "You know him, then!" He pulled a little away from her on the bed, as though he thought she might have Culpepper hidden under the covers, Kathryn thought.

"No, no," she hastened to say. "Or only a very little. You see, he is my cousin. My distant cousin, upon my mother's side, my mother's name before marriage being Jocasta Culpepper. But I haven't seen Thomas since I was a very little girl." She thought of him holding her in his arms, as he twirled her round and round.

In her memory he was a very tall man and more powerful than any she'd ever met since, able to hold her and twirl her, and do with her as he pleased. She was sure this was but because her memory of him came from when she was very small. She had grown since. She wondered what he would look like to her now.

"And he promised you strawberries?" Dereham frowned at her, his expression puzzled, as though he were making a desperate effort at understanding.

"Aye. He said he would come visit and bring me strawberries. But he never did."

"You see," Dereham said, smiling. She could tell from his smile that he was imagining her as a much smaller girl than a mere four years ago. "You cannot go and join your fate to such an oath breaker."

"Indeed, I cannot," Kathryn said, and smiled back, thinking that in her mind the whole event seemed as though it had happened many, many years ago, and why should it not be so? Why should she tell Dereham anything that would distress him? What good would come of it? But her heart beat just a little faster. If she were to find herself betrothed to Thomas Culpepper by the force and will of both families, how could she avoid it? How could she even oppose it? It was very well of Dereham to say that she should say nay, or else say she was pre-contracted, but how would any take their contract seriously?

Oh, true, and she'd heard this, in cases when a husband decided to put his wife away or else claim the marriage had never happened, contracts such as theirs—no more than two children pledging troth in dark, with no sanction from any authority—were used as an excuse. But that's all they were ever used as—an excuse. There was nothing more in it, and she didn't remember a single case when authorities bowed to the pre-contract of two mere lovers.

"But you . . . can't you offer for me, Francis?" she asked softly. "Then we could be contracted to be married, and no one could separate us."

"We are contracted to be married, and no one can separate us," Dereham said.

She shook her head. "We are contracted, it is true. But—"

The dark eyes acquired a dangerous shine. She'd seen it before when Dereham looked hard at a man whom he thought was disputing his word or contesting his place. Sometimes he even looked that way at his friend Edward Waldgrave. "Mean you to play me false?" he asked. "To forget our contract as though it had never happened. I warn you, Kathryn—"

She didn't want to know of what he warned her. She cut in with, "No, no. I mean to play you true. I mean to be your wife in law as I am in troth, but, Francis—"

"Do you not *but* me, Kathryn Howard, for of sure fact you are plighted to me in the eyes of God and if you were to lay with any other man, it would be adultery."

His voice had risen so much that Kathryn was sure it would be heard all through the dormitory. She thought that the other sounds, out there, of laughter and voices and kisses, had stopped. She thought everyone out there was eagerly listening to them. She swore they were even holding their breath as they listened to their argument.

She put her finger to her lips then spoke in a whisper, "Calm yourself, Francis. I never mean to lay with another, ever. You are my husband and I am your wife." Even as she said it she felt a little shiver, for she'd never meant to tie herself to a man who'd ill-treat her or behave as if he owned her, and from the dark look in Dereham's eyes, it seemed to her that he was just one such. How had she never seen it before? He'd always seemed so easygoing, such a gentle lover.

"But you said," he reminded her, his voice somewhat lower, "that you might have to marry whomever your family decides."

She shook her head. "It is not like that. Only that . . . Surely you understand my wishes are never made much of. And then, you know, no woman gets much say in whom she marries . . ."

"You just tell them that you're pre-contracted," he said. "And they cannot force you." But he must have caught the look of fear on her face, because he ran his hand gently down her cheek. "Ah, Kathryn," he said. "What a foolish girl you are. If you are already married, how can they make you marry another?"

She sighed. "Only, I'd feel much better," she said, desperately thinking of another way to tell him her thoughts, one that would not cause him to upbraid her for unfaithfulness or lack of love, "if you could ask my grandmother for my hand. Sure she'd give it to you, for she likes you well. And then we could be married in the eyes of the world, as well, and you could kiss me in public if you so wished."

He laughed, a laughter that sounded sad at the same time. "Ah,

Kathryn. If only it were that simple. Oh, it is true that the dowager likes me well enough . . . How well, I don't know, but she grants me much indulgence. I've long suspected she knew how it was between us, too, for when my uncle came looking for me, he says she told him that if he could not find me anywhere else, he should look in Kathryn Howard's chamber." He shook his head, slightly, as though considering the strangeness of his elders.

"But she hasn't punished us," Kathryn said. "You see, she approves of you!"

Francis laughed again, that odd, broken laughter that seemed amused at itself. "Of me, perhaps, Kathryn, but not of my fortune. My birth is well enough, I'll give you that, as is my means . . . but not enough to marry the daughter of a Howard."

"But I am the daughter of a penniless Howard," she said, softly. "My father . . . if only you knew it. He lived on my mother's fortune and then the fortune of his next wife and then . . . I heard that he had died, or at least the duchess talks of him as though he'd died, so perhaps his last wife, Dame Margaret, managed to keep some of the money she brought into the union. But between his marriages, we lodged at common boarding houses, or else we presented ourselves, all ten ill-dressed children, at the door of better-heeled relatives and made ourselves guests there for as long as we could before they turned us out. My clothes were small and much mended, my food was scant, and there was never any money for masters . . ."

He shook his head. "And yet all that matters not, for you are still a Howard and still the granddaughter of a duke. If you were begging in the gutter, yet you would be above my means. I misdoubt your grandmother will let you go to anyone with less than a manor at their command, and I don't have that, nor will I have it, unless my uncle dies and dies childless."

"What then?" Kathryn said. "Yes, yes, I can tell them I am pre-contracted, but you know they have means to make me obey."

She was afraid he'd be angry again, but this time he wasn't. Instead, he seemed to be deep in thought. He shrugged at her. "Well," he said. "We will . . . There is perhaps an enterprise I may join, off the coast of Ireland. It involves . . . some business in which it is possible to make enough money to amass a fortune overnight."

"Privateer?" she asked, having heard of some of these enterprises.

He shrugged. "Something like," he said. "But not quite." He frowned, his features becoming for a moment cold and dark and distant. "I do not care what risks I run, nor even if I die, Kathryn, only you stay faithful to me till I come back."

And then, as though he were a man dying of thirst, who'd been lost in the desert a long time, he tore at her shirt, pulling it up in a passion till he had her wholly naked upon the bed. And then he fell on her, kissing her—her forehead, her eyelids, her lips, her chin, her neck with light butterfly kisses; her breasts with kisses so rough and hard that she cried out; and then continued kissing down her stomach and her legs to her feet, and then back up again.

When his face was close to hers, she was shocked to see that he was crying, great tears falling down his face and dripping from his well-trimmed beard. "Ah, Kathryn, the thought that I might lose you makes me want to end my life, entire. Ah, Kathryn."

She squirmed under his touch, and she could tell that he was serious, and she could tell that he was passionate and indeed that he was starving for her touch and her kisses and her love.

But for the first time in their lovemaking, she felt much as she had with Manox—something had put a distance between them. His display of temper, she thought, and the way he had looked at her, as though he might crush her in the pursuit of his desires. It seemed to her that there was another Francis Dereham beneath the man she knew, one that she'd never encountered, one that she was not absolutely sure that she wanted to be exposed to.

It was this Francis, she thought, who was ravaging her now, for his lips and hands were rougher than they need be, and he seemed to be slacking his appetites on her more than caring if she enjoyed it or, indeed, if she experienced any pleasure in his touch.

His hands moved only to feel her, and his lips kissed her hard and rough, and now his fingers were between her thighs, probing at her most secret place, but he hadn't noticed that she just lay back or that her body was perfectly unresponsive to his probing. He didn't seem to know or care if she were as inflamed with his passion as he was. Not even as he entered her and called her name, softly, many times.

She felt the rise and fall of the rhythms of passion in her body as though it were happening to someone else. Her head turned, she was looking through the thick, dark, bed curtains, and seeing the candles flicker out there and the candle flames move, as someone wished more light for what he was doing.

The lute played plangently, and she heard someone laugh loudly—she thought it was Dorothy Barwick. And then a murmur of voices. Dereham was panting, as he thrust into her. How could she feel so distant from it all? Was he not her husband before God? Had she not pledged her troth to him? And why did some part of her very much hope that wasn't true, even if it meant that by allowing him this liberty, she was a slut.

Dereham whispered once more, with feeling, "Kathryn!" and collapsed upon her, his weight only prevented from crushing her by his taking his weight upon his elbows.

"Sluts, slatterns, abandoned women," a voice yelled and for a moment—for the time of a breath—Kathryn thought that it was her conscience that was upbraiding her.

Then Dereham jumped and started frantically doing up his codpiece, and she realized the voice had sounded from outside and, in fact, was no other voice than Mary Lassells. "What a pretty party to be having here, when her ladyship is abed and your dormitory is supposed to be locked!" Mary Lassells yelled. "Sweetmeats and wine and all. What a pretty pastime for ladies and gentlemen to be meeting thus in this place, like common thieves and gluttons."

There was a pause. Kathryn could hear shuffling and movement out there, and one or two girls were crying, but she could not imagine what was happening from the sound of it. She pulled her knees up and into her, and hugged them fiercely, while she closed her eyes and prayed with all her might that God might protect her, and that Lassells and whoever else was out there—for she doubted that Lassells alone would cause that much consternation—would simply think that she was asleep.

Dereham must have thought the same thing, for he rolled off the bed, and she could hear him squeezing himself into the dusty space underneath.

Confirming Kathryn's worst fears, the duchess's voice sounded, loud and ominous. "Put all those foodstuffs into that basket there. I doubt not you've been raiding my pantry, for else, where would you have got such. Mistress Alice Restwold, you may pack your things separately from those of us who will be going to Lambeth, for you will be returning to your father's household upon daybreak with a full account of what I saw with mine own eyes between you and Master Waldgrave. How your father deals with you, it is his choice, though I've been told it was you who stole my key and had it copied, and were you mine I would have you beaten then sent abroad to some foreign convent. But you're your father's daughter, and he may do with you as you please."

Kathryn shivered, and she prayed harder. She could hear steps out there, but she didn't realize anyone was approaching her bed, till the curtain was torn open, and she found Mary Lassells staring at her. Then she heard the *tap-tap* of the duchess's walking stick, and she thought that it would presently fall upon her, but instead, the duchess said, sharply, in a tone that made it clear she was being sarcastic, "Oh, and look. Here is my virtuous granddaughter, sitting all alone amidst the debauchery. Be it not that she sleeps naked, she could be the most honorable maiden in the kingdom."

Kathryn looked at the duchess with piteous eyes, trying to form a lie in her mind, but none would come. The only words that came to her mouth were, "Oh, please—"

At that moment a sneeze sounded from beneath the bed. In less time than it takes to say it, the duchess had fallen upon her knees with quickness that should be impossible for a lady so advanced in years, and she was thrusting her stick under the bed.

There was a loud yelp, and then Dereham shot out the other side on his hands and knees.

The candles had gone out, and so, though Kathryn could see he was grabbed by two tall men, she could not tell who the men were. She gave them no thought, at any rate, sure they were the sort of men that her grandmother kept around her whenever she needed strength and muscle. "Take him away," the duchess said drily. "And teach him a lesson he won't soon forget for daring to meddle with a Howard."

She looked back at Kathryn. "As for you, you must come with me and we must talk."

Kathryn, in expectation of the stick falling upon her, tried to grab at her shirt but failed, and instead got the sheet. This she wrapped around her as her grandmother herded her with the walking stick out of the room and into the silent hallway and stairwell, leaving Mary Lassells and however many strong men behind to deal with the rest of the unruly dormitory.

Twenty-six

KATHRYN was crying by the time they arrived at the duchess's chambers, clutching her sheet around her and trying to look as though she had been innocent, though she rather suspected from what had passed that her grandmother knew far too much to be taken in such a way by mere pretending.

The duchess pushed Kathryn onto a chair and only then did Kathryn notice several things: that the room was well illuminated, with multiple candles on several locations, both on the wall and at various tables. And second, that two people were sitting on chairs, on either side of the one onto which Kathryn had been pushed.

The people, she saw but could not understand, were her uncle the Duke of Norfolk, Thomas Howard, and his wife, Elizabeth.

Since it was well known that the duke and his wife lived at daggers drawn with each other over the fact that the duke had taken a mere laundress for his mistress and sired several children upon her, it seemed odd to see them both in the same place at the same time. The dowager duchess herself had told Kathryn more than once that she had rarely seen the two in the same room and sometimes she thought they had divided the house in such a way that they need not run into each other.

Even now, they were not looking at each other, and only slowly turned to look at her, even as the duchess circled around the three to go sit in front of them, facing them, as though she were a judge evaluating their sins.

"I had a letter today," she started, after she sat down, speaking in that brusque manner she had, as though she were continuing an interrupted conversation and everyone should know what she'd said before that. "That displeased me much. It was left at my seat in the chapel during the evening mass, and you may judge how it distracted me from my prayers when I read its contents." She nodded. "It told me that my granddaughter, Kathryn Howard, a wench I brought into my household out of the goodness of my heart and to lighten the burden of her father, Edmund, may God rest his errant soul, had not only been entertaining Master Francis Dereham, but she had, if you please, pledged her troth to him. Like that, with no blessing and no permission. And they've been calling themselves husband and wife, as though all were proper in their relationship."

She paused and looked at Kathryn. "Right well I knew that something was forward between Master Dereham and Mistress Kathryn Howard, for I am no fool, and I can see well enough. And I knew he went into the dormitory, sometimes. I have, in truth, told his uncle to seek him in her chambers, hoping this would give him the understanding he needed to talk with his nephew and stop anything that might be excessive. Alas, this did not happen, and alas it seems to me the affair was far more advanced than I believed.

"For once I questioned one of the wenches, Joan Bulmer, she right away told me everything I needed to know. How Alice Restwold had made free of my key and had it copied by a cunning artificer, and how each of the girls had been admitting lovers in to disport with them, long after they should have been asleep. How those lovers brought many good dainties to eat. And she particularly told me how Francis Dereham—who before Kathryn was a devotee of Joan Bulmer herself—had spent more than a hundred nights in my granddaughter's bed."

Kathryn was crying. She realized it because she felt the tears falling down her cheeks, but she did not dare say anything or make any sound, as she was quite sure that her grandmother was working up to banish her forever from the house. Why else make reference to having taken her by charity and to relieve Edmund of her care? And where would she go, now?

She didn't dare look toward the duchess, so she looked toward her uncle who was sitting at her right side.

The duke gave her a pale smile. "And someone wrote Your Grace about it?" he said, and smiled broader and winked at Kathryn. "What madcap wenches you are," he said. "Can't you just make merry among yourselves without these fallings-out?"

"It wasn't a wench who wrote me," the duchess said, ponderously. "It was that Henry Manox who used to be Kathryn's music teacher."

A long silence stretched, during which Kathryn had time to realize that both her uncle and her aunt were as aware of her past indiscretions with Manox as her grandmother was.

Her aunt cleared her throat at long last and said, "Well, girl, beshrew my soul. You should be careful about this. Were these parties every night?"

Kathryn looked over at her aunt and nodded a meek yes.

"Well, then," Elizabeth Howard said, heatedly. "You should be careful, for you must know that so much eating every night will injure your figure. Only look you to Dorothy Barwick and—"

The dowager duchess coughed. "Well, let us hope, Elizabeth, that what she's been doing with Dereham hasn't already injured her figure."

The adults fell quiet till Kathryn suddenly realizing what those words tended toward said, "Oh, no! For we knew a way where we could . . ." She went red in the face. "Where no child would result."

The duke moaned softly, as though his worst suspicions had been confirmed and the dowager duchess said, "Mean you it truly went so far?"

"We were married," Kathryn said, hysterically. "Or at least we thought ourselves so, for we'd pledged our troth, and does not the law count that as married?" Her tears started again, on hearing the thin, desperate note in her voice, and she covered her face with her hands.

Nothing was said in the room, but she had the odd sense that the duke and the dowager duchess, his stepmother, who normally did not see things the same way, were looking at each other and forming some understanding.

At long last, the duke's fingers touched her arm. "Kathryn, listen, child, this never happened."

She rubbed her eyes to clear the tears, then looked at him. "But it did, milord. We pledged our troth, both of us, in my bed when he—"

"No, Kathryn, listen, it never happened." The duke looked intently at her. "Those words were never said, and he was never in your bed with you."

"But—"

"Child," the dowager duchess said. "I have told you before, and I will say it again. Do not be more stupid than you can help. Who is there to say any of this happened?"

"The . . . the other maids!"

The duchess made a gesture dismissing the other maids. "Unless they were in the bed with you, faith, they cannot know what you said, and besides, Kathryn, they cannot know what you did, not if you kept the bed curtains closed."

"Oh," Kathryn said, as the hope of escape presented itself to her. "There is . . ." she said, "Francis."

The dowager made a clicking sound with her tongue. "Some of my gentlemen are having a talk with Master Dereham and, Kathryn, when they're done, he'll have no inclination at all to claim better acquaintance with you than of what can be seen between your dress and your bonnet."

"But . . ." Kathryn squirmed. Into her knowledge of what passed between her and Francis went her fascination with him and her love for him, or what she thought had been love. But had it truly? She thought of that moment in her bed, when he'd thought she'd changed her mind on her promises and how suddenly dangerous and ugly he looked, and she shivered, as though a window had opened somewhere, letting a cool breeze in. "But I did give him my promise. Of my own free will."

The duchess shook her head. "He knows more than you do, Kathryn, and he used you as he pleased. I would not doubt—not for a moment—that he has had such a string of broken promises at his back. He's a beautiful gentleman, is Francis Dereham, and he has a good head on his shoulders, generally, but . . . He's young, and I'm sure he hasn't reached his present age without pledging his troth to a half dozen maids, promises that he forgot when they were no longer convenient. This is why one doesn't do it without consent and not without proper witness."

"And sometimes even then," Elizabeth Howard said, "it is not all clear."

"No," the dowager said. "So, Kathryn, your uncle is right and this never happened. It was a dream you had and nothing more. We will talk to the other girls, also. Even Mistress Restwold will be given a chance at reprieve if they learn to hold their tongues."

"And if Francis is still inclined to talk . . ." the dowager said. "Well, there are other things that can be done. Things of a more permanent sort that will ensure he never again blackens your name."

"Indeed," the duke said. "You cannot let a mere scallywag like Francis, with hardly a feather to fly with, stand in your way. Not when you're so beautiful and talented at dance and music and . . ."

"And other arts which gentlemen love," his stepmother finished. "Only, listen, remember what I once told you about this. Remember that as far as your husband—once you marry—is concerned, these arts are a closed book to you. Let him teach you, so that he can feel sure that he is always the most important, the central person in your life."

It seemed to Kathryn that her Aunt Elizabeth snorted, but all Kathryn did was nod.

"Good," the duchess said. "You shall go to your room and put your shirt on and go to sleep. And tomorrow we will pack to go to Lambeth in London. For we have arranged for you a most glittering marriage."

"With Thomas Culpepper," the duke said.

"My cousin?"

"Well . . ." the dowager said, "I believe he is some form of cousin to you, though distant, but the more important thing here is that he is a well-set-up gentleman and has been raised, as it were, in the king's chambers and in the king's favors. Being well set and smart, there is nowhere he might not rise."

"Only, of course, he cannot marry you while you remain wholly provincial," the duke said. "So we've arranged it so that before your marriage is announced, you shall go to court."

"To court, but . . ."

"Oh, there will be a queen soon enough, and the king is giving signs of reorganizing the ladies so that the queen might have attendants. So we'll go to Lambeth and from there it will be easy to put in an application—which I believe your uncle has already made—that you should become one of the queen's maids-in-waiting."

"So you see, my poppet," her uncle said, patting her awkwardly on the arm, "how important it is that you be clean living and innocent with your maidenhead still intact and that you never have pledged your troth with any man."

"Yes, indeed," the duchess said. "It is a good thing you've been brought up so carefully. Otherwise, Lady Rutland, who oversees the ladies-in-waiting at court would never allow you in, for she's very strict about morality and upholding all such just standards."

Kathryn inclined her head. She still felt as though Francis Dereham were being unjustly treated, but it seemed as though, for his safety as well as hers, she must treat their love as though it had never happened.

Twenty-seven

BEFORE leaving, Kathryn went to the stable to say her good-byes to the horse she'd ridden. Strangely, though she was not sure about her love with Francis nor anything that had passed between them, she remembered those rides fondly and wished that they'd stayed only at those rides.

She patted the horse and gave it an apple as a treat and then as she was crossing the yard toward the house, one of the stable boys intercepted her. He stopped in front of her, with his hat removed, and his head downcast, and she thought the man had lost his mind or else was so lost in some form of thought that he did not see her.

Annoyed at his impertinence, she made to skirt him. But his hand shot out—a large hand, at the end of a muscular arm, a hand she knew all too well, and it held her by the wrist. "Stay, sweetheart. Stay."

Fearful she looked up at this man, who was clearly not a stable boy but Dereham: a Dereham with his hair in disarray, a thick stubble of dark beard upon all of his face, and, she noted as he smiled at her, two black eyes and a bruise covering all of the left side of his face.

Kathryn realized she must have made a sound of shock when he smiled at her and said, "It looks worse than it is, Kathryn. Worry not. It is nothing but a bruise, and I'd endure a thousand such for you."

She started to open her mouth to tell him that he must not speak like that. To tell him, for their safety, never to speak again about their betrothal.

But he shook his head. He looked hastily one way then the other, then whispered heatedly, "No, Kathryn, there's no time for that, and no time for long and sad good-byes, either. I am off, as I told you I might be, to the coast of Ireland on that enterprise I spoke to you about." As she started to open her mouth, he seemed to rush to speak. "Do not you worry. I'll take good care to keep my head upon my shoulders, and to keep myself hale and well so I can come back to my sweetheart. This thing with Culpepper, from what I understand, will take time to arrange. One of those slow negotiations between two old families. If God be with me, I should be able to make my fortune before then and come for you. And then, if your family still won't give their yes, we'll have the money so that we can go somewhere—perhaps France—and live without hardship. So wish me well, my sweet, and I shall be gone, to get both our futures."

Again, he looked both ways, and then he extended a tied bundle to her. It seemed like a very grubby handkerchief. "While I'm gone, keep this safe. If things come to an extremity and they're ready to drag you to a contract with this Culpepper, this money will allow you to run and hide yourself, and keep yourself safe till I come for you."

She opened her mouth, but she couldn't really refuse the money, which he was thrusting into her hand, without calling attention to their interaction. So far the only other people in the yard were stable boys and though one or two had looked curiously their way, none seemed disposed to interrupt them. In fact, Kathryn would lay a bet that Dereham had bribed them not to see them. But if she made any loud sound or argued, she was sure other people within the house at the other end of the yard would come to see what was happening or, at least, look out their windows.

Dereham said, "God bless you, Kathryn Howard, and keep you safe till I return for you."

Before he could quite go away, Kathryn heard words come out of her own lips, in a whisper that was slightly more than a sigh. "Take me with you!"

He turned around to look at her, and smiled, "What, my dear? So loath to part?"

She nodded and felt tears come to her eyes. She wasn't sure herself that she understood what her crying was about. Part of her was enthralled with the idea of going to London. The court and her memories of Thomas Culpepper conspired to paint a glittering picture of what lay ahead for her—even if Thomas had never brought her strawberries.

And yet something else inside of her thought of Dereham and the coast of Ireland, and it seemed to her as a blessed refuge. It was, she realized, that she had never seen the court and her one meeting with Thomas Culpepper was so short as to qualify as none. She couldn't imagine putting herself in the hands of this man she knew not at all and making him her god on Earth.

And she was sure the court would be as bewildering as the duchess's household had first been—rules and events she didn't understand, all of it happening in a way no one would bother to explain. It was as though she were leaving her father's house once more.

In Father's care, she might have suffered hunger and deprivations. She might have been ill kept and her clothes too short and too worn. But she'd known her father and her siblings, and understood the rules of living with them. In the duchess's household, she was not sure she understood all that was happening, even yet. And now she was about to step forward into a bigger and more complex household.

"Take me with you," she said in a rush. "I'd rather endure privations and danger by your side than stay here." And it was true, because though she probably would know nothing on shipboard, yet she would be with Francis Dereham whom, temper or not, she knew as well as she knew anyone.

But Francis only laughed at her, a bitter laugh deep in his throat. "It cannot be, my sweet, for women are held to be ill luck aboard ship, and besides, I'm not such a cad that I'd expose you to the mortal dangers I will face." He squared his shoulders, and she perceived he was doing his best to look powerful and strong. "Only you remain brave and faithful," he said. "And you shall see that before very long, I shall come and claim you."

And then he put his very disreputable cap back on his head and was gone amid the other barn cleaners and horse tenders.

She shook herself a little and went on toward the house, hoping no one had seen her.

What foolishness that had been. Why had her mind seized upon what seemed suddenly to be a vista of freedom? Had she really thought that Francis would take her with him in what amounted to no more than the life of a privateer?

And she was looking forward to the life in Lambeth and then, at length, in the court, whenever the new queen chanced to come. She could imagine it in her mind's eye—new clothes and music and dancing. She would amuse herself as she never had so far, and everyone would be enthralled by her.

But all the same, she shivered, clutching Dereham's cash bundled in a filthy handkerchief. She felt, in some inexplicable way, as though she were taking a step in the dark, where her foot would meet with nothing when it landed, and she would tumble, headlong, into an abyss.

What foolishness, she thought to herself, again.

Later that night, when she was alone, she opened the handkerchief to see what sum Dereham had thought could save her from an unwanted marriage, if it came to that pass.

Inside the kerchief was a hundred pounds, an amount that Kathryn had never seen all together in one place before, in various currencies from various lands, but all of it good.

She put it where she had put other treasures in the past—under a loose board beneath her bed.

It wasn't until she was well on her way to Lambeth that she remembered she had never retrieved it, but she reasoned that she would collect it when next she came to Horsham again.

The Rose without a Thorn

Twenty-eight

KATHRYN could hardly sleep for the excitement the last night she spent at the duchess's palace at Lambeth before going on to the palace to take her place as a future lady-in-waiting to the queen.

Queen Anne. How strange it was that when last Kathryn had been in Lambeth, it had been to see the coronation of a Queen Anne, her own cousin. And now, she was in Lambeth again, and about to become maid of honor to Queen Anne. This Queen Anne was very different, though the word in the court was that she was very beautiful and that all the potentates of Europe had vied for her hand, which King Henry had won only at great cost.

She was the sister of a German prince, and the King's own painter, Hans Holbein, had been sent to paint a portrait of her, which, when shown at court, had caused many a gallant to sigh and vow that he'd never seen a better-looking lady.

Only the duchess had held out upon the idea that one Queen Anne who'd been a beauty was enough, and that this Queen Anne "is very well set up, no doubt about it. Beautiful eyes and a very straight nose. But to my mind, those German women don't look like our kind. And her face is heavy and set . . . well, like that of a cow. She's not a patch on your late cousin, girl, and she never could be. But then, neither could any woman."

Yet the king, at least in rumor, was half mad in love with the portrait and the report of this Anne of Cleves, and waited in impatience for her appearance. The queen's household was forming in all possible speed, and it included a full complement of maids-of-honor—two hundred. As many as had served the late Queen Jane, whom the duchess had finally stopped calling "that whey-faced wench," perhaps in deference to the dignity of death, or perhaps because the queen was, after all, the mother of the prince heir.

In early August, Kathryn had been dressed in her best and taken to be seen by Lady Rutland, who had looked her over from head to toe and nodded approvingly. "She is a very small lady," she'd said, talking above Kathryn's head to the duchess. "Though very beautiful."

"Although she be small," the duchess said, "she's fair vivacious and always full of fun. She'll bring joy and life to the court."

Lady Rutland had looked doubtful at this, but after she'd asked Kathryn to play the lute and sing, she had sighed and said, "Do you speak French, child? Or German?"

Kathryn had curtseyed in the exact way she'd been taught to and said, "If it please you, my lady, neither, for my kind grandmother doesn't think it good that women should be too educated or too clever."

At this the two older women had traded a look over Kathryn's head, and Lady Rutland had nodded once. "A good thing, that," she said. "For a repeat of that is not needed."

"No," the duchess said. "And you know, it was only Thomas Boleyn's fancy to educate that girl as though she were a princess. Everyone in their place, I always say."

Lady Rutland had conceded the wisdom of this and inclined her head. "Well, and mind you," she said. "The only good thing about her speaking German would be that she might be able to talk to our new queen, for I have heard that the dear lady speaks nothing but German. Not one word of English."

And with that the two women traded a look over Kathryn's head again, and something seemed to be understood between them that neither took the time to explain to Kathryn.

Lady Rutland had given the duchess a long list of clothes that Kathryn must have—a seemingly unending number of dresses in the French fashion, as well as coifs and undergarments, which must be made of lawn and not of the linen that Kathryn had worn her whole life. There were even lists of how many pearls and other adornments must be sewn to what garment till Kathryn was sure that the duchess must refuse—for she'd never even heard of such a rich trousseau, much less wearing one.

But the duchess had smiled and told Kathryn that the Duke of Norfolk had contributed a fair amount to his niece's elevation and that everything should be done according to the best possible manner and in the most expensive and easiest way.

For the first time in Kathryn's life, such promises were true, and the next few months were spent very pleasurably, indeed, choosing material and jewels, and having things done the way she'd always dreamed they should be: This she desired, and it was given to her. That she craved, and it was handed over. She had only to say a word, and things would be showered on her.

In Lambeth, this time, she slept not in the maids dormitory—in fact, since that infamous night, she'd been kept almost completely away from her peers—but in the antechamber to Her Grace's room, and Her Grace took care to show Kathryn how to array herself and what to do to make herself attractive, as well as imparting to her a thousand small tips about how to go on in the presence of any nobleman, even the king.

"You've been too easy with your smiles and your favors, so far, my girl," the duchess would say. "Far be it from me to impair that natural friendliness, which is one of your principal attractions, but at court you cannot go on like that."

Fortunately, though she'd never been schooled, Kathryn found she had a natural quickness for gestures and words, for orders of precedence, for how far one curtseyed for an earl, a marquess, and even the king himself.

"Mind you," the duchess said, "don't you go into the palace starry eyed and full of nonsense, for that is a sure way to your doom. As married as often as Harry has been, he is an old reprobate and as likely to tumble a pretty young thing as not. Mind you the fate of Bessie Blount, got with child and then married off to Lord Clinton, who never, ever forgave her indiscretion, even though it was with the king and even though Clinton benefited by it in honors and lands. Mind you that, my dear, as well as the fact that your cousin Thomas is a proud man and is not likely to take used goods, even from the king."

"But how am I to respond?" Kathryn said, perturbed. "If the king importune me?" So far she hadn't done so very well at refusing the attentions of far lesser gentlemen, much less the king.

The duchess had seemed to understand that. She had smiled wryly and said, "For all the king's vices, he has never yet imposed on the unwilling. Tell him you are honored, of course, and prostate yourself, but always remind him that you are a poor maid, whose only form of riches are in your honor—and that you have nothing else to tempt a husband with. Which, mind you, is near enough to the truth, considering how your poor father left you penniless. You must tell the king that and also that you trust in him not to do you violence. And also—" Here the duchess's smile became yet more broad and yet more wry, as though she could well imagine what was going on in Kathryn's head. "If he tells you how much he is suffering and what a great need of you he has, you are to tell him that you hate to give him pain, but you cannot give in, because your future as well as the well-being of your soul depends on it. Promise to remember that!"

Kathryn could well promise it, since that last had come with a light blow to the head to make sure the knowledge penetrated and was well received. She was doubtful, as she was not very sure she, who was the smallest of his subjects, could truly refuse the sovereign.

But then, she called to mind the other words that the duchess had said often while she prepared Kathryn to become a maid-of-honor. "Mind you, my girl," she said, "the fate of your cousin Anne Boleyn."

This injunction was used in respect to her becoming swollen up with pride at her new clothes and jewels. It was offered about her practicing the lute and becoming too sure of herself in respect to the playing of it. It was said again and again, as the duchess reminded her to mind to whom she gave her favors. "And preferably," the duchess had said wryly, "that should be only to your husband, once those negotiations are concluded. Before him and after him, to none. I would think you have had enough adventure for a lifetime."

And so, by pleasant days, they had come to the last night that Kathryn was supposed to spend in the antechamber to the duchess's chamber. She lay there, in the little space between curtain and door, not really sleeping, though she dozed, her mind full of the delights ahead and yet misgivings about what traps might lay hidden in what seemed to be a glittering future.

She hadn't heard anyone go by and thought that only Lassells was in the chamber with the duchess, but she must have slept while someone else went past, because she woke with a man's voice rumbling from the duchess's chamber.

"It is a dangerous game," he said. "And for all we know, this German queen will live many long years and give him a passel of children. I've heard that these Germans are nothing if not fertile."

Kathryn recognized the duke's voice and blinked a little in puzzlement.

"Pshaw," the duchess said. "You have always been a thin-blooded coward, Thomas Howard. Nothing to your father, who was one of the bravest men who ever—"

"A bravery, which, alas, brought no reward."

"Bravery is its own reward. Sometimes you have to gamble with the chips you have."

Thomas Howard laughed. "What, my mother, was my brother Edmund your natural son? For those words could have come from him. He always gambled and, alas . . . he always lost."

"We shall not lose," the duchess said. "Think you I don't have any spies? I have it on good authority that Cramner made sure that portrait looked the very best it could, and that no wonder, mind you, as she's not a patch on our Anne."

"Who is, alas, dead."

"Indeed, but we aren't. And while we remain alive, it is our lot to continue striving for advancement. Or would you prefer, Thomas Howard, the quiet of the tomb?"

"Madam, I—"

"You will let me play my hand for once. You will do your best to help with it, too, for if I win, it is to the good of the whole family and even, dare I say, to the good of the kingdom."

Thomas had cleared his throat and spoken in the aggrieved tones of a stingy man. "I have already contributed, have I not? Money for dresses and fripperies."

"Dresses and fripperies that will bring back their weight in gold," the duchess said.

"Perhaps. If this queen doesn't outlast him."

"She will not. My spies say she's heavy of tongue and heavier of figure, a great woman with a bovine understanding of the social graces. She is no Howard girl."

"Let's not forget what happened to the last Howard girl to try for the glittering crown."

"No. But this one is nothing like her. Where Anne was bold, she is mild, and where Anne could torment, she's kindhearted."

"Perhaps too kindhearted?"

"I have instructed her well."

"Let us hope so, my dear mother-in-law, for you know the wrath of kings is death."

Unable to comprehend any of it, Kathryn decided this must all be a very strange dream and, turning, pulled the blanket over herself and fell asleep, this time deeply. So deeply that if the duke had truly been in the duchess's chamber, his departure failed to rouse Kathryn.

Twenty-nine

THOUGH Kathryn had joined the queen's maids in August, it was well into December before there was a queen, or at least before the woman who was to be queen arrived in England.

Anne of Cleves having got to Calais in August was there delayed by bad weather till the day after Christmas, when she was finally able to make her crossing.

At the palace without a queen, life had fallen into an easy rhythm. The ladies-in-waiting were trained in how to serve the queen when she was in. For the Christmas holidays, they had fun in a quiet way.

Kathryn found herself a great favorite, as the ladies asked her to sing and play for them in the evenings while they were at their work. Her voice was praised, as was her skill with the music. If she had any sorrow at all, it was that, so far, she had not yet seen Thomas Culpepper.

His being in the king's household, and there being not a queen, there were no amusements that joined men and women. She had heard from the other ladies that he was fair and nimble in the dance, and that he had a good voice, but there the knowledge ended.

Kathryn had come to accept that, unlike her memories of him in youth, he was not a very tall man nor endowed with particular strength. And there her hearing about Culpepper must rest till the queen arrived, a fact that made Kathryn very anxious for the queen to arrive.

Every day she would walk in the gardens and climb a small hillock from the top of which she would look out at the sky and hope that fair weather in London foretold fair weather at sea.

It was one day as she was doing that, that she heard an exclamation behind her, and turning around, she saw a dark woman standing stock-still with her hand to her face. As Kathryn turned around, she realized the woman was very pale, as though she had lost all strength or perhaps as though she were about to lose consciousness.

Kathryn started down the hillock toward her saying, "Are you well? You look so ill."

At the sound of her voice and seeing her close, the woman lowered her hand from her face, revealing a mouth puckered in what seemed to be a permanent frown of worry. Then her mouth opened, and she said, "Oh, I am sorry. It is only that as I approached you from the back, you looked like her . . ."

"Her?" Kathryn said.

"My . . . my name is Jane Boleyn," the lady said. "Lady Rochefort."

"Oh," Kathryn said and curtseyed, then realized which "her" it had to be that Lady Rochefort had confused Kathryn with. "Oh, you mean I look like my cousin Anne!"

"I see her sometimes," Lady Rochefort said, looking at the sky over Kathryn's head. "But never so clear and never so . . . so present. When I saw you there, I thought that she . . ."

She looked at Kathryn, and Kathryn thought she saw shadows

march behind the unremarkable brown of Jane Boleyn's eyes. There was pain there, a pain that she could not quite understand. Jane Boleyn looked back at Kathryn for a moment and then sighed. "Do you think," she said, "that the dead can pardon the living? Do you think they do? That they . . . that they can pardon and . . . and come to love the living?"

"I don't know," Kathryn said, simply. "My mother died, but . . . I barely remember what she looked like. And my father . . ." She tried to remember whether she wanted her father to forgive her for anything, but she couldn't find anything in her mind to reproach herself with. After all, she'd done the best she could while she lived with him. And he was the one who had sent her off. "I am Kathryn Howard," she said. "And people have told me before that I have a turn of my cousin's . . . Nothing . . . nothing like her, but I give an air of her."

"Like the note that lingers in the air after a song," Jane said. "You know, she used to sing all the time. Even when she was in the tower she composed songs. He loved her so much."

"The king?"

"No." Lady Rochefort shook her head. "No, my husband." She nodded, as though confirming suspicions that Kathryn should have held. "George Boleyn. They were very close."

Kathryn remembered something from way back about how there were some accusations against Anne Boleyn that couldn't be repeated. And she remembered the duchess saying, "George? I don't believe it."

Now Kathryn could say, also, "I heard that she and . . . but . . . but we didn't believe it."

"You shouldn't have believed it," Lady Rochefort said, and she scanned the sky above her head, as if she expected at any moment to see the sky open and the multitudes of the dead ride out, whether in anger or forgiveness, Kathryn couldn't tell. "It was all in my mind. He didn't notice me . . . and I loved him so much."

She looked back at Kathryn and now her eyes were just suffering—pure suffering distilled and given form. "I thought if she were dead . . ." Lady Rochefort said. "And then I realized if she were dead, he would never notice me still. So then I thought if he were dead, he would let me go. But he would not. An' I could not. I still dream about him, every night. He comes and looks at me, with those sad, sad eyes. And then he undoes his collar and shows me the red mark at his neck." She shivered.

And Kathryn, who could not see suffering but wish to ameliorate it and who did not know how to console a woman who carried the kind of grief now crushing Jane, did the only thing she knew how to do. She stretched her hand to the other woman, "Come, Lady Rochefort. You are shivering. Me thinketh you are cold. Perhaps we should walk toward the house."

They walked along the path for a moment and presently Kathryn said, "Do you think the queen will be able to sail soon? I so hope she'll be here for the Christmas celebrations! It would grieve me beyond speaking if we were robbed of our celebrations because of the weather at Calais."

"I think that one cannot count upon the weather at the channel," Lady Rochefort said. "I've heard of boats stopped there for many months together. And you cannot be more impatient than the king, but neither will the king let such precious cargo make a perilous crossing."

After that the two spoke perfectly sensibly together. And many times, in the coming days, Kathryn sought out Jane Boleyn for walks or talks in the evenings. It wasn't so much that she appreciated the lady's company—for in truth their conversation rarely went beyond the merest platitudes and the sort of talk that Kathryn could have with anyone at all. It was because when Jane was left too long alone, Kathryn could see her eyes darting about, looking here and there, as though she could see things that no one else saw. Kathryn could not stand the idea of the woman suffering so greatly among people who paid her little mind.

"Do you know who the woman is to whom you talk so much?" Elizabeth Basset asked Kathryn the next day, catching her between the dormitory and the gardens.

"Lady Rochefort?"

"Indeed. Do you know who she is?"

"The widow of George Boleyn, is she not?" Kathryn asked.

"The widow . . . And quite responsible for his death. Her deposition got him beheaded, along with your cousin Anne Boleyn."

"I know that," Kathryn said. "Or rather, no one has ever told it to me, but I suspected it from things I heard at the Dowager Duchess of Norfolk's."

"And yet you talk to her!"

Kathryn had done a lot of thinking since first starting to talk to Jane Boleyn. She thought of her own sins most of all. After all she'd pledged troth with Francis Dereham, but then she'd let him go as though he were nothing at all when her grandmother had ordered her to do so. And though she didn't think Francis was dead, his expedition to Ireland entailed great danger, and it might very well mean he was dead now, in which case his death was upon her conscience as sure as George Boleyn's death was upon Jane Boleyn's.

For though Kathryn had never felt the kind of love that Jane had felt for her husband, she could imagine what that would be like. She had seen that kind of pained, distorted love in Henry Manox's eyes. And Henry Manox, just like Jane Boleyn had done to her husband, would do Kathryn a bad turn if he could. She tried to imagine that kind of love. Painful love, she thought. Love that bit deep into the heart and would not let go. And she was awash in pity for those who felt it.

"I don't presume to judge," she said at last. "Have you never made any mistakes, Mistress Basset, that you feel heartily sorry for?"

Elizabeth Basset sniffed and shook her head. "Mistakes perhaps," she said. "But I have never committed so monstrous a crime."

And on that, she walked ahead of Kathryn, leaving her behind.

It seemed to Kathryn that she had made an enemy there, but she did not care. There was always any number of people who would mislike her, but there was a very large number of people who liked her, as well. She was quick of understanding and always willing to help, and that meant she soon became a great favorite with the ladies around her.

Still it was a surprise to her to be chosen among the fifty English ladies who were to receive the queen—who was sailing to England at last—at Canterbury. The other ladies chosen were older than her and of much greater stature at court, but Kathryn was the only one who showed her pleasure by doing a little dance, bringing a smile to Lady Rutland's face. "Mark ye," she said. "How proud and happy Kathryn Howard is to do her duty by king and queen. Ye should all be so happy."

Only on the day proper, Kathryn was not sure she was so happy. It was sleeting hard and bitterly cold. They traveled in carriages, well wrapped in blankets, but it was so cold that there was no opportunity for merrymaking or even for singing, as she usually did to while the time away. Only for wrapping yourself tight in furs and hoping you wouldn't catch a mortal chill before meeting the queen. And in Kathryn's case, hoping as well that she would not die of some dread disease before she even got to meet her intended, Thomas Culpepper.

But at long last, they arrived at Canterbury and there, in the guest house of the great monastery of St. Augustine, the ladies were served a light supper by a great warming fire, and then outfitted in matching velvet hoods and disposed in the queen's chambers to await Anne of Cleve's arrival.

It was some hours before the queen—or she who was to be queen, though they always called her queen to each other, in their conversations—arrived, and when she did, she looked nothing like Kathryn expected. She'd seen the portrait. Indeed, all of them had. And there was a faint—very faint—resemblance between the portrait and the woman. Only the queen's features were not nearly so regular as they'd been painted, and they were thinner and bonier—though perhaps she'd lost weight during her months of exile in Calais, waiting for the sea to allow her crossing. And she had a long nose, not visible in the portrait that showed her frontally. Her eyes were hooded and nowhere near as open or expressive as they'd been in the portrait.

The result was that she looked older than she'd seemed, and also more imperious and less gentle.

She spoke no English, and when she spoke, it was in a harsh tongue, which went with her harsher features. She gave vent to that tongue now, while the women all stared at her, in various expressions of surprise.

"Her Majesty says," a thin woman said, when the queen was done, advancing and speaking volubly in a terrible accent, "she says that she's very glad to be here, but that of everything that's been done for her in England, from gun salutes to great gifts, this is the best thing yet, for it shows that her subjects are as anxious to be acquainted with her as she is to be acquainted with them, and of that she's glad."

The queen smiled, and her thin features were quite transformed, of a sudden, seeming younger and happier than she'd been before, and in that moment Kathryn could not help liking her. What must it be like, she wondered, to be cast adrift like that, far from one's home and everything she knows? For if she looks strange to us, for certain we look strange to her. And if her tongue sounds odd to us, surely our tongue . . . She shook her head. What a terrible thing this was. She could not but feel pity for the woman, despite her ungainly features and the horrible gown she was wearing, a German thing with far too much fabric that showed off her figure as much as a tent would.

Kathryn rushed forward to help the queen get ready for dinner, by washing her hands and face and changing her gown—for another gown that looked just as bad. Her gowns all had a strange musty smell, as though she'd been keeping them in trunks too long in the damp climate of Calais and no one had told her to air them. Fine gowns they were, too, and very beautiful, but in a style that could make no woman— or indeed anything—look well.

And yet, the two or three times that Kathryn became the recipient of a dazzling royal smile, she thought that Queen Anne was really not that bad-looking.

Which was why she was shocked—as she came back from a lengthy errand to the kitchen to tell the cook to prepare warmed bricks for the queen's bed, where the bricks could not be found and the cook could not seem to understand what she was supposed to do to warm them—by hearing words harshly pronounced from somewhere ahead of her. "The king likes her not, milord. You mark my words. Of all the attributes of women that he likes, she has none. And of those he dislikes, she has them all."

"Think you that it is quite that bad?" a man's voice answered.

Now, looking closer, Kathryn could tell that the voices came from a room ahead, where the door was open only the barest crack, just enough to allow sound to escape.

The first voice spoke again, and she recognized in it the voice of Lady Browne, though she'd heard it only once, welcoming them to this guesthouse. "I think it is perhaps worse," she said slowly. "Not only will the king not like it, but because she's not his subject and is the sister of a powerful prince herself . . . well, I ask you." She shook her head. "You mark my words, someone is going to lose his head for this."

"The painter Hans Holbein," the male voice said, and now Kathryn realized it was the voice of her uncle.

"Perhaps, but I believe not. Because Holbein is an artist, and the king knows that and will know that Holbein's way of seeing things is different. Influenced by his artistic eye. He'll probably forgive him. Cromwell now . . . This marriage is Cromwell's devising."

There was a long silence. And then the Duke of Norfolk said, his voice heavy with thought. "I wonder if the king will go on with it. If he will marry her at all, if she turns out not to his liking . . ."

"I suspect he'll find a way to get rid of her. I saw the little wench, by the by. Beautiful girl and so full of life."

"Is she not? And there's something about her of . . . you know . . . my other niece."

"Indeed, there is. I wonder how long until she catches his eye."

The words made a monstrous meaning in Kathryn's mind, a meaning that she was loathe to credit or believe. She was going to marry Thomas Culpepper. She'd been brought to court to marry

Thomas Culpepper. She'd not think ought else. She'd not let aught else come into her mind. She was going to marry Thomas Culpepper.

She started running before she realized she was doing it. Running toward the queen's chambers.

Without thinking or listening for whom might be in the rooms, she threw the door open into the antechamber. And stopped.

Thirty

In the room there were two men. One of them was tall and thin, with dark hair and the sort of features that made him look as though he'd grown careworn before his time. "Broken to harness" the dowager duchess called that look, where the features collapsed around the bare, supporting bones and left in their place only a firm, zeal-burned certainty that the possessor of the face would do his best and work his hardest and would, by all that that was right and meet, die on his post rather than default.

Kathryn knew that as the face of Sir Anthony Browne from when they'd been received into the guesthouse. She'd thought of him rather as a saint of old in a painting, his face longer than broad and framed in dark, dark hair and beard, with the eyes too large and too full of intention. He'd looked worried then. Now he looked scared.

The reason he looked scared, Kathryn thought, was the other man in the room. Kathryn had seen him once or twice, glimpsing him from a distance while she was in Greenwich Palace. Sometimes she saw him in the gardens. Sometimes she saw him across the hallways. He always had a number of men with him, and always Kathryn froze in place and came no nearer for it was no part of her duties to disturb His Majesty, the king of England.

Now she saw him up close, his presence overwhelming in the crowded room.

He wore a suit of gilded cloth and over it a cape made of furs. His hair had white amid its auburn glory, and he'd grown stout with years—so she heard. In the palace she'd heard that he never jousted nor hunted anymore.

But he was also a head taller than any other man and, standing there, sparkling in his golden suit, it seemed to Kathryn that he filled the whole room.

She said "oh" under her breath and froze in place. Neither man saw her, as they were both well away in a confrontation of their own.

The king paced back and forth in the narrow room that was but a receiving area to the queen's chambers. Behind it was the place where the ladies-in-waiting had greeted their new sovereign, and behind that still the dining room where they had served her dinner. Anne of Cleves was now at the other end of the apartments, where she would be getting undressed and washed and ready for bed.

Doubtless it was his knowing that he couldn't be heard that allowed His Majesty to give full vent to his temper. He was pacing from one end of the room to the other, yelling as he did so. "I have never been so struck with consternation as when I was shown this woman who is supposed to be my queen, I tell you!" He scowled and frowned and added, "I see nothing to this woman as men report of her," he said, and paced some more.

Sir Anthony Browne cowered and muttered something that could not readily be understood, and the king shook his head at him. Standing next to the hapless Lord Browne, the king seemed yet more a giant of a man or perhaps—as Kathryn had heard tell in stories—like those gods who, in Greek and Roman times, descending from their mountaintop fastness to fulminate mortals for errors they did not know they were committing.

"Tell me, sir," the king said. "Do you see anything of her as men report? Is she then so beautiful as to dazzle the eye? Think you, sir, that many other men, many potentates, have vied for her hand?"

Lord Browne shrugged. "I think, Sire," he said, "that she wears very unbecoming clothes in the German style and that wearing them masks her true figure, making her seem not to Your Majesty's liking."

"And why wears she these clothes?" the king said. "Surely she had some idea what would be worn in England. And surely, having this idea, she would have done something about it? Made sure to make her clothes in the style of gowns that she knows I like. It betrays very little liking for or interest in my taste and opinion," he said.

"I think, Sire, if I might venture to say, that she is so unschooled . . ."

"If by unschooled, you mean dull, I've already perceived that myself," he said. "Why, she can't even speak English, but can only make those guttural sounds from her own country. And I can't find that she speaks French, either."

To this, Lord Browne made no comment, but the king reacted yet as if the nobleman had objected and said, "Anne Boleyn, my wife, could speak French and German as well as English."

This seemed to be too much for the gentleman, because he said something under his breath, from which the words, "is dead" could be distinguished.

"Aye, dead she is. And I am constrained to marry this woman . . ." He opened his arms on either side. "I like her not."

"I perceive that, Sire," Sir Anthony Browne said, his eyes intent, his cheeks flushed.

"Why did you not tell me she would not be to my taste?"

"How could I, Sire? My own commission was to receive her and do her honor, and I did that knowing full well I was receiving my future queen. Would you expect me to do her insult or to insult Your Majesty's taste with it? If she were good enough to please other men, I think she might have pleased Your Majesty, and that my saying then that she was too brown or that her features were not to my taste would only have compounded insult to yourself."

The king nodded. "Perhaps you have reason, in this. Yes, yes, I can see the fault is not with you. But I like her not. I am ashamed that men have praised her as they have done, and I love her not."

He covered his face with his hands. "I must be gotten out of this contract, Lord Browne. I must."

"Well," Lord Browne said, his voice even, as though this royal plight were perfectly normal. "Well, then, Your Majesty has clever lawyers and bright jurists. They should be able to find, among themselves, some way you can get out of the contract."

The king stared at Sir Anthony a moment, and then nodded. "Very well, Lord Browne, very well. And so they will. Cromwell had best find . . ." He shook his head.

It was apparent to Kathryn the interview was at an end, and she realized at any minute, one or both of the men might realize she had overheard them. She could not stand the idea. She might not get punished for eavesdropping—for how could she be, when they'd been speaking so loudly in an unlocked room—but her presence would not be welcomed.

She backed from the room slowly and out to the hallway and then paused. She should hide, so she wouldn't be in the hallway when the king came this way. From inside the room, she heard the king say, "I was so distracted that I forgot to give her the furs I brought for her as a New Year's gift. Would you please—"

Kathryn had just decided that she would knit herself by the door, so the king would not remark her presence, when the king came out of the chamber.

She froze in the middle of the hallway. He frowned at her, distracted, then started to go the other way. At the same time, she had decided she must go that way to avoid him. As she realized he was going that way, she stepped the other way, at the same time he stepped that way also, and she found herself staring at the expanse of royal gold cloth doublet.

"Madam!" the king said, sounding much put out.

Kathryn did the only thing she knew how to do, the thing she had been taught to do and prepared to do for all these long months. She sank to the floor in a deep curtsey, then bowed her head low.

"Your Majesty," she said. "I beg your pardon. I am so addled with your glory that I—"

This brought a chuckle from the king's majesty, which, in the way of such things, grew into a guffaw. "Rise, rise, then," he said. His hands on Kathryn's shoulders pulled her up, and she rose to look at him.

He looked at her a long time, his eyes narrowing, then widening, as if he found something new in her features or something else that he wished explained. He looked—Kathryn thought—caught somewhere between surprise and anger, between recognition and pleasure.

At long last he spoke, "You're one of the queen's ladies-in-waiting, I suppose?" he said.

"Yes, and it please Your Majesty."

"It pleases my majesty very much," he answered, his voice suddenly soft and velvety. "And you have been at court much? You seem like a very little girl."

She shook her head. "I've only just come to court," she said. "I was brought," she said, "to be part of the queen's establishment."

The king made a face. "Ah, the queen. I like her not."

Kathryn, thinking that it was no business of hers to criticize the queen, merely bowed at his words.

"And that smell about her . . . It quite overpowers me."

"It is her gowns," Kathryn said. "They have not been aired, and they smell musty. Her land must be very cold and not sunny, and clothes must be kept at the bottom of trunks with a lot of camphor."

The king visibly shuddered. "I like it not," he said again, and getting no answer from Kathryn, he sighed. "She's not a clean, pleasant thing as you are, my dear. As . . . as English maids are." He nodded and seemed about to walk around her but turned around, "What is your name, my dear?"

"Kathryn Howard, Your Majesty," she said, and curtseyed deep again.

When she looked up once more, the king was quite gone. And Kathryn thought that her uncle, if indeed he had any foolish plans of using her to attract the king, had been quite wrong. The king cared not for her charms or for her beauty. He cared only to tell someone—anyone—how much he disliked his queen.

Feeling sorry for the lonely foreigner with the lovely smile, Kathryn walked into the chambers to perform her duty to the one who was, for now, her rightful mistress.

Thirty-one

KATHRYN had been surprised that the king married the queen after all, but perhaps she shouldn't have been, she thought.

After all she'd heard—even then, the marriage had been arranged among countries. It wasn't like a man jilting his betrothed, to whom he'd promised the world, in the woods by the river. The king had entered into a contract with another country as much as in an engagement with this woman, Anne of Cleves.

It was clear the king didn't like it. He complained to all he could find. Kathryn didn't see him again after that day in Canterbury, so she did not hear him complain to her, but she could well imagine that he would, given a chance, because everyone else reported it to Anne.

That day, Kathryn found herself listening to the wild confidences of Lady Rochefort, as she came from the garden into the house. Jane Boleyn had caught up with her and accompanied her, talking. "They say," she said, "that he said she cannot be a maiden. That he felt her breasts and her stomach and they are not those of a maiden." Jane was pale and excited, her eyes shining as they did when she was moved by some internal impulse that—Kathryn had come to know—had very little to do with what was happening externally around her and far more with what was happening internally in Jane's own mind.

In the rising and falling tides of her own madness, her guilt, the remaining hopeless love for her long-dead husband, Jane moved and talked, and often needed but little encouragement from reality to latch on to something that was passing around her and talk about it with burning passion.

"What think you it means, Kathryn?"

Kathryn shrugged. "Ah, but what can it mean?" she said. "Nothing at all, Jane, save that the king doesn't like her."

Jane had seized Kathryn's arm and drawn closer. "They say," she said, "that the king went to her in Canterbury, you know, without announcement, hoping that she would recognize him, even in his plain form, which would show him that their love was true."

Kathryn had heard the same and had wondered at the king who could imagine that there would be love between himself and this woman he'd never met. Oh, Kathryn had heard all the legends and stories, where children who had never known their parents instantly recognized them from something natural in the blood. And she'd heard the stories where lovers who were meant to be fell upon each other on first meeting as though they'd known each other from birth and craved each other above all.

Having lived in the world a number of years, though she was unfortunately not sure whether that number be fifteen or seventeen, Kathryn thought this was all nonsense. How could people feel anything for someone they'd never seen? "If the king thought that . . ." Kathryn said, and then had the good sense to keep her mouth shut, because what went on in her mind was that for a man so much older than her, and far more experienced in life and love, to believe in such tales showed a credulity almost bordering on childishness.

She didn't say it, but Jane Boleyn must have guessed it, because she laughed. "Isn't it just like a man?" she said. "They live like that, from tales of youth, and they understand themselves and others very little. For all women are more dependent on love and the fruition of the heart, they believe it more . . ." She was silent a moment. "If I had known what was in George's mind . . ." But she said no more, nor did Kathryn pursue the subject.

Instead they walked in through the side door and up to the queen's chambers. It was their duty to be present at the making of the queen's bed, though they weren't quite of enough rank to make her bed themselves.

When Kathryn got in, the mattress had been unrolled over the bed. The heaviest of the ladies-in-waiting, a stout German who had come with Anne from her homeland, took the duty of rolling upon the mattress to test it for hidden daggers or other traps. Next the feather bed was laid upon the mattress and the ritual repeated.

Then came the linen sheets, examined for the presence of some cunning hidden poison. Finally the ladies who had made the bed kissed the places where their hands had touched, and just at that moment, Anne of Cleves came into the room to retire.

She came with her own maids, who helped her remove her elaborate and bewildering German hood, and her various layers of dress.

While they were doing it, one of them said, "How nice it is that to think that the king's majesty himself will be lying and sleeping on this bed we just made."

The queen's serious countenance flashed into that smile that made her look almost beautiful, and she said brightly, "Is it not?" Her accent was still thick, but—for her short time in England—she was making remarkable progress in English. "I think I have the kindest and best husband in the world. Aye, and the most devoted, too."

Her words struck the ten or so women in the room with the kind of silence that betrays unexpressed thoughts. They looked at each other and none said anything, and the queen was suffered to continue in her bright, easy voice. "Every night he comes and sleeps with me. He lies next to me and says, 'Good night, sweetheart.' And then in the morning, he kisses me and he says, 'Fare thee well, sweetheart.'"

The silence stretched a little longer, and then someone said, in the kind of horribly bright voice people employ when they are saying something that they think might be reported and perhaps cost them their lives but which needs be said anyway. Kathryn could not see who spoke, but it must be someone behind, near the bedstead ornamented with a god with an enormous erection chasing a flimsy-clad goddess. "Why, madam, that's all very well, but it is what he does between good night and fare thee well that counts."

"Why?" the queen said, and looked momentarily puzzled. "What should he do? What mean you?"

Jane Boleyn cleared her throat and spoke with the madcap impulsiveness of one who already lives in hell. "Why, madam, I believe she simply wishes to know whether you might be pregnant, for it's a conclusion the entire country prays for daily."

"Nay," the queen said, sitting herself down while two of her German maids combed her fair hair. "Nay. I know well I'm not."

"But how can you know you're not?" another lady said.

And then, with growing courage, Lady Edgecombe put in, "Me thinketh that our lady is still a maiden."

This brought about laughter from the queen and a puzzled look, following the laughter. "How can I be a maiden?" she asked.

"When I sleep every night with the king?" She looked around the chamber, at all the silent women. "Is this not enough?"

Lady Rutland, the chief of the maids-in-waiting, sighed heavily, "Your Majesty, there must be more than this, or we shall never have the Duke of York that all the country is sick with longing for."

Anne shook her head. "But no. It's enough. I am quite contented." She looked bewilderedly at her ladies-in-waiting, as though she suspected that something had been lost in their use of the language and her understanding of it that made them speak of different things.

Lady Rutland sighed. Kathryn thought she saw in the lady's eyes, the thought, quickly abandoned, that someone should explain the facts of life to this poor innocent and that perhaps, by rights, that someone should be Lady Rutland herself. But she could not, between the language difference and the queen's sheltered upbringing conceive of how to bring an understanding about.

Instead she shook her head. "Maybe you should speak with Mother Lowe about this," she said. Mother Lowe was the chief of the German ladies-in-waiting, who had come with Queen Anne from her native land. If Mother Lowe could not contrive to explain the facts of life to her mistress, then, faith, no one could.

But the queen only smiled the bewildered smile that she had in common with those very young or very deaf—the smile of complete lack of understanding—and shook her head. "Nay, I am contented as it is. I know no more."

"Still," Lady Rutland said, "I think you must tell Mother Lowe that the king has neglected you, madam, and not performed his conjugal duties!"

But all the queen would do was incline her head and say with that internal steel that belied her exterior mildness, "But I receive quite as much of His Majesty's attention as I wish."

Kathryn understood this to mean the conversation was over, and wondered if the poor woman at all understood what had happened and how precarious her position was.

But at the very moment she was trying to frame her mind to put words to it, she felt a hand pluck at her sleeve. Turning she saw a young boy, of the sort who belonged to the king's household and served as a page, sent here and there in the palace to take messages or packages.

"If you please, madam, are you Mistress Kathryn Howard?"

Kathryn looked at him and nodded once. Wild ideas went through her mind. That Dereham had found her and wanted back his hundred pounds, which she'd stupidly left at its hideout at Horsham. Or perhaps that her marriage with Thomas Culpepper had finally been arranged, and she was being called now to make her promises.

Instead, when she followed the page out to the hall, the page bowed to her. "If you are Mistress Kathryn Howard, the king's majesty would like you to come and play the virginal for him, for he is troubled in his mind and would like to calm himself down before he sleeps."

Kathryn took a step to follow the page, and then remembered what her grandmother had said about the king, the king's appetites, and what he was likely to try if he were not restrained. Trembling, because she knew not obeying royal orders could bring about the king's wrath as much as anything else, she said, "Wait . . . please. Please, wait a moment."

Back in the royal chamber, she touched Jane Boleyn's arm, and when the lady looked in her direction, Kathryn whispered, "Please, come with me."

That Jane followed her without asking why was either a measure of her confidence in Kathryn or how few friends she had and how much she'd come to trust in Kathryn.

She followed Kathryn all the way to where the page led them. The page opened the door, and they went in, to find the king sitting upon a chair, next to a very lovely, ornate virginal. He looked startled at them. "I sent for a song bird," he said, and forced a smile over what seemed to be a peevish expression. "And I got two. Lady Rochefort, I didn't know you sang."

Kathryn sank to her knees in her curtsey and stayed that. "I beg Your Majesty's pardon," she said, "if I have done wrong. But I know Your Majesty did not intend to injure a poor maiden's reputation by having me alone with Your Majesty in here. While I am sure this, the least of your subjects, could trust her virtue to you as she could to her own father, I will recall to you that my father, that Edmund Howard who bled in Flodden Fields in the service of Your Majesty's honor, is now gone. I have no one but myself, and no protector. Your Majesty would wish the wicked tongues at court to speak ill of one so young as I?"

For a moment it hung in the balance. Henry's mouth moved in and out, in a sort of a moue, as though it could not decide whether or not to show displeasure. And then he sighed, like a child denied a treat. He shifted his leg. He frowned. "No. You are correct." He looked at her. "Oh, stop looking so scared, child. Am I then, to you, such a terrible dragon that you should fear me so much?"

"Not afraid," Kathryn said. "But overwhelmed. It is strange to think that I am here in this room with Your Majesty. That the power and might of England, the head of the Church itself, is here with me, and I so insignificant."

This brought a little cackle from the king. He patted his leg in a movement that would probably have been a slap had he been fully overcome by amusement. "Well, well," he said. "You are a pretty child, and you may rise. One doesn't wish always to be . . . Harry with the crown. Sometimes one just wants to be Harry the man. And for now, we'll be Harry the man, who has a headache and hopes your pretty playing can soothe it." He spared a look at Jane Boleyn, who was kneeling on the other side of him, still staring at the floor. "And you also, Lady Rochefort, rise. You are welcome here. Take a seat. You can make sure this pretty child is quite secure in my presence and that I'm not tempted to play the seducer." He seemed to think this very funny and laughed a great deal at his own joke.

Kathryn perceived the sadness behind the joke, and all of a sudden she understood that this powerful man, so large, so ungainly, was suffering from sadness at the loss of youth, which he could never recover. She'd heard about him in the palace. How he had once been considered the most handsome, the most beautiful prince in all Christendom.

Now his youth was gone, and he was still king, but he wished—as he had told her—that Harry himself without the crown were still capable of seducing her, or any maiden he set his eye on.

She felt his sadness, and though she'd tried to follow the duchess's instructions and not attempt to carry all the weight of other's sorrows upon her shoulders, still she could not help trying to alleviate the very great sorrow of this man who was so big and so great, and yet so lost and so helpless in face of his own desires. Of her own impulse, she rose from her curtsey and neared him, and kissed him—a peck on the side of the face—and said, quickly, for fear that if she lingered her voice would betray her lie. "I am afraid," she said, "that I somewhat deceive Your Majesty. Lady Jane Rochefort is here not to ensure that you don't try to seduce me, but to ensure I don't lose my head and succumb to your considerable charm."

She knew she had done well when she saw his mouth turn up at the corners. For a moment, very brief, she was afraid that it was an ironical smile and that he would expose her striving to impress him. But instead, the smile became fuller, and his eyes shone. "Is that so, then?" he asked. "You find Harry the man someone who might seduce you without trying?"

She inclined her head, hiding the flame in her cheeks. "Your Majesty won't be so ungallant as to tempt me out of my modesty and make me repeat what I said. Oh, I should never have said it. But there it is. Harry with the crown is too great, too strong, too much for me, a poor maiden, and he would wholly overpower me. Harry the man, now . . . Harry the man . . ." She stepped back. "He can still overwhelm but in another way." She forced herself to smile at him.

He grinned at her. "Bless you, my child. What a pretty child you are. For all that, I'll sleep better tonight, I'm sure, after your playing. Sit you at the virginal and show me what you can do, for I have heard all over the palace that there is not any other musician at court to equal you."

"Your Majesty does me great honor," Kathryn said, and sat down. She took a deep breath and she played. It wasn't difficult at all. As always, once she found herself in front of the virginal, the music just flowed as though it came from deep wellsprings within her.

"Bless you, my dear," the king said. "How prettily you blush. Like a rose. A rose without a thorn."

As she rose from the virginal, he took both her hands and kissed them with his moist, hot lips. "Bless you, my dear, for being kind to Harry himself, Harry without the crown." He turned to Lady Rochefort. "And thank you, Lady Rochefort. Bring me this child again, will you? Tomorrow? That she might play me her fair lullabies, and I may sleep."

Thirty-two

"COME, my dear, and play for me," the king said, and Kathryn came. It was the tenth time she'd been called to the king's chambers in as many nights. She played, and Lady Rochefort watched her play and nodded off now and then.

Kathryn didn't mind that the lady should nod off, for she imagined the pain and the guilt the woman lived with during the day were quite enough to exhaust her. Her being there was enough to grant Kathryn some protection from the tongues that wagged in her direction.

Already, she noticed something strange happening in that she saw people give her odd looks, but at the same time other people approached her. Ladies-in-waiting of far higher rank, who had never paid any attention to Kathryn, now gave her jewels or gifts of fabric, or simply complimented her on her taste, her looks, her smile.

It seemed to Kathryn that each day brought a new surprise.

She was not stupid. Well she understood the treatment she received came from these people's belief that she was either the king's mistress and therefore had his ear, or that she was the woman the king loved and therefore she had his ear.

The pageants and ceremonies of introducing Anne of Cleves as queen to the Englishmen went on, but every day another person would approach Kathryn and say, "They say the king likes her not." Or "They say she is still a maiden." Or yet "They say that he is trying to get a divorce."

Cromwell, the architect of the Cleves marriage was in the Tower and people said he had been ordered to find a way out of this marriage for the king. They wondered whether it would save his head, or if it would fall like the heads of other favorites before him and be exposed on London Bridge for the horror of passersby.

That night after she played, the king looked down for a long time. When he rose, Kathryn looked toward Lady Rochefort, but the lady was asleep and snoring.

The king must have seen her look, for he smiled. "Ah, Kathryn, fear me not. I was attracted to your cleanliness, your maidenly modesty. I would neither seduce you nor allow you to be seduced by me."

He walked slowly and limped a little. She had heard he had a wound on his leg, sustained in a joust, which made him hurt and which ran continuously with some foul humors. Sometimes, she'd heard, the wound closed, and then the king would lay in great pain until all of him, even his face, turned black with the pent-up humors. No one had told her but it was implicit that one day he would die of that foul wound.

Only right now, it did not seem so very bad. He had a silver-plated stick with its head an elaborate Tudor Rose, and Kathryn thought that it was of very little more import than the walking stick of the duchess that was more used to hit others than to support her.

As if to prove her point, he left his walking stick against the chair as he limped to her. He smelled of perfume, and his beard tickled the side of her face as he leaned over and said, "Kathryn, I would like to know—if by some miracle I were free of this sham of a marriage . . . would you have me?"

Her breath stopped, and it would not come. In her head, as if in a dream, futures clashed. Her small self lost at the coronation of Anne Boleyn. Thomas Culpepper, whom she had not seen since that day but was to marry her, or so the Dowager Duchess of Norfolk said. Unless, of course, it were all a trap designed to catch the king and to make the family powerful again, as it had been in the days of Anne. Thomas, who had never brought her strawberries. And then there was Harry. Harry with the crown. Harry without the crown . . . well, she felt sorry for him. At least as sorry as she had felt for Manox when he was her teacher.

In Henry's eyes she read the same hunger for her, the same desire, only this was not some man, some private Englishman who might have his way with a maiden in the dark space behind the stairs of some anonymous chapel and never suffer for it, or it never be known. No. This was the king and master of England, and every eye on him.

And yet for all his power, he had been married against his will, and now he bent over her, breathing hard. "Would you have me, pretty Kathryn, if I were free?"

Kathryn saw herself with the crown. She thought of her dream long ago, when she'd first come to Lambeth, that she'd marry some foreign king and be the center of everyone's attention. She thought of the game in the dormitory so many years ago. The bit of lace hitting the dusty ground, forming incomprehensible scrolls, and Alice's voice calling out, "There, it's Henry. You'll marry a Henry."

Henry with the crown. Henry whose wound would close one of these days and carry him off. And then the woman he left, if she had a son by him, that woman would be the regent. She would be as good as a king in her own right.

Behind her mind, this went on. It was like a grand procession going down the street of a city, but in the building in front of which the procession passes, the real business goes forward.

And the real business was that Kathryn, looking up, read eagerness and sorrow in the king's eyes. Desire. And, though he be the king, half a certainty that he would be rejected.

She could not stand it. She dropped from the stool on which she'd sat while playing and laid herself prostrate upon the ground, her face against the floorboards. "Your Majesty," she said. "Your Majesty, how can you offer me this? Can you not know that I am not worthy of the king?"

From above came a big gasp, as though Henry had tried to sigh but were overwhelmed, and then his voice very softly, "I am not asking you to be the king's wife, my dear. To the king you can be his dear queen and sit beside him in the throne room and bring forth, if God be willing, a Duke of York to our majesty's joy.

"But to Harry without the crown will you be his wife? And be his rose without a thorn for all your days and play your pretty music for him and laugh your pretty laugh and bring a ray of light into his dark, dark days, my dear? Will you be the youth he sees fleeing before him?"

She felt her heart beat upon her throat. What choice did she have, truly? What choice? Oh, it was very easy to say, and many would say it, that she could say no. That she could walk out of here and marry Thomas Culpepper and live the life of a country gentlewoman. Praying, working, and praying again, and bringing up children to be fair and strong. Obeying her husband. Her country squire husband.

But it was not like that. She couldn't put it in words so much, but she was sure as she was sure one day of dying and meeting her maker, that it wasn't that simple. She had talked to many people since she'd come to Greenwich, and she had heard the story of the king's pursuing of Anne Boleyn.

It was said, though Kathryn was not sure how much truth there might be in it, that Anne had in her youth been in love with the Duke of Suffolk. Only the king had been in love with Anne, and he had made sure that Suffolk was married to someone else, speedily. A woman who had plagued his days into an early grave.

And meanwhile, the king had laid siege to Anne, going round and round like a hungry wolf around a farmhouse in the dead of winter, pursuing and pursuing and pursuing until Anne had nowhere else left to go and nothing else left to do but marry him.

Perhaps there, too, had lain the seeds of her destruction, for by the time that Anne had married him, the seeds of resentment had been sown, and the seeds of hatred and the seeds of sorrow. Perhaps by that time he resented her so much that all he could do was turn on her.

It was a small balance, Kathryn thought, between Harry with the crown and Harry without. Harry without the crown, faith, wanted to be loved for who he was. But he would not forget Harry with the crown, and that Harry might come out at any minute and demand his royal rights.

She could not say no. And when she looked up and saw his worried look, she did not want to. "Aye, Sire. Aye, if you were free, I would be yours. And gladly, too. I think"—she smiled a little—

"that your youth not be fled as far as you think, Your Majesty. It seems to me that I would bring back your youth, and together we'd rejoice in it, aye, and have a Duke of York, yes, and many other fair and strong brothers and sisters for him."

He reached down and lifted her, laughing all the while. And he held her close, her face pressed against his heavy brocaded doublet. "You are my rose without a thorn," he said. "My rose without a thorn. After so many years, I have at last deserved you."

Kathryn felt some moisture on her head, and looking up, she realized that the king was crying upon her. Confused, she reached up. She tried to stop the royal tears, which horrified her. "No, Your Majesty, no. This must not be. You must not be unhappy."

"I am not unhappy," he said, with a catch in his voice. "And you must call me Harry, my dear, when we're alone. Even if I must be Harry with the crown and do many a foolish thing as king's must do—things you don't understand nor care about, setting about armies to put down rebellion, closing down dissolute monasteries, and caring about the doings of other kings the world over—for you, my dear, I would always be your husband, Harry."

"My Lord Harry," she said.

He leaned down and kissed her softly. Her forehead. Her eyes. Her lips. His great big hands held her close. He murmured things she didn't readily understand about roses and thorns and a perfect love.

She was afraid that next he would drop to his knees and raise her skirts, this was so much like what Manox had done. But before anything so unfortunate could happen, there was a scream, and the king sprang away from her, fumbling.

He must have put all his weight upon his lame leg, for he screamed and tripped and finally fell heavily upon his chair.

Kathryn stood there, her hair disheveled and her coif askew. The scream stopped and was followed by a heavy panting, and then Lady Rochefort's voice, seeming to come from somewhere quite far away. "There was blood. There was blood all over. It was the Tower."

The king's hand clasped tight on the silver rose above his stick. Kathryn had the idea that were it not for his fear that he would scare her, he would have taken the stick and possibly broken it across Jane's head. Instead, he spoke, slowly, "Aye, Jane. Aye, the Tower and the blood, but that's all in the past now."

He looked at Kathryn then and smiled. "Mistress Howard, it would please me greatly if you would retire from the palace for a few weeks."

It was so unexpected that Kathryn failed to understand it. Only when some lady had done something wrong was she sent away from the palace, usually back to her family. What had she done, then? Had her answer to him been the wrong one? She didn't believe so, and when she looked at him, she found him smiling. But why would he be sending her away, then?

"Have I done aught," she asked, "to displease Your Majesty?"

He smiled. "No, Mistress Howard. You have pleased me greatly. But I would enjoin you to go down river awhile and to lodge with your uncle Norfolk. Tomorrow I shall send for him and ask him to make suitable apartments ready for you. It is best, for propriety's sake, that you be removed from the queen and from the palace and from my presence all together. Norfolk will do the thing prettily."

Her face must have shown her confusion, for his great big hand came forth and caressed her cheek. "Fear not, my moppet, that you have to be without me for very long. This shall not happen. I will come visit that you might play me your lullabies. But now, go you to bed and dream pretty dreams, my Kathryn."

Kathryn had gone from the chamber, not sure whether she was on her feet or on her head. Out in the hallway, Jane got close to her and whispered, "Kathryn, did he ask you . . . does he wish you to become his mistress?"

Kathryn shook her head. "No. It is all very strange, but . . . I think he means to have a divorce. He said he means to marry me. Surely," she said, thinking of the foreign lady with the sweet smile, "surely he can't mean to have her executed, can he? For she hasn't done anything."

"No, surely not," Jane said. "It's not just that she's innocent," Jane said, in the tone of one who didn't put much trust in innocence itself as a protection from the king's wrath, "but that her brother is a prince abroad. The king would not want to set himself wrong with the Protestant princes of Germany."

"No," Kathryn said, and was almost sure that she said right. "He asked if he were free, would I marry him. But . . . why would he have me removed from the palace?" she asked in confusion.

"Oh, that much is clear," Jane said. "It is that if he means to marry you, he means that not even a suspicion of scandal should attach to you."

"But . . ." Kathryn said. In her mind there was her affair with Manox, of which the duchess had told her all the maids knew, and then her much worse affair with Dereham, and what would people say if she became queen. But then she thought that if she became queen the king's own majesty would be wrapped up in her virtue. If he loved her well . . . If he loved her well, surely he would not believe anyone who besmirched her. Nor would he let anyone speak about her honor. Certainly not if she were the mother of his child.

Sure, he had Anne Boleyn executed, but—Kathryn thought,

having listened to people in the palace—he'd had Anne Boleyn executed not because he believed she had been unfaithful, though he might in fact have believed it, but because he had found it impossible to live with her. She'd been by turns demanding and commanding, and Henry wouldn't like that, not with all his power, to find himself submitting to a woman.

No. Kathryn must do this, and of a certain surety she saw no way out of it. In fact she was sure her grandmother and almost everyone she knew would think Kathryn a great zany for even considering escaping becoming queen. If Kathryn was to do this, then let it be that she was the mildest and sweetest of wives, ever ready to bend to his will, treating Harry without the crown as though he were Harry with the crown, and making him—what was it that the duchess had told her, so many years ago—making him believe he was her king, her sovereign deity, and that she existed only for him.

"He wants sweetness," she said, hoping that her words would make it so, and when Jane didn't answer but only looked at her with wide eyes, she added. "It is funny, you know, for so many years ago, in the dormitory at Horsham, we were playing this game with bits of lace, throwing it on the ground to form the name of the man we'd marry. Just a silly game. And my bit of lace formed Henry."

Jane was quiet a long time, then sighed. "Yes. I had a portent like that once." But the way she spoke and the way she looked ahead as though at horrors untold . . . Kathryn couldn't find the power in her to ask her what she meant by that.

Thirty-three

"My dear, dear Kathryn," the dowager duchess said. She was waiting in the duke's palace in the very sumptuous apartments set aside for Kathryn. "I always knew how it would be."

She stood in the middle of the painted rooms, which were hung all over with precious embroidery and extended both hands to Kathryn while the stick fell, unheeded from her hand to the floor. Kathryn grasped her grandmother's hands and curtseyed prettily. The hands felt papery, dry, and cool under her own, but the duchess laughed. "I knew that no man could see you and resist you. You have a look of her, my dear. That you do. And though it went badly in the end, she was the great love of his life, you mark my words. He has missed her terribly since she has gone.

"They say that right after this sham marriage of his, her daughter, dear little Elizabeth wrote to Queen Anne, if such ye call her, and told her she would be glad to come to court and meet her new mother, the king ordered Cramner write to Elizabeth and tell her that she had a mother so different as to this one that she had no business at court and this one was not mother of hers and that"—she gave Kathryn an intent glance—"I will tell you, didn't mean he thought that this present creature was better than our Anne."

Kathryn nodded. She felt it an ill omen that on this day they should be talking of her cousin, who had walked the same path and married the same king. She resisted an impulse to cross herself in order to ward off Anne Boleyn's sad fate. "The king has been all that's kind to me, madam," she said. "And His Majesty's attention to me has been like the sun coming out on an overcast day and transforming everything."

The duchess smiled. "He has been very kind to all Howards. Your uncle Norfolk is very pleased with you, my dear. For though his son tried to convince Norfolk's daughter to catch the king's fancy and be his mistress, she said she would have none. Which, mark my words, is just as well, for the girl has no spirit, and mistress is the most she could aspire to, only to be discarded like Bessie Blount. But you . . . you my dear have a fire that can't be denied, and I shall see you yet wear the crown. I hope to bear your train at your coronation, just as I bore your cousin's once."

Kathryn nodded. Again the ill omen. She clasped her little head in a fist and claimed tiredness to be allowed to lie down upon the bed in these most luxurious apartments. She had a feather mattress, as she'd never enjoyed before, and a featherbed and feather eiderdown. Lying amid it all, she felt as if she were in a cloud in heaven, dreaming.

Lying down was, however, the only way she could avoid the attention of everyone in the household. She could never understand how many servants had been assigned to her. It seemed every time she turned around there was a new one, prostrate on her knees, offering wine or ale, or else water to wash her hands, strawberries, grapes, oranges, and all manner of good things.

Someone was always standing by in case she found her bed too hot or too cold, desired her fire built up or cool rose water brought up to bathe her forehead and wrists.

Lying down was the only way she could escape them all. Lying down and closing her eyes. Very often, she found herself between imagination and dream seeing herself as a little girl on London streets, walking with Thomas Culpepper, who made sure that no one molested her or hurt her.

She walked through the streets again, but this time when she caught a glimpse of the queen in procession between the Tower and the place where she would be crowned, the face that peeked at her from beneath the hood ornamented with fur was her own.

This was usually when she woke up screaming, panting, her forehead breaking out in sweat, her hands shaking.

This had just happened on her second week in the house when she found a maid kneeling by her bed, extending her a folded paper. She looked at the maid, as though the maid had taken leave of her senses, then tried to collect her own memory. Had she sent for a paper? She was sure she hadn't.

Then, her eyes clearing from their sleep confusion, she realized that the paper was folded over and that it bore a melted seal upon it.

She extended her hand for it and took it, and broke the seal and read. It came from Joan Bulmer. She'd married a small lord with a manor in the north. She recalled herself to Kathryn's attention by reminding her that she was used to serving as Kathryn's secretary—which was true for the very few letters that Kathryn had need of writing while she lived at Lambeth. One or two of them to Dereham, she recalled with a shiver. And though Anne said nothing at all in those letters that could be considered dangerous, she was sure that Joan alluded to the deeper relationship that the whole dormitory knew existed between her and Dereham when she said that she had kept Kathryn's secrets and had no intention of divulging them.

With difficulty for, though she read better than she wrote, Kathryn hadn't often read very much, Kathryn looked at the rest of the letter. It seemed Joan had found herself living with a man she liked not and who exerted over her that full power a husband could have over his wife.

She wanted away from him and his rough treatment. She begged Kathryn, of her kind mercy, to make her one of her maids and bring her to London. "For it is said that the king means to put you in that position from which he is now endeavoring to remove the foreigner. And if it be so and if he do good things for you, I hope you will remember your secretary and devoted friend, Joan Bulmer."

Of all the girls in the dormitory, Kathryn had loved Joan the least. She suspected that Joan had been an accomplice of Manox's in getting the letter about Dereham to the duchess. And yet, that had ended well, had it not? And perhaps Joan Bulmer was not such a bad sort. She had after all been upset that she'd been supplanted by Kathryn in Dereham's affections. And then she'd had the bad luck to make an awful marriage.

If Kathryn received her with kindness, surely she'd see that Kathryn was her true friend and she herself would deal well with Kathryn. Surely.

"Bring me pen and paper," she told the servant. "And ink and sand."

Before the words were well out of her hand, the objects were presented to her. She took them in her shaking hand and wrote a reply.

It was only a few words for, secretary or not, Kathryn had never found much use in enmeshing herself in excessive wordage. She told Joan if such came to pass and if it were her great good fortune to receive such bounty from His Majesty, then she would make sure to summon Joan to court and to her own household.

Thirty-four

THE king came in a small rowboat, rowed by two of his servants, crossing the silent river in the dead of night, and was received in estate at Norfolk House. There were dainties and card games and talk, but most of all there was Kathryn and her music.

With great care and continuous vigilance, the duchess tried to prepare the way. "We'll leave you alone as much as we can, but not alone in the room, for we'll not want Harry taking advantage, will we? We'll leave you alone with him, though, to talk privy like. Be ye always kind and careful with him, and remember that he is too old to enjoy argumentation and disputes." She stopped for a moment, as though thinking something over. "If indeed he ever enjoyed it, which I doubt. I think Anne managed to cajole him into it, but he did not really like it, if you take my meaning, much less enjoy it.

"No, best you pattern yourself after Jane Seymour, whey-faced though she might have been. But she obeyed him in all things, and by obeying him, she attached his affections true and proper, though her face was nothing to recommend her. An' if she had lived," the duchess said, "she would have been regent after his death. He had already made documents to that intent. You do that, too, my dear, and only think, he has not very long to live."

Kathryn didn't like it when her grandmother spoke of the king's advanced age or that, for sure, he could not be long for this Earth. She knew this was true, or suspected it might be. And, of course, part of her mind knew she was marrying him because he was the king. Were it not for that, she would have at least thought of saying no.

But marriage was all a chance, and she'd drawn the king of England, and she'd endeavor to serve him as her true master. She did not want to think of widowhood.

The first time the duchess spoke like this, though, Kathryn said, "Madam, you said I was to go to court to become polished, so I might marry my cousin Thomas Culpepper who was court raised. Was it all then a ruse?"

The duchess had looked at her puzzled. "No, oh, no. We were in the midst of negotiations for that marriage, only we realized what way the wind was likely to blow and you know, my dear, common men—or women—who stand in the way of royal caprice get blown to pieces and nothing remains of them. Best then to set our sails so they're full of royal favor."

The duchess had patted her and left her to entertain the king with her music. They spoke very little, when they spoke. The king did not seem to know what might interest her, and force, she did not know what might interest the king.

Music was the only thing she knew that they had in common, only, sometimes, at the duchess's suggestion, she and some of the other girls practiced their dances for the king's amusement. But that was all.

Two weeks after she'd left the palace, and when Kathryn was starting to suspect she'd dreamed the king's declaration and his question, Henry had approached her, when she was still sitting at the virginal, after playing.

As though of a common accord, the Duke of Norfolk, his wife, the dowager, and all who were standing about attending on them moved to the other end of the room.

"The thing is done," the king said. "And now, will ye be my wife, Kathryn?"

"The thing?" Kathryn felt a surge of panic, and took her hand to her throat. The way the king said it, it seemed to her that Anne of Cleves would now be lying dead. Dead to make her way for Kathryn. How odd it was that he had got rid of Catherine of Aragon for Anne Boleyn and now . . .

"Divorce," he said. "Oh, do not look so scared. She agreed to it all and made the thing very easy, indeed. I promised her four thousand pounds in stipend every year, three properties, which I'll sign over for her, and the right to call herself my sister." He nodded. "I'd have given her ten times more to rid myself of her presence, and to be able to have you, Kathryn." He took a deep breath. "But she took my offer and is contented with it. I don't think Cleves can be a very rich estate so eagerly did she take it."

"And now I am thus free to marry you, if you will have me."

"I will have you, my lord," she said. "Conscious of the great honor you do me."

Tudor Rose

Thirty-five

Kathryn had never thought much upon her wedding, always having thought it would be a simple affair with some country esquire. But if she could have cast just one desire for that day that would decide her life, it would be that it should be a fair day and warm.

It was not to be.

Though it was August and the day promised warmth late in the afternoon, she left Lambeth for Hampton Court in a carriage just after dawn, and there was fog all about, obscuring the roads and the gardens as the carriage departed.

She was alone in the carriage save for the duchess, who, it turned out, wished to spend this last opportunity in lecturing Kathryn about what she should do and the intricacies of marriage.

Perhaps her delicacy prevented the duchess's remembering that her granddaughter, the future queen, had already some understanding of the relations between men and women, but the duchess spent a great deal of time in explaining those and in such an odd way that it seemed to Kathryn that this woman, who'd been married twice and had—it was rumored—used her seductive power as her weapon an equal number of times in the shifting sands of the

Wars of the Roses, didn't know anything about men or the wishes of men or yet how things happened between men and women.

"You will mind," the duchess said. "To always take care of his pleasure first and make sure that he is pleased in you. It is not important whether you experience pleasure or not, though if he asks you, you are to express yourself wholly fulsome on the great pleasure he gives you and how much you enjoy his ministrations. Is that clear girl?"

Kathryn inclined her head and told the duchess it was clear. It seemed to her very silly, really. Perhaps the intimate part of her life with Henry wouldn't be wholly pleasurable or not pleasurable in its own right. She remembered her encounters with Manox, where he was the one pursuing his pleasure and she'd never fully enjoyed it.

But even then, in her worry that they'd be discovered and the worst consequences that could come of it, Kathryn had found some enjoyment of the mere physical pleasure. She could not see how it would be different with the king.

Oh, surely, he was old. And the duchess expounded on his physical repulsiveness at great length. "I swear," she said. "Harry has gotten so fat that the three largest men that could be found could easily fit in his doublet and with room to spare."

And then, after a moment, "And they say, you know, that the wound on his leg does stink, like a corpse that is three days rotting. Fortunately, he has his physicians and his assistants, not like some gentleman in the country where you might be called to minister to him. It cannot be a pleasant job for those who have to change his bandage." She shook her head. "I understand they fill the bandages with perfumes and many pleasant odors. But if you should notice any smell, pretend not to. In fact, I would advise you, before you go to bed, to take you a kerchief and soak it in perfume. This, breathe you in. Some strong scent, like camphor. Breathe deeply till all your sense of smell be dead, and then you will not risk making a face should the smell from his wound come to your nostrils."

Kathryn nodded again, dismayed. It seemed to her the more she heard, the more pity she felt for King Henry. Everyone trembled at him, and everyone was scared of his might. And well might they bed. The duchess also reminded her that, "Even now, it is said, that Cromwell is in the Tower, waiting to be parted from his head tomorrow. Pay heed, child. The man you are marrying is very powerful and can raise you high above the rank of all mortals. But he also can rain death on you. As he told your poor, ill-fated cousin, he makes you and he can unmake you just as fast, and your unmaking will be stronger than your making, and will take everyone who supports you down with it.

"Be you meek and clean, properly behaved and gentle. Show him never a frowning face. Defer to him in all things, for Harry is a man who likes being tended to. The motto you chose—no other wish but his—is a good beginning. Hold you fast by it, and you will come out well and have a good roll at becoming the most powerful woman this kingdom has ever seen."

While the duchess lost herself in dreams that included "Oh, Kathryn, his other wives will be as nothing to you in your power," Kathryn's mind went on.

It was a sad thing not to be able to tell one's mind be quiet, or bid it be still and not think about the things people said and the feelings behind what they said or what other people must feel and suffer in consequence. Kathryn didn't know when she'd become aware that her mind was more unquiet than most. She thought it must have been when she heard the other ladies in the dormitory talk about their beaus and their suitors.

It was always what great conquest they'd made and what great gifts they could get. Kathryn understood this to a point. She had felt very proud when she held Dereham's affections. In a way, she thought, deep inside, she'd thought of it as a game in that he'd been the most desirable of all the men sniffing around the maid's chambers. With his dark, flashing eyes, his dark hair, his expression that could look as though it would consume you with his hunger, he'd been desired by all the women. Often, Kathryn would see another of the maids look at him or else do something to attract his attention, and she would smile for she knew how secure he was and that never would he stray or look at another woman.

But then there was the other side of it. She'd worried about what he felt, even at the end when he'd threatened her and she'd realized he was not the man she thought he was. And even as repulsed as she was by Manox and his attempt to besmirch her name, she remembered him, that time she'd seen him in the yard, thin looking and haggard, as if he'd not been sleeping.

And she remembered Jane Boleyn telling her how it hurt her to love her husband and love him madly and yet to not have that love returned. It occurred to Kathryn that she was very fortunate indeed not to know what love was. Oh, she'd thought she had known, but now that she looked back, she could see that all she'd felt for Dereham was a strong liking. She couldn't imagine loving him like Lady Rochefort loved her late husband—a love that even now would not leave her and drove her mind to madness, making her, in a way, enamored with the grave. Nor could she imagine loving him as Manox had seemed to love her—craving more and more of her every time and never satisfied with what he got. She could not imagine loving someone so much she'd destroy him—or herself—rather than let them go.

As though reading her mind, the duchess, who'd been watching her, said, tartly, "It is a good thing you are not in love with him. I think Anne was by the time she married him, and that's what made her so shrewish. The same with his wife, the first Catherine. Look you how long she dragged the divorce and how painful she made it when, had she agreed to it, we'd have none of this nonsense of breaking from Rome and no turmoil in the land." The duchess was strongly Catholic, though these days she spoke not of her loyalties. "What could she expect to get from opposing him? Men never give in when you're arguing with them and reminding them they have treated you badly. But Catherine was in love with him, and love is grasping and irrational. She tried to hold him when he would flee. And Anne noticed his affair with Jane Seymour, and was jealous and treated him badly. Learn from their mistakes. If she had continued being sweet with him, forgiving all, likely he would not have moved against her, or if he had, he'd have divorced her, not had her killed. This Queen Anne, too, mark how sensible she was, because she loved him not. And she did very well by it and is her own mistress for the first time in her life and, I doubt not, vastly pleased with it all. So, be you happy you're not in love with him. Treat him always with equal kindness and even gentleness, and he will hark to you above all others. And if he has affairs—something I doubt me, considering his age and infirmity—do you as others have done and pretend to see nothing."

Kathryn inclined her head again. And all the while, she felt sorry for the king. What must it be like to have the power of life and death over his subjects—to be able to raise them or sink them with a word and, with another, send them to the block or the gallows, and yet not be loved.

Oh, she knew that in churches throughout the land and even in the faraway lands, people prayed for the king's health and that he was seemingly loved, but yet she doubted it. At least she doubted they loved the man beneath the crown.

She'd seen the pageants to Queen Anne of Cleves, where people looked at Henry and flinched a little. The older people talked about the beautiful king they'd known—the young man who was vigorous and athletic and whom, one day, his own humble subjects had undressed in a fit of adoration. She couldn't imagine it now.

The dowager duchess herself elderly and often, like today, dressed in the ridiculous attire of a much younger woman—her face painted in a way that highlighted her wrinkles, her dress all red velvets and strong golds, which made the faded skin of age look yet older—spoke of King Henry with distaste. Kathryn wondered if, given a chance, the duchess would marry the king herself and somehow doubted it. But, of course, the king commanded, and you did not say no.

As she was thinking this, she realized that if she was going to be queen, and if she had no way of avoiding it, she might at any rate attempt to make the king feel better about himself and more loved. Perhaps, she told herself, if he didn't feel that most people despised him, he would be more contented, and the kingdom happier withal.

The carriage had stopped, and the duchess said, "Are you sleeping, girl?" even as the door was thrown open.

Kathryn looked out the door at two gentlemen who were holding the door open. Her uncle was extending his hand to her to help her down, and what seemed like a sea of ladies and gentlemen were bowing to her. She covered her mouth. For just a moment the greatest desire to laugh overcame her. How ridiculous it all was.

These people had known her for months, some of them for years, and never had they felt like doing so much as nodding to her. But now because the king loved her, they would bow to her and prostrate themselves, their faces in the dirt to welcome her.

A quick pang that this must be what King Henry experienced, this reverence empty of true love, made her lose all desire to laugh, and she set her hand in her uncle's and stepped out of the carriage, while the duchess helped carry her short train.

She was dressed in a gown that the king had himself sent her—a fair gold and red brocade figured all over with ripe open roses. Around her neck, she wore a necklace she had last seen upon Anne of Cleves—a tablet of gold with hanging pearls.

The duchess had exclaimed when she saw it and had told Kathryn that it had once been Anne Boleyn's and that a B used to hang at the bottom of it among the pearls, but Kathryn refused to believe it was ill omened. After all, all the other queens had worn it since her late cousin, so it was more of a jewel of power, like the crown, than something she'd got from the ill-fated queen.

Kathryn followed a gravel path, while the ladies who lined it fell on their knees and bowed. Most of them she knew from her own time as a lady-in-waiting to Anne of Cleves, and she tried to smile at them, but they all looked down and pressed their faces to the ground.

The palace itself was the most handsome that Kathryn had ever seen. She was led through a bewildering succession of rooms, each more magnificent than the last, all gold and painted walls, all columns and hangings, till she was, at last, in the queen's room. She marked with a frown that the initials for the king and the queen in gold upon the wall seemed to have been changed hastily. It seemed to Kathryn, if she squinted, she could see an *A* under the C that was the Latinized version of her name, and under that a *J*.

But most of all she was overawed by the beauty and riches all around. How had come she, Kathryn Howard—youngest daughter of the youngest son of the Duke of Norfolk, the son who had only ever been able to keep his family in penury and want—to this estate? What did it all mean? Was it just the ability to catch the king's eye?

It seemed like a dream, as people bowed her through an open door, past the bed, and then down a flight of steps, to the queen's closet.

The closet wasn't one, or not precisely. It was part of the queen's apartments, but it overlooked the chapel at Hampton Court. from it's depths. Through a screen, you could see the altar with its candles lit.

A mass started almost as soon as Kathryn came into the closet, even though Henry joined her only some minutes later. It was a solemn mass of thanks, with the Te Deum sang by a choir that made the music more beautiful and soaring than Kathryn had ever heard it. Lost in it, she almost forgot until she heard the priest pray for the king and his lady, Kathryn, that God send them issue and plentiful.

Then it was time to say the vows, which were quick and simple, and just as any couple on the street might say them: *With this ring, I thee wed, with my body I thee worship, with half my worldly goods, I thee endow.*

The king said them eagerly, and Kathryn said hers carefully, unwilling to make a mistake. She thought how ridiculous it was that she should be endowing the king with goods. What would they be? Her gowns? Or perhaps the hundred pounds from Francis

Dereham that were left, forgotten, under the lose board of the dormitory at Horsham.

She smiled at the thought and in smiling, caused the king to smile at her. He leaned over to kiss her and whispered, "I am glad you are happy, sweetheart. I await anxiously the time to go to bed and take you, fully and well, as my wife."

Thirty-six

DURING the dinner that followed, while entertainers came to play, Kathryn caught people giving her curious and pitying looks. They were so clear, she could almost read them.

They wondered how she would take to the king's person, gross and immense as he had grown; what she would think of his bandaged leg; and if perhaps she wouldn't run screaming from the deformed, aging monarch.

Kathryn smiled at the looks, because she thought it was all very much beside the point. She already knew she could endure physical intercourse where she was not very much interested, and besides, in this she found herself in full agreement with the dowager duchess. Her interest here, and all her care, was to see that the king was satisfied and made happy. He had given her so much. How could she but help give him what she had.

At length it was decent enough for her to retire to bed. She said her good-byes to the courtiers who had come to the celebratory banquet. She curtseyed to the duke, her uncle, and embraced the dowager duchess, who pressed into her hand a soaked handkerchief, which turned out to be full of rose water.

Part of Kathryn disdained it and wanted to fling it away. But part of her knew that she didn't realize the full extent of the king's malady and that she might in fact find herself flinching from the odor. With this in mind—and knowing the duchess, in this at least, had Kathryn's best interests at heart—Kathryn smelled the kerchief deeply, then left it on her bedside table while her chamberers undressed her and helped her prepare for bed.

The bed was already, as Kathryn had seen it made so many times, prepared for the queen, all properly tidy and clean. She wondered which heavyset woman they'd got to roll on it and test it for hidden daggers now that the German ladies had left with Anne of Cleves for her retreat at Richmond.

But she was more concerned with being undressed, then attired in a chemise of simple cut but covered all over in exquisite embroidery, all lover's knots with hers and the king's initials intertwined.

And then her maids retreated and she waited. She did not wait long. A moment later the king arrived, already undressed for bed, and wearing a chemise, himself, of cloth as fine as hers and covered all over with as much embroidery.

Either in vanity or because his feelings on the occasion overcame the infirmities of his body, he did not have his walking stick with him but walked in under his own power, talking and joking with his entourage.

It seemed to her he might have drunk a little too much, as though to give himself courage, and she realized in that moment that even the king himself expected her to be repulsed by him and to flinch from his size, his girth, his smell.

She resolved, right there, not to do that. It would have been, she thought, like kicking a cowering dog or torturing a friendly cat. It would be adding pain where only good had been received.

Forcing a smile onto her face, she watched her husband sit on the side of the bed. Henry. It had been this Henry all along. How odd it was and how she would have laughed all those years ago if anyone had told her the king was to whom the divination referred.

She shook her head at her own foolishness and smiled at him. The king smiled back her, looking somewhat surprised. Then he turned around and told his entourage in a happy manner that Kathryn had never heard from him, "What, you laggards? What do you, lingering about in my room where I mean to take my rest with my wife? Think ye to stop us from conceiving a Duke of York?"

There were protests from the entourage, some of them accompanied by half laughter, as though they reacted to the king's playful tone more than to his words.

"Well, fie with you, then, and be off, for bright and early in the morning, I mean to go hunting for the deer in my thickets." He grinned. "Tonight I have other thickets to plunder."

The men filed out, all too quickly, taking their lighted tapers with them. She could tell from the looks they exchanged that none of them expected to actually go hunting with the king in the morning. She knew that the king hadn't gone hunting in many years, not since the pain in his leg had grown such as to stop his enjoyment in the sport.

But she had other concerns, as the king gave her a very soft kiss and said, "Hello, sweetheart. Did I make you wait long?"

"It seemed a very long time," she said. "Me thought perhaps Your Majesty had changed your mind and realized you did not want me, after all."

"Not want you!" he said, and laughed. "Never."

He undid her chemise, and quested about with his hands, shocking her a little with his clumsy touches, his awkward explorations. It seemed to her that Dereham, and even Manox, much younger than the king and, for sure, much less experienced, had a care and a manner about them that the king seemed to lack.

How could he not have learned it with his four wives, his mistresses?

And then she realized it was because Dereham, and even Manox, had had to learn to please the woman or else she would not let them continue. But the king of England had no such concerns. He could do as he pleased him and shame the devil. Which woman would be foolish enough to tell him nay?

He kissed her again and again, and he felt her body all over, but she could tell—his breath didn't quicken, and he gave no signs of nearing that point of madness that Dereham reached before he took her—that his body had not responded as it should have.

Also his touch was maddening her and not in the way that Dereham's touch had inflamed her. It was not a pleasurable touch, but it seemed to stop just short of anything that could lead to her pleasure.

His large, clumsy hands, very dry and cold, felt now her sides, then squeezed her breasts, touched her thigh, then squeezed her belly, all of it in haphazard manner. It was—Kathryn thought—like the efforts of an untutored and tune-deaf girl when first faced with a virginal, pounding the keys at random and hoping, somehow, that from the discord music would emerge.

She surprised herself with the thought that if this marriage were to work at all, she was going to have to teach the king to play her body as it should be played. But she understood enough of men to know that she couldn't seem to teach him. And certainly not tonight.

Well she minded the duchess's injunction that the man she married should think he was the first, if not the only, and thinking he was the first, he could not be shown that his wife knew more than he did.

No, she would have to teach him little by little with small touches, smaller gestures, and most of all with the expression of her pleasure. Only if she did that, would she be able to teach him without hurting his pride.

As for tonight, something else must be done, and the something else she elected to do was to let her own hands roam over the king's body, from his face—lingering on the red beard that was starting to show traces of grey—down his strong neck to caress his shoulders, then his chest, then trace their path down to his member.

It was smaller than Dereham's but not by much, and when she touched it, it was just as soft and velvety as Dereham's had been. She felt it hardening under her hands and made sure not to grip it in such a way that would betray her experience, but to touch it again and again, over and over, just like she'd done to Dereham when, perhaps, he'd drunk too much or perhaps was too tired for his manhood to spring to life instantly.

Leaning close to the king, she kissed his cheek, again and again and again. "How strong you are, my lord," she said, making sure that her eyes and her voice and everything confirmed her admiration. "How wonderful your body is, so virile, so manly, compared to me who am so slight and so weak."

Her words did it, and his manhood sprang to full life under her hands.

He took her upon the soft feather mattress and the feather bed. It seemed to her that it lasted very little—as little as her first joining with Dereham. And yet the king looked satiated and satisfied as he leaned over to kiss her. "My rose without a thorn," he said. "In your arms I feel young again.

Thirty-seven

KATHRYN woke up in an empty bed, staring at an embroidered canopy. Light came through the wrought linen of the bed curtains, and from outside she could hear people moving.

She knew, from serving Anne of Cleves, that well before the queen woke, her chamberers and maids would be busy in the room: warming the queen's clothes by the fire, preparing water for her washing, getting everything ready to spare Her Majesty the smallest discomfort.

Save the discomfort, of course, of having her entire life take place in front of strangers; she was always on display.

Pulling her chemise around her, she sat up in bed and made to open the curtains, which were brought fully open by Lady Margaret Douglas. Lady Margaret was the king's twenty-five-year-old niece, a woman of such headstrong character that four years ago she had secretly married Lord Thomas Howard. The affair had ended with Lord Howard in the Tower and then his death, for daring to marry without the king's permission.

But she had been one of Anne of Cleves ladies-in-waiting and met Kathryn, and Kathryn had done her best to draw this odd royal widow out. Now, Lady Douglas seemed to be enjoying life in a quiet way and had become the chief of Kathryn's ladies, holding the same position as Lady Rutland had held under Jane Seymour and Anne of Cleves.

"Good morning, Your Majesty," she said.

"Good morning, Lady Douglas," Kathryn said, and, looking confused, added, "How late is it?"

"Why, dawn has barely broken, Your Majesty."

"But . . . where is the king, my husband?" she asked, of a sudden fearful that in her embraces, the king had detected that bit of experience that told him he was not the only and certainly not the first and that even now he was somewhere, plotting to have her seized, perhaps to have her executed. For was it not treason to not let the king know you were not a virgin?

But Lady Douglas only laughed. "His Majesty is out, with his gentlemen, my lady, for bright and early did he ride to the hounds."

"The hounds?"

"He went hunting, milady," Lady Douglas said, and smiled. "He said he felt most marvelous refreshed and as though he were as young as you are."

Kathryn blushed, but got up and submitted to the ministrations of her various maids as she had once watched Anne of Cleves do it. As she did so, Lady Douglas, standing a little aside, talked to her.

"Your Majesty has received several petitions," she said. "For advancement or else for a post at court."

"Do we have vacancies, then?" she asked. "In my household?"

Lady Douglas smiled. "The Lady of Cleve's German maids have left to go with her to Richmond, and that left some openings. But more than that, my lady, it is customary for the new queen to give posts in her household to friends and relatives."

"But—" Kathryn started, meaning to say she had no friends or relatives in need of such bounty.

She was interrupted by Lady Douglas. "Your mother, now widowed, has asked, of your goodness, whether she might not join your household."

"My mother!" Kathryn said, thinking she might be dreaming. She could but dimly remember that Jocasta Culpepper, who had been her mother, but she did know that Jocasta had died giving birth to yet another child, who had died himself aborning.

"Your father's third wife, Lady Margaret Howard, Lady Margaret Jennings, as was."

Kathryn remembered Dame Margaret more clearly. She remembered her coming into the household and making her rules and buying Kathryn a very pretty gown and . . . sending her off to become someone else's responsibility. She barely prevented herself from protesting that Dame Margaret had never so much as given her the promised strawberries, but instead she closed her eyes.

It would be so easy to take revenge. Much too easy. She understood now why people would go in trembling from fear of the king, who could not only separate their heads from their bodies, but also deny them posts and advancement. She might be able to have people killed—from what she understood, Anne had, though it required much more work than simply ordering it done.

However, because she could have people put to death did not mean she need to do so. In fact, perhaps it meant she shouldn't for such a power could be its own undoing. She couldn't avoid one part of being a queen: that no one would show her a real face or a true emotion; that no one would tell her, "I like thee not," even if it were true. What she could avoid was the other part. She could avoid knowingly and by her actions giving people reason to like her not or cause them to hate her in secret till they could do her a wrong.

She remembered all too well the closed-in feuds in the dormitory at Horsham. How one girl could hate another forever over a stolen hair ribbon or a man's attention.

But those at least had been open feuds, not the sort of dark, closed-in feelings where someone hated you but would not let you know. Where the hatred festered and grew till . . . Till like Jane Boleyn's hatred and jealousy of Anne Boleyn erupted in absurd accusations of incest, which in her madness, she might have believed at the time.

No. Kathryn would not tread hard upon the halls of power. She inclined her head. She had two hundred women. She wouldn't even notice her stepmother among the lot. And then, if she did, what did it mean? She doubted Dame Margaret hated her or even despised her. Doubtless sending Kathryn away had just been what any woman in her circumstances would do, trying to lessen the expenses of a spendthrift and all too fertile husband.

"Tell Lady Margaret Howard," she said, gently, "That I will be glad to find her a place in my household, and then, pray, do you so, Lady Douglas, as I am none too sure how the household is arranged yet."

"Certainly, Your Majesty," Lady Douglas said, even as the chamberers were lowering Kathryn's overgown over her head and cinching it in place.

"And while at it, does Lady Rochefort have a place in my household?"

Lady Douglas hesitated. "Your . . . your grandmother, Lady Howard, she said—"

Kathryn could well imagine what she'd said. Poor Jane had very few friends since everyone knew she had as good as murdered her husband, even if she'd used the block and the executioner's ax to do it. But if that one sin were held against her all her life . . . and besides, she'd suffered more from her crime than anyone else, arguably perhaps even more than the man she'd killed. "Send word to Lady Rochefort that I'll always have a place for her in my household. She might be what she is, but she's always been a good friend to me."

"If Your Majesty so wishes," Lady Douglas said, and bowed her head. "But . . ."

"I know. But I do so wish."

Lady Douglas sighed. In this, too, Kathryn realized, she was different now. No one would offer her unwanted advice. No one would push upon her their own opinions. All she had to do was say "I do so wish" or "I do so intend" and all resistance would melt.

"I should also tell Your Majesty that we've received a very ill-spelt letter from a woman who calls herself your old friend and dormitory fellow Mary Tilney, who also wishes for a place in your household."

"Mary Tilney!" Kathryn said, this time with nothing but pleasure. "Of course. Please, find her a place where I can see her often and we can reminisce of our days as girls together. You see, she was the person who showed me around my grandmother's house and . . . and helped me with everything when I first joined."

With that Lady Douglas was dismissed, and the queen left her chamber in the midst of a group of her ladies to hear mass.

The king didn't return till the evening.

He came in, bluff and hail, his walking stick quite forgotten, full of sparkling stories about his hunt. By the light of the tapers placed upon the table next to them, he looked younger and almost handsome.

Kathryn knew well enough from hearing Dereham tell of his exploits, few of which interested her at all, how to keep gentlemen talking, even if she were on the verge of falling asleep from sheer disinterest. There was the smile and the touch and the admiring exclamation.

All of them worked on the king just as though he had been the most inexperienced of courtiers, quite unready for female admiration. He talked fast and happily of stags missed and stags brought to earth and of his dogs and horses, which were in dire need of exercise.

"I've been a laggard, sweetheart. I see now," he said. "Jane's death so took the joy out of my life that I did not have the strength to do anything and, therefore, let myself get old before my time. But you know, I am not yet quite half a century. That's not so bad, is it?"

And Kathryn, suppressing a quick, lancing pain at the thought that she herself was still far short of a quarter century, said loudly and well, hoping she heard it herself and believed it, "Certainly not!"

The king's eyes sparkled as he smiled at her. "Aye, my rose, I know I am older than you, but the thing is, when you touch me, I feel as though I were young again. I regret only that I can't be truly your age, and live my lifelong with you and sire many children."

"Your Majesty will live many long years yet," she said, laughing. "Perhaps another half century. And we shall see many strong children grow to manhood."

He got out of his seat nimbly, like a young man, and knelt at her feet, kissing both her hands. "May it be as you say, sweetheart," he said, as his eyes sparkled at her, full of love.

That night, by small touches and directions, she started teaching him how to pleasure a woman.

Thirty-eight

In August they moved to Windsor. Kathryn traveled in comfort in a curtained litter with a company of ladies. Strangely, the only ones she felt comfortable with were Mary Tilney and Jane Boleyn. The first because Kathryn had known Mary so long, and even if Mary tried not to tell her the truth, Kathryn could read it in Mary's eyes and expressions. The second because Jane was mad, and being mad she could always say what she pleased, even if often she said it while speaking to the clear air or to that shade of George Boleyn that seemed never to be very far from her thoughts or her sight.

It hadn't been a merry trip like the ones that Kathryn had made with her fellows from the dormitory when she was single. Without being told she guessed it would be unseemly for the queen to sing and make merry jests while in her litter with her ladies-in-waiting.

She did play a little on her lute to pass the time. But most of all, she looked out through a slight opening in the curtains at the dun-colored fields. Here and there, she saw cattle lying about and from the smell perceived they were dead. Men and women lined the roads she passed, their caps removed, their heads bowed. They didn't call her whore or harlot, as they'd called out to poor Anne Boleyn on the night of her coronation, but the voices in which they called out, "Long live Your Majesty" and "God bless Queen Kathryn," were more subdued than not.

It wasn't till they arrived in Windsor, while she was washing away the dust from travel in warm water in front of the fireplace, that she could ask Lady Douglas, "What is it? The plague?"

Lady Douglas shook her head. "Faith," she said. "There are rumors of the plague in London, and that is why the king's majesty doesn't see fit to take you there. But that is not what causes this in the countryside."

"What is it, then?" Kathryn said. "For I have traveled before," she said, as if all her trips between Horsham and Lambeth made her a world-weary traveler. "And I have never seen such dun fields, so many dead cattle, or people so dispirited. Do they dislike me for their queen then?"

"Oh, no, Your Majesty," Lady Douglas said, while helping rinse dust from Kathryn's long auburn hair. "There are, maybe," she said, "some as do but not that many. The ones who resent you at all do so because they loved Lady Anne excessively and wished her to be queen. But she herself having accepted the divorce so mildly gives them no force to pursue her rights for her." She shook her head. "No, milady. What ails the kingdom is this long, hot, dry summer, the lack of rain. The crops die in the field and the cattle for lack of fodder."

What an omen! Kathryn shivered, afraid that this would be held to her account, but Lady Douglas, as though reading her thoughts, shook her head. "No, milady, I don't think we can hold it to your account. It has happened before in this kingdom, and it will again. My grandfather always said there was no accounting for the weather or for the rage of princes." And as though realizing how her words could be taken, she laughed a little. "You see," she said, "he had lived through the Wars of the Roses with all their shifting alliances, and he thought that princes could not be trusted not to make war at will and with no regard."

She dried Kathryn's hair upon a linen towel and commenced brushing it. Normally this was the work of other experienced, specialized attendants, but Lady Douglas seemed to wish to talk to Kathryn in semiprivacy—there were only two women standing near the fireplace—and, therefore, undertook this work herself.

"I thank God every day," she said, "that I was born in this time and not my grandfather's, and that I grew up under the rule of such a good king as our King Henry, because he's kept us from having war in the kingdom, everyone's hand against everyone's else's till it seemed it would be the end days, just as the Bible foretold."

She brushed Kathryn's hair carefully. "There is a letter, Your Majesty, from the Dowager Duchess of Norfolk."

Kathryn stiffened a little but tried not to look alarmed. "My grandmother? Is aught wrong? You said that there is plague in London, and Lambeth is not that far away. I know the king has physicians. Should I—" As she spoke, she started to rise from her seat.

"Nothing is wrong with your grandmother, Your Majesty," Lady Douglas said. "Only she writes to you to ask you a favor for someone she said was an old friend."

Kathryn looked puzzled. Lady Douglas continued, "She has heard from a man called Francis Dereham."

"Francis!" Kathryn said, surprised. The name came to her as

the name of one dead, no more to be pronounced between the living.

"You know him, then, Your Majesty?"

"He was . . . He was one of the gentlemen of honor at the house of my grandmother," she said. "And I have spoken to him in the past. He was, I heard, gone to Ireland to make his fortune in some enterprise of privateering."

"It seems," Lady Douglas said, "that his enterprise prospers not, and that he's determined to come to court and has applied for a post in your household."

"In my household?" Kathryn asked. "But why cannot my grandmother give him a place in her house?"

Lady Douglas shrugged. "I know not. Save that your grandmother said that he would make you a good secretary and that she's sure that he would be a comfort to you to have so near."

Kathryn did not know what her grandmother could be about, nor yet why Lady Douglas looked so pensive. She shook her head. "And yet, he is not in our country, yet," she said. "And I do not wish to make a decision or to think overmuch on this. When he comes onto our land and is ready to make a proper application to my household, I'll see how I feel about it. Why my grandmother thought this one thing—of all things—would give me comfort, I know not."

The look of Lady Douglas's face, which had been closed and grave, seemed to ease up of its own accord. "Ah, my lady," she said at last. "Elderly people have such odd fancies, do they not? Who knows what she can have been thinking."

"Indeed, who knows?" Kathryn said. "Perhaps she was thinking of her own youth and how much pleasure it would give her, now, to see someone from that time. But I'm not so old that my time at Horsham makes me misty eyed."

Lady Douglas smiled and shook her head. "Your Majesty is not old at all." Then she bowed. "If you please, I will now call your maids to help dress you, that you may not be late to dinner with His Majesty, the king."

Thirty-nine

THE long, hot, dry summer continued. They moved from Windsor to Ampthill in Bedfordshire. The king talked of taking Kathryn to London and having a reception in her honor, but it seemed the plague lingered there and the king—for all his renewed vigor—retained a great fear of any illness he might catch.

Instead, they had banquets and parties; he went hunting and sometimes took the queen.

Kathryn was vaguely aware that foreign ambassadors were kept waiting, that ministers grew impatient with documents to be signed in the king's chambers. She knew that the business of the kingdom seemed to have come to a standstill while the king took his ease and enjoyed his honeymoon.

But everyone in her household smiled, and said how renewed the king was and how he seemed to have got his joy in life back. And none accounted it an ill if the business of ruling had to wait yet awhile. So Kathryn determined to enjoy herself.

She had a dim, vague idea that there would be more serious business in her future. She knew that once she went into London there would be delegations and petitions, people wishing for favors from her, and people wishing her to intercede with the king for them. Already some local nobles had attempted this, but she had told them—and truthfully, too—that for all the king's kindness and love toward her, she had very little influence over his decisions. Well she minded the example of Jane Seymour, who had only come close to losing her lord's favor when she'd tried to ask him to spare the lives of the northern rebels. Kathryn, younger than Jane and not carrying the heir to the throne, thought it best not to attempt any such thing.

Instead, she immersed herself in the whirlwind of celebrations. She arranged to have new clothes in the French fashion, having noticed that those were the king's favorites. She accompanied him in the hunt but made quite sure not to out ride him. She let him lead just as she let him win his card games with her.

At night, she sometimes played for him before they went to bed. And the bed itself, though it would never be the same as the passion she'd at first experienced with Dereham, was pleasant enough. She didn't, at least, suffer from the fear of being caught that she'd lived through with Manox.

It was at Ampthill that Kathryn noticed that Margaret Douglas was acting very oddly. She blushed and smiled and seemed at once ten years older and far sillier than she'd ever been.

To her amazement, by dint of much observation, at banquets and dances—where the king danced but little, yet enjoyed watching his wife amuse herself—she realized that Margaret Douglas's eyes, and often her whole attention, fell upon Kathryn's own brother Charles.

Charles and Tom—Henry had, after all, died—as well as Mary had come to join Kathryn's household as soon as it was formed. She liked them well enough but had found them so different from the brothers and sister she remembered as a girl that she could not fully give up on her mourning for the siblings she had known nor rejoice, like Joseph in Egypt, at the recovery of her errant family. Instead, she'd arranged for them to have places at court—as she should have, since they were her own blood—as she had for some of her Leigh brothers and sisters and left them to their own devices otherwise.

But though Charles had grown tall and strong, a black-browed man who was quick with his words and quicker at the dance, she was still used to thinking of him as that overstretched, russet-haired young man to whom she'd bid good-bye when she'd been the one chosen to live with the duchess at Horsham. Or at least, she saw nothing attractive about him.

If she had been looking before, she realized, she'd have been aware that many of the ladies in court were making plays for Charles and that he, either out of genuine love or calculation, was playing for the highest born of them all, the king's niece herself.

Kathryn remembered how the lady's last marriage had happened, and she trembled for her brother. But Lady Margaret Douglas seemed so happy and her brother seemed to be treating her so kindly that she dared not say anything.

Month long, she watched the lovers. She was aware—how could she not be—when Lady Margaret Douglas was late to attend her and suspected sometimes from Lady Margaret's panting and disheveled state that she came from Charles's bed. And she feared for Charles's life and his position, but she couldn't find it in her heart to blight their love. Well she remembered being caught at her own loves, and the shock and horror of it, even when she hadn't been in love with Manox.

She watched in a growing sense of fear, and then woke one morning to a voice like thunder outside the curtains in her room.

It was screaming so loudly that she could not make out what it said. After putting on her chemise, she wrapped a blanket about her shoulders and opened the curtains.

Her heart was racing madly, and her head was spinning in all directions at once. Had the king found out about Manox and Dereham? Perhaps Joan Bulmer, whom she still took care to see as little as possible, had told. Or perhaps it had been that luckless creature Dereham himself.

But instead, when she opened the curtains, she found the king screaming at a man and a woman who were surrounded by the king's gentlemen.

"Impudent, disobedient wretch," he said to the woman in whose disheveled, crying-marred countenance, Kathryn could only with great difficulty recognize the features of the king's niece, Lady Margaret Douglas. "Twice you seek to play this trick on me." He glared at Charles, who was being held by two men, next to his lover. "As for you, sir, I should send you to the Tower and let you rot there, as another Howard has before you!"

He wheeled around, as though sensing that Kathryn had opened the curtains. He could not have heard her, he was shouting so loudly. As he turned to her, Kathryn almost didn't recognize him. He was red faced and seemed to have swollen, causing his eyes to become tiny, hard pits on his face. He looked more like a devil of the pantomime than like her bridegroom. "Do not interfere, madam," he said. "For I will not be moved in this."

Kathryn looked at her brother's desperate expression, his eyes fixed upon her face in a mute appeal for her intercession. But what did he think she could do, except perhaps end up arrested beside him? Did he not know the king and the king's wrath, which could be death?

She looked at her husband and at her brother, and the king thundered, "They were caught, if you please, in the wretch's chamber in full and complete intercourse, as though they were married."

Kathryn didn't even know which of the wretch's chambers the king meant nor, she realized, did it matter. Instead, she inclined her head to his wrath. "Then Your Majesty should deal with them as your heart commands," she said, even as she felt a stab of fear that this would end with Charles dead in the Tower. They'd been children together. True, since she'd been left at Horsham, he'd not written her, but he'd never been one to write much to anyone. But he was her brother, and they'd loved each other when they were little, in their innocence—even living out of boarding houses and in utter penury. But what could she do for him? Her pleading was more likely to hurt him more and destroy her. "For you are the king," she said, submissively, "and you know better than anyone how to govern your kingdom. I am only a small, weak woman, and though he be my brother, he is first your subject."

The effect of her words surprised her. They caused the king's face to calm down on the instant, as it was said that the waters of the Sea of Galilee had calmed at the voice of the Christ. Like that, the red blotches were smoothed, and his face resumed its normal appearance, though it still looked stern.

He said, "You are, as always, the most excellent of women," then turned to his niece. "As for you, madam, you are to be taken to the old Abbey at Syon and there be kept, in seclusion, while you meditate upon your sins. You are to consider whether your continuous rebellion is what is due of my majesty and the excessive kindness with which I have treated you." Then he turned to Charles, and it seemed to Kathryn that she saw fear clench tight at the bottom of Charles's eyes, making his pupils into tight, dark pinpoints. "You will not contact my niece in any way. Not through letter and not through messenger, and never go yourself and speak to her. She is to be for you, from this day forward, as one dead. For now, in love of my dear wife, your sister, I am holding myself in forbearance and not sending you to the Tower or to that well-deserved traitor's death that comes to those who court my near relatives without my consent. But my hand will not be stayed again should you sin once more. Is that clear?"

Charles, clearly still unquiet in his mind, had given his babbling assent that he indeed would never see Margaret again, and he thanked the king's majesty more than he could express and marked well the goodness of His Majesty toward the wretch that he was.

It seemed to Kathryn that, as he spoke, she saw a look of disdain on Margaret's face. It was sure that her feelings had been true and that she felt betrayed by the lover who so quickly disavowed them. But she didn't know yet how authentic her brother's feelings had been, and she didn't have a chance to talk to him for some weeks.

The chance came when both of them stepped out of a crowded room during a dance and found themselves alone in a little place in the garden between two statues. Kathryn had smiled and he had nodded, and she didn't know from where her question came. "Do you miss her terribly, Charles?" she asked.

He had looked at her in full surprise, then had spoken very softly, "Margaret, you mean?"

She'd nodded. "Margaret Douglas."

"I only miss her as I'd miss my own heart had it been torn from my chest," he said. The way he said it, each word carefully enunciated, made Kathryn realize that his seeming lack of feeling wasn't, in fact, because he'd not cared about his paramour but that he cared so much that he dared not say anything, for fear that once it flowed out he'd not be able to stop.

He was tightly controlling a roiling pit of emotion trying to burst out, but she had to ask him, "What made you do it, then? I know she would be a great catch, but sure you know the king would never let you have her! Surely you know it would be death to attempt her. You're lucky to have escaped with your life."

His answer had been a laugh, short and hollow, like the tolling of a bell telling of death. "Lucky, little Kathryn? Lucky? Know you not that being dead is much easier than living with a broken heart."

"Charles!"

He shook his head and looked ahead of him at the darkness of the trees in the garden. A little wind had started up, stirring dust from the long-dry ground and hitting upon Kathryn's exposed face and hands like tiny stinging slaps.

"I would do it again, you know," Charles said. "Tomorrow if opportunity presented."

"But why, if you knew you could never marry her?"

"Ah, for the time with her, that's why. Even if it had been no more than a few hours . . ." He shook his head and looked at her. "You've never loved, have you, Kathryn? Not loved like that, not loved madly. If you had, you would understand. When two souls knit together at first sight, any risk is worth it for one minute, one hour with the one you love. Even if you know that you must die for it."

Forty

In October they came to London, and Kathryn glided into town at night on a very grand barge surrounded by her own people. At a banquet, afterward, all the worthy of London paid their respects to her.

In the morning, the king asked her if she felt equal to receiving Anne of Cleves. "For I promised her," he said, "that she'd come to court whenever she so wished, and if I keep her at bay, people will invent some infamy or other and her party will go. It must be seen, my lady, that you two are friends and like sisters." He looked at Kathryn with a worried expression. "But I know you have so open and frank a nature and are so shy of dissimulation that I am afraid of asking you to undertake this and in public yet."

Kathryn was forced to smile. She could not imagine why the king thought she needed dissimulation, except that during these months she'd come to know him somewhat. He joined to his fear that people would find him, himself not the king—Harry without the crown, as he called his natural self—repulsive, a strange and great illusion that every woman on whom he deigned to rest his favor came to love him madly. She thought that was what he thought—that she must be jealous of Anne of Cleves because Anne of Cleves had spent all those nights by his side and, therefore—even if she'd left him as good a maiden as she'd arrived—Kathryn might resent her.

She forced her smile and bowed her head and tried to reassure him without lying too openly and without offending him. "It is true," she said, "that I find it very hard to pretend that which I do not feel, but Your Majesty knows my sole care is for your happiness and to make you rejoice that you chose me as your wife. If Your Majesty needs me to be kind and gracious and to behave to my Lady of Cleves as though we were close friends, then we shall do so." Latching on to a memory of the past and knowing that the two of them had most often talked during walks in the garden or while petting the royal court's excessively large number of pet cats and dogs, she added, "Only perhaps, if it were possible to procure two young spaniels of the kind the ladies at the court favor, for my Lady of Cleves loved them exceedingly and I do not think that she took any of them with her. A good breeding pair, perhaps, so she can treasure them and enjoy the company of their offspring."

The king had smiled. "You are graciousness itself, Kathryn. I shall arrange for my gentlemen to seek those dogs out. Also, if you will permit me, my sweetheart, I will arrange for two gentlemen to attend you and her, should you wish to dance or in otherwise to do as will amuse you with music or dainties or whatever you ladies do in private. If I spend overmuch time with her, people will say that I am contemplating bringing her back into my bed. It is best you two be seen to be as close as sisters."

And so it was that Anne of Cleves came to court. While Kathryn felt no trepidation at all over the reception of the queen she had displaced, yet the situation must be awkward. She did not know how Anne of Cleves felt. She remembered the former queen's innocent joy in her position, her certainty that the king loved her, though he never made love to her, and she wondered if perhaps the older woman resented her.

On the appointed day Kathryn waited in her chamber, seated upon a chair that wasn't a throne and yet gave the impression of one, and surrounded by her closest maids when the door opened and Anne of Cleve's was announced.

Kathryn didn't know what she expected, but she did not expect for the other woman to fall upon her knees and, on her knees, approach the throne.

It was partly because she wanted to obey the king and be seen to love this woman as her sister, but partly because she felt a horrified sense that this was wrong, that Kathryn jumped up and met Anne of Cleves halfway up the chamber, taking her by the hands, kissing her on each cheek—which with the taller woman on her knees was at a very convenient height indeed. "Rise, Lady of Cleves, rise, for you embarrass me. You must not be so humble before me. What am I, but the most humble of your maids? And you the daughter of a prince and the adopted sister of my lord. Rise, please, rise."

Hesitantly, as though shocked at such emotion from her hostess, Anne of Cleves rose slowly and spoke in English that was no longer halting, even if it was marred still by a strong German accent. "Your Majesty," she said, "must understand that I was very afraid of offending you."

"Offending me, you? You, who had ten times the reason to be angry at me?"

"But why would I be angry at you?" Anne of Cleves asked, confused. "For well I know that you did nothing to replace me. It was only that the king preferred you to me, and we all know what men are." She smiled a little at that, as Katherine led her back to the chair that had now been set beside the one Kathryn had occupied. "You can no more control them than I could. I am glad the king, who was a gracious and kind lord to me in all but that he could not love me, has found a lady so suited to his temper, and I vow I hope for the longest and happiest life for both of you, and many children to gladden the kingdom."

After that, Kathryn had dismissed her maids, and she had sat with Anne of Cleves and talked. It should have been awkward, and they should have found their conversation halting and slow. But instead, Kathryn found that she was speaking to the one woman in the world who knew exactly the life she was living and who understood her frustrations and distress at being always on display.

Before they fully realized it, they were discussing the embarrassment of everyone prostrating themselves at their approach and the natural shame of having such things as their monthly cycles known to all.

There was only one moment of sadness when the former queen asked Kathryn if she was quite sure that the king behaved to her as he should to a wife. Kathryn understood this to mean that Anne of Cleves was asking her if she was quite sure that she was no longer a maiden. Kathryn assured her of this and a fleeting shadow crossed Anne of Cleves's face. Then she smiled and said, "I find it unlikely that I will ever marry, but I have asked the king if I can have the Lady Elizabeth with me at Richmond, for I feel like she's as a daughter to me, and I've seen her there often."

From that they'd talked about the king's children—that goodly babe, Edward, fussed over by an army of nurses and maids; Elizabeth, precocious, inquisitive and already showing signs of what the dowager duchess would doubtless call the Howard charm; Mary, proud and reserved. "I do not think," Kathryn said, "she gives me the deference due her mother."

At this Anne of Cleves had laughed. "But how can she, Your Majesty, when she is older than you?" And Kathryn's humor, catching on that, made her laugh at her own pretensions. "I owe I'd not thought of it that way."

"She's well enough, is Mary," Anne of Cleves said. "We correspond and meet sometimes. She likes to speak of books and theology, and the theology she learned is so different from the one I learned that we find we have everything to talk about."

At that moment the two puppies were brought in, and Kathryn presented them to Anne of Cleves. They were full young, just removed from their mothers and very beautiful, with large, liquid eyes. Anne's reaction was all Kathryn had hoped and for a while they played with and petted the puppies.

"I think I'll call this one William," Anne said, at last, seizing hold of the little male. "Wilhelm. See how his mouth is set in such a scowl? He looks exactly like my brother when I displeased him, which I'm afraid happened very often. Though the puppy," she continued as the little animal licked her, "seems by far the more affectionate."

They were both laughing over this when the king came in. Kathryn quickly asked a servant to take the puppies away for now, until my Lady of Cleves required them, then rose to greet the sovereign. He embraced her and kissed her, then embraced and kissed Anne of Cleves with perhaps more warmth than Kathryn had ever seen him show that lady.

The three of them sat together at supper, and a right merry supper it was. Now that Anne knew enough English to make jokes, she proved a very suitable conversationalist. And now that the king was no longer forced to be married to her and thus kept from his heart's desire, he seemed to genuinely enjoy her company.

But after dinner he left them, saying he was too old to dance—an amusement both girls had expressed an interest in—and that he would send in two of his gentlemen to partner them. He ignored Kathryn's protests that "Fie, my lord is not too old," kissed them and embraced them, then left them.

Musicians came in and set up their instruments.

And then two gentlemen came in and bowed to them. One of them was Charles Howard, Kathryn's brother. The other one . . .

Momentarily, Kathryn couldn't breathe. He was a tall man with hair as red as the king's own hair must have been in his spring. His features were perfectly regular and pleasant. His eyes oval, well cut, and expressive beneath his arched eyebrows. And his lips were sensuous and seemed to come to a resting position in a little smile. He was shapely of body, too, with muscular legs and a well-built chest that could not be hidden even by the richly broidered and ornamented doublet he wore.

But describing him meant nothing. He was all that, yes, but he was so much more. The effect of him compassed his presence, something that could not be described, nor seen, but could surely be felt. And he moved like a cat, with ease and naturalness.

Her hands clenched upon her skirt, her throat closed. She was aware of Anne of Cleves giving her an odd look and her brother Charles a knowing one. After which Charles drew Anne of Cleves into conversation, probably, Kathryn thought, to save her from seeing how stricken Kathryn was.

Knowing she was stricken allowed her to conquer it, though. She drew herself up proudly. "My lord," she said, though her voice might be a croak.

He gave her a very deep bow, and she thought that the bow was as much out of respect as to hide a smile of the deepest mischief, a trace of which remained upon his lips as he straightened.

"My lady queen," he said. "I am your cousin, Thomas Culpepper, and I believe we've met once before."

Now she felt her color come up in waves upon her face, but she had an excuse and seized upon it. She laughed, a shaky, unsteady laughter. "We have indeed," she said. "How well I remember. And I was seized with embarrassment remembering how that young Kathryn must have annoyed you and kept you from the natural entertainments of a gentleman on a coronation night."

He laughed easily. "I don't think you kept me from anything," he said. "Save only perhaps getting very drunk on the free wine flowing from all the fountains."

"I am sure you would not have gotten drunk," she said, and turned to Charles, so blinded by her confusion that she seemed to see him as through a mist. Even through the mist, she realized how concerned her brother looked and how much she must sound unlike herself, but she tried to force herself to be normal and said, "Charles, I met Thomas at the coronation of our cousin Anne. I'm afraid I'd got quite lost, separated from our grandmother's ladies, and he found me wandering about in a most disreputable manner."

"Not disreputable," he said. "Only lost."

"Disreputable. And he devoted the rest of the night to playing squire to a little girl. Though it will shock you to learn that when he left me at our grandmother's, he promised me he would be back to visit me and give me strawberries, and he never did."

"That doesn't surprise me at all," Charles said, hiding his alarm well beneath a veil of amusement but not so well that Kathryn didn't perceive it. "Thomas is well known for disappointing ladies' expectations." He smiled brightly at both Kathryn and Anne of Cleves. "And now, my ladies, shall we dance?"

They'd danced, all four of them a very long time. First the traditional dances and then more modern ones and finally some dances from her country that Anne of Cleves taught them. She'd never got to dance them in her country, she said, since her brother was so strict, but she had seen them danced and now that she was her own mistress, she'd been learning them alone in her room.

After Kathryn got used to Thomas Culpepper's presence, some of her awkwardness vanished. Not the odd sensation that looking at him gave her. She still felt as though one look at him made her unable to breathe, caused her heart to clench in her chest, and made her quite unable to think clearly.

But as with wine or strong beer, more exposure lent some immunity. She could look at him without showing her interest and treat him like the cousin he was without causing Charles to give her odd looks.

"It is amazing I've never seen you before at court," she said between dances, while Anne tried to get clear in her mind the steps she meant to teach them. "For sure I would have remembered our former acquaintance earlier."

"Not so amazing," he said. "I did not go on the progress. And before that, I never got to accompany the king's majesty when he went to visit you." He smiled a little. "Truth be told, I have a great fear of the dowager duchess and her walking stick."

She'd laughed and talked about how the dowager used her walking stick on unsuspecting heads, and sometimes suspecting ones, all without referring to her own past adventures.

Toward the end of the night, Culpepper excused himself from

the room for a few minutes. When next he partnered Kathryn for a dance, in the middle of a twirl and disguised by it, he slipped something into her bosom.

She felt it, papery, against her breasts and looked up at him to find his expression such a mixture of amusement, hope, and fear, that she said nothing.

It wasn't till she was in her room—for once the king was not spending the night with her, having retired to bed long before the dances were done—that she had time to pull the object from her bosom and examine it.

It was a long folded paper, sealed with red wax and a seal she didn't know. Breaking the seal, she found pointy, exact handwriting, which was not hard to read, not even to her inexperienced eyes.

Your Majesty, My Queen, the letter read.

How odd it is to have to refer to you in this way, when the minute my eyes saw you I realized you were my own true love and the one I was born to marry. How odd that we are to be divided in this way by my own feckless neglect and the desire of a king.

My fecklessness lies not only in having forgotten my promise to visit you and bring you strawberries, but also in my not having gone along when the matter of our possible marriage was bruited. You see, I mistrusted the dowager and was afraid she meant to shackle me to someone no one else wanted. So I took myself to the country and made myself scarce to my great chagrin now that I have met you.

The moment I saw you, I fell instantly in love. I cannot explain it, as I've never loved in the past and, in fact, have always made much sport of those who claimed to love at first site. But your look, your voice, will always be in my heart, and I'll always be the fool who failed to seize upon the most wonderful love that could have been on this Earth.

Yours, in hope of paradise,
Thomas Culpepper

In the bottom of the letter, hastily written, a line begged her to burn the letter, since *"neither you nor I can withstand His Majesty's wrath."*

It hurt her to burn the letter, as much as it gratified her to know that his thoughts and reactions had been the same as her thoughts and reactions—instant, unavoidable love, as though their hearts had knit together in the one instant.

She shed a tear as she put the letter in the fire, and it had just gone up in flames when the king came in through the door. "I could not sleep without you," he said, then, marking her tears, "Cry you, sweetheart. Cry no more. Your Henry is here."

Forty-one

THINGS could never be the same, though she tried. It vexed her because there was no sense in it. Why should she be so drawn to Thomas Culpepper, with whom she'd talked a bare two times, with whom she'd danced one evening.

She could not explain it. And she hated not being able to explain it. The thought kept returning to her that this must have been how Manox felt about her, how Jane Boleyn felt about her late husband. She tried to imagine what it would be like—what form of horrible suffering it would be—to endure this attraction without its being returned. She could not. And then she doubted that it was a worse suffering than enduring the attraction, knowing it returned and not being able to express it.

Early in the morning she woke up thinking of Thomas Culpepper, wondering how he was doing and what occupied his mind. She thought of him all day long. At night, while she lay in bed with the king of England or while the king made his still-clumsy love to her, she imagined what Thomas Culpepper might be doing, and with whom.

Without knowing if he were sleeping with the maidens of the court, she imagined that, of course, he was, such were the morals and manners of the royal court, and in retaliation, she hated all of her maids. She imagined each of them kissing Thomas Culpepper or sighing in his arms or lost in pleasure with him in bed, and she grew waspish and demanding with them all.

She overheard them say it was because she was so indulged by the king and how her power had gone to her head, and she couldn't tell them it was none of that but only that she was afraid each and every one of them was her rival for the love of Thomas Culpepper. The love she could not have.

The king smiled at her short temper—always short-lived, as she remembered the king's own temper could be lethal—and gave her dainties and land, jewelry and clothes. It took Kathryn some time to understand that the king hoped her temper meant that she was with child. And for all she knew, she might be, as the normal flux of her cycles had stopped. There were whispers at court, and her ladies cast her hopeful glances.

And days slid, one into the other. And nothing changed. There was the hunt and the banquets, the dancing, the king's indulgent love—and Kathryn's desperate, hopeless longing for Thomas Culpepper.

She started changing her route so that she crossed paths with him or else saw him cross the corridor ahead of her. She learned when he practiced jousting in the yard and would go to a window to watch him below.

Sometimes he caught her looking and smiled up at her.

Of these moments her days were woven.

In the middle of all this, she received a letter from the dowager. Francis Dereham was back in England, penniless and scarred. She asked Kathryn to make him her secretary.

Kathryn demurred. Oh, she understood Francis's plight and now,

now that she understood love, she felt guilty about the way she'd treated him. She'd not toyed with him on purpose, rather she'd not understood her own emotions. But all the same, she feared that Francis Dereham had reason to be resentful of her and to think she'd broken her promise, and it wasn't just the money she'd taken from him and so blithely forgotten under a loose floorboard at Horsham.

But she thought—remembering Dereham's temper and his quick retorts—that it would be better if he were not at court, and his temper were not tried by seeing her married to the king and grown great beyond his reach. More important, she was afraid that his quick gaze would discern how she felt about Culpepper and would make some move to avenge himself. What that was, she did not know, but she was sure he would do something that would injure her and possibly put Thomas in jeopardy.

Diffidently, and not daring to commit her true reasons to paper, she wrote a letter to the duchess, telling her that she did not think Francis should come to court.

The next day she got a letter from Lady Bridgewater, her aunt Elizabeth Howard, who was married to the Duke of Norfolk, and another letter from the duchess, begging her to take Francis Dereham—that poor boy, so beaten by fate and his adventures—into her household.

This time, not daring write to her grandmother, she had herself rowed across the Thames to Lambeth to speak to Her Grace.

Forty-two

"But why will you not have him?" the dowager asked.

Kathryn had entered the duchess's apartments and closed the door behind herself, as well as making sure there was no one about, not even in the chambers leading up to the one in which they were.

The duchess obviously knew what this was about, but looked utterly baffled, all the same. "But I thought you were such good friends."

"Good friends we were," Kathryn said. "And perhaps it would be better if the king never heard aught about this friendship."

"But . . ." The dowager looked puzzled. "I thought you loved Master Dereham."

"By honor, madam, and by my vows, I am bound to love the king, my master, and no other." She kept her voice low, all the while wondering how she could possibly have misunderstood the duchess. After all, she had always thought the old lady was as shrewd as any and far more shrewd than most. How could she have so misunderstood her that the duchess seemed innocent about the dangers of forcing Dereham upon Kathryn?

Now the duchess sighed, and she sat upon her chair—paying no heed to the fact that she was not supposed to sit in the front of the queen without permission. Well she knew that Kathryn was far too kindhearted to demand she stand.

She looked up at Kathryn with a cool, speculative gaze that looked all the more intimidating for coming from within a nest of wrinkles that Kathryn didn't remember being there the last time she'd seen the dowager. "Child, child! Far be it from me to tell you to neglect your duty or to not fulfill your obligations to your husband, but have you thought of what will happen should the king die and you without issue?"

"Why . . ." Kathryn said. "The same that will happen have I issue, is it not? I will be the regent until the prince attains majority."

The duchess sighed again. "You might be," she said. "But think you on this: the king leaves behind an infant son and two daughters that he has made illegitimate. Your family is neither meek nor mild, and I avow your uncle and I will give you what support we can, but, child, we are only one of the great families in this land. The Seymours stride the land yet and try to get back to their prior position of power. If you are left as our queen dowager, they can do that by either marrying you—you'll become the spoil of the strongest man—or by accusing you of some heinous crime and having you killed."

Kathryn swallowed. Until this moment she hadn't thought of it that way, but she supposed that it was always indicated. "I suppose," she said, slowly. "That I am more like my father than I had thought."

The dowager gave her a quizzical look, and Kathryn laughed. "Remember, madam, how you asked me once if I were likely to grow my father's fondness for the gaming tables, and I told you I didn't believe so. But I guess I have the same attraction for the danger and the glory that gaming gives. It is a game, is it not, madam. All or nothing? Now I think about it, you, too, and my uncle, must have the same attraction to gaming, since you must admit you used me as your pawn."

The duchess sighed. "All of life is a gamble," she said. "And there is no such thing as a sure bet."

"But I still do not understand, madam," Kathryn said, "what this can have to do with Francis Dereham that makes it so urgent for you to make him my secretary."

The duchess was quiet a long time. "Well, madam?"

"Tell me this, chit. Does Harry . . . that is, how does he perform the office?"

It took Kathryn a moment to realize of what the duchess spoke, and in the end she thought of it only because of the sly look in the duchess's eyes. Her first thought was that she was being asked how Harry attended mass. It was only on second thought that she realized she was being asked how Harry performed in bed. "Every night and eagerly," she said, and got an odd look.

The duchess raised her eyebrows. "Are you with child? There are rumors."

"My flow has stopped two months ago."

"Is it Harry's?"

Kathryn should have been offended but wasn't. It was said simply in the way of a reasonable enquiry. She nodded. "It could be no one else's."

"Well then, I congratulate you, and I hope for your sake that it takes, they rarely do, you know, Harry's children. All his wives have lost more than they keep. If this should happen to you . . ."

Kathryn finally understood what the duchess was tapping around. "Madam," she said. "Do you mean that I should have children by Dereham and pretend they were Henry's?"

The duchess shook her head. "Some things, my dear, should never be said aloud, even if one is sure no one but our friends are listening. But you know, my dear, if you should need help, you'll have a friend at your right hand."

"Madam," Kathryn said, drawing herself up, aware that in her case the height to which she could draw herself was inconsequential. "Surely you don't think I would to that."

"An' that's the spirit," she said. "And so you shouldn't. But you will take him as your secretary, will you not?"

"What? To perform the office for me? No, I will not, madam, and I am shocked, in fact, that all these women in my family, all these ladies that wish me well, should want me to have Dereham so close. What if he talks?"

The duchess gave her a long, wise look. "What is more likely, child? That he will do you a bad turn if he depends on you for his advancement and his support—he's fairly on the rocks after his adventures in Ireland—or if he is outside, cast about, knowing you no longer care what becomes of him? In which case do you believe he will seek to do you a bad turn."

A bad turn. Kathryn remembered Dereham boasting of what he would do if anyone replaced him in her affections. What would he not do if he thought she had cast him entirely out?

Oh, she hated this, and there was no way out of this. "Very well, madam, if it must be so, send Dereham to me. Before he comes, though, pray remind him that he is to be my secretary and nothing more. One foot wrong, one word in the wrong ear, madam, and we're both lost, he and I. Pray tell him that it's not just my life he'd destroy."

But all the while in the boat, back to the palace, she wondered if it would make any difference to Dereham. She wondered if he were not rotten with the sort of love that Jane Boleyn had nurtured for her late husband. The sort of love that would rather kill than allow the beloved one to go on and be happy with someone else.

She felt as though a chill had come upon her and closed her eyes, listening to the water beating against the boat beneath her.

She would have to pray and hope, just like the gambler between casting the die and watching them land.

Kathryn had turned out just like her father.

Forty-three

THAT night Kathryn lay awake till late, waiting for the king, but the king did not come. She wondered if someone had her heard her talk with the duchess, and woke up feeling battered and bruised and weakened inside in a way she couldn't describe.

It was as though, she thought, something inside her were speeding up—something that wasn't her heart or, indeed, any organ she could name, but something that was part of her, nonetheless. Speeding, speeding, rushing, until it presently would go so fast that she would lose consciousness or perhaps go all to pieces, like all those gods in Rome and Greece who got taken to pieces and thrown all over the sky.

She didn't want to ask her chamberers, and she didn't want to ask her maids if they knew where her husband was. Her grandmother's advice came to her, if Henry played on her, she should pretend not to see it, as others before her had.

But pretending not to see it and in fact not seeing it were different things. And Kathryn feared that if some other woman should attract his attention . . . Why had Anne Boleyn died? Because she was headstrong and made the king's life difficult? Or because the king preferred that "whey-faced wench" Jane Seymour? Kathryn couldn't answer, and she doubted anyone could.

She sped out of her chambers as soon as she was attired, ignoring her maids requests that she wait or that she take company with her. She could half hear the noise of feet behind her, catching up with her. One or two, perhaps three, of her ladies-in-waiting were following her. She didn't care.

She ran like a mad woman through the hallways. She ran as though she were not the queen of England, but still Kathryn Howard, the youngest maid of honor to the queen. She ran headlong and heedless, along paths she hadn't taken since she'd come to the king's quarters, every night, to play for him.

What would she do if she found another woman playing for him? Did she want to see this? Did she intend to make a scene?

Oh, she wasn't jealous of the king, though perhaps she was—she was jealous of the affection, of the attentions of Harry with the crown, of the things he could give, and more important, of the importance he bestowed on whomever he loved.

She wasn't jealous of Harry without the crown—his clumsy caresses, his confused attempts at pleasuring her.

But the thing was this, wherever Harry without the crown went, Harry with the crown followed. The two were one being only and linked to each other in ways that could never be prized apart.

Panting, her heart beating in her chest as though it would crack out of her rib cage, she made it into the king's quarters. Out of breath, out of hope, out of patience, she entered the first room—the antechamber, where a few of his gentlemen were playing at dice.

"Henry!" she said. And looking blindly at the men, not recognizing any, "Where is the king, my husband?"

Two men rose. One of them said, "Kathryn? Are you well? Kathryn!" She recognized the voice of her brother, but she couldn't see him clearly. There was nausea clenched in her throat, her heart was beating fit to tear her chest. Her breath came in ragged, painful gasps.

But worse of all was the pain in her stomach. Fear and anxiety it must be. She remembered her stomach hurting a few times, when she was first at the duchess's. She remembered the clenching pain of not knowing what to do, not knowing where to go and being quite sure that everything she might do was wrong.

She clasped both hands around her stomach. Those times, at the duchess's, it had never hurt as though a sharp-fanged, evil-clawed beast had seized hold of her middle and was tearing at it with ravenous hunger, seeking to tear her apart. It had never felt like this. Never felt as though she might die from it.

"Madam," another voice said. Two pairs of hands grasped her, one hand at the arm, another supporting her back. "Your Majesty looks quite ill."

There was a feeling of moisture upon her thighs and for a moment she wondered if she'd forgotten herself so far as to lose control of her bladder, but none of it mattered very much.

What mattered, instead, was that the king had failed to come to her last night. The king was already tired of her. What did anything else matter? It wasn't just the king's wrath that could kill you. The king's lack of love could also.

"My husband," she said. "My lord husband, the king? Where is he? Is he within? Who is with him? Does he . . . does he love another?"

"No," the voice she only now identified as Thomas Culpepper's said. He sounded as though he were only denying it perfunctorily, though, as though it didn't matter very much and something else were holding his attention. "No, no, Your Majesty. His Majesty suffers from a blocked wound upon his leg—he is in great suffering."

"I must see him," Kathryn said, and tried to take a step forward, only it felt as though the entire room were swimming—as though she had drunk too much and couldn't see, couldn't feel things right. The floor under her feet seemed quite fluid, and her knees bent as she tried to walk, and the pain in her middle was worse than ever. "Let me see my husband," she said, trying to flail at the two men on either side of her. She knew one of them was Thomas Culpepper, and she yelled at him, intemperately, "Let me see my husband, Master Culpepper. If he's suffering, I must go to him."

"Kathryn," the other man said. "Don't play the fool. The king ordered his door barred against you. He doesn't wish you to see him in this state."

"Charles," she said. "Charles," and she clutched at her brother's sleeve with desperation. She remembered the conversation with the dowager just the day before about what would happen if the king died before she gave him a child. How she would become either a pawn or would be killed so that one of the rival factions could take power. "Charles, the king must not die. The king's majesty must stay alive. He must stay well, Charles!"

"We are doing all we can, sister. His physicians are closeted with him, and they are a cunning lot. His wound has stopped flowing, and it is said the humors have turned him all black. Sister, he is in great pain, but this has happened before, and he survived. Don't disturb yourself. You truly don't look well."

Her ears were buzzing, loudly. Through the noise, she heard Thomas Culpepper's voice, as from a long distance away. "Howard, I think the queen is bleeding. Look you on the floor."

She tried to deny that she was bleeding, but she had not strength to do it. She felt them lift her bodily, between them. She heard them scream, "The queen is bleeding. Send for her women. Send for a physician."

She tried to protest that she wasn't bleeding, that she couldn't be bleeding. Her flux had stopped. She was pregnant with the king's child. The Duke of York. She would be the mother of the Duke of York and the regent.

"Beshrew my soul!" Jane Boleyn's loud and shocked voice. "I believe Her Majesty is miscarrying."

Forty-four

SHE woke up in her room between the soft sheets. She felt tired and somehow distant, as though the entire world had departed her, going to some place remote and far away and leaving her, Kathryn, here in this soft island of safety.

Lying on the feather mattress, the feather bed, she imagined to herself that she was lying upon a cloud of heaven and sighed softly. For a moment it came to her how lovely it would be to be dead, far from everything, not caring. No more to battle in the joust of life. No more to try to stay safe and ahead of those forces that would destroy her.

But the problem was that she had never believed very much in another life. Oh, it wasn't that she disbelieved. They told her in church that there was another life after this, and she didn't see very much reason to disbelieve it.

It was like the tales that travelers brought of distant lands where strange people lived and strange fruits grew. Why would anyone bother making them up if they weren't true?

In the same way, she believed it might be possible that the life after this one was true. After all, everyone told of it. And there were stories of ghosts and demons, of angels and holy apparitions, coming down from heaven to encourage the faithful and punish the wicked.

But did those tales tell the truth—had anyone ever really come back?

And what if they hadn't? Then there was not very much after death. Only the tomb, dusty and deep, and being forgotten forever.

There would not be dancing or music or love. And she would never see Thomas Culpepper again. And though seeing Thomas Culpepper hurt her—though even thinking of seeing Thomas Culpepper hurt her—the idea of never again seeing him hurt her yet more, and she feared that somehow she would go on suffering after death in that life that didn't exist.

Suppose for a moment that this afterlife existed, somehow. And that she neither got to heaven—which she had some vague idea required more holiness than she possessed—nor was quite so wicked as to merit hell? Then where would she end up? Could she perhaps remain a ghost, haunting the vast corridors of Greenwich Palace?

And would that ghost see Thomas Culpepper, long to touch him, and be unable to?

She heard a sound and rather thought that she had exclaimed, an exclamation of fear and sadness. In response to it, the curtains of the bed were open, and she found herself staring at Lady Rutland's motherly countenance. She had come back to manage the queen's household when Lady Margaret Douglas was sent to Syon.

"I see you are awake, my lady. How feel you?"

"Tired," Kathryn said. "So tired."

"Well, that is only to be understood, when you realize how much blood you have lost."

"Blood?" she said. "But I . . ."

"You lost the child," she said. "It happens sometimes. You worried too much about the king's majesty and his infirmity. It is not good to worry too much."

"The king," Kathryn snatched, convulsively onto her covers, holding them tight, and trying to rise, as though the pliable coverlet could give her enough support to get on her trembling feet. "The king. How is the king, is he . . . ?"

Lady Rutland only shook her head. "He is the same way, madam. The wound won't flow and the humors are poisoning his body. More than that I don't know, as only his physicians and his chamberers are allowed to go in and see him. Even his gentlemen must stay in the chamber outside his room and get their news from those allowed inside."

"The king mustn't die. He mustn't."

"Praise God's mercy," Lady Rutland said, "he shall not. He'll be preserved to be a husband to you for many years yet."

Kathryn murmured again, "The king mustn't die," as she fell back upon the bed.

She'd never know if she'd fallen asleep or lost consciousness. For the next few days, her memory was a confusion of half-understood words and of things being done to her rather than by her. She felt people raise her, and people clean her, and she had some idea that she had been force-fed some bitter-tasting concoctions.

After a long time, feeling as though she'd been running a long race or perhaps lost in a labyrinth unable to find the way out, she woke up.

Her bed, and she herself, smelled of sickness and sweat. She woke up with a starting cry, as though it had surprised her to find her way out of her nightmare. Then she blinked. The air on her face felt very cool. She opened her eyes. It was dark but not completely. The sort of dark before the full light of dawn, or else the sort of penumbra you get when night is falling. She sighed as she turned, then started a little, as she realized the king was by her side, looking down at her.

He looked sad, perhaps disappointed. "There, sweetheart, there," he said softly. "They tell me you miscarried a child."

"Was it a son?" she asked. She remembered, vaguely, from long ago that her cousin Anne Boleyn had miscarried her son and that everyone had said she'd had a miscarriage of her savior. Her savior.

"It was too early to tell," Henry said. "You should not have worried so much. This leg of mine . . . sometimes it stops, but then it starts again. I have no intention of dying, sweetheart. It's very important that you worry not. A child that is growing within the womb is very sensitive to this sort of upset."

Kathryn started apologizing. She felt as though she were a little girl being scolded, and she cried and begged and implored the king not to take back Anne of Cleves. She held with both hands onto the clumsy, rough hand that was attempting to smooth her hair, "Your Majesty, give me another chance. Do you not discard me, yet. I can give you a Duke of York, I can."

There was a chuckle from the king, and then the soft voice, speaking, "An' you do not, you will still remain our entirely beloved wife." He patted her hair. "I don't know why you'd think I'd ever take back Anne. I never intended to. I never want anyone but you, my Kathryn. It is fit perhaps that my first queen should be Catherine and also the last. Come, do not cry. I will not die, and if God wills, we shall have fruit to our union. Little princesses who look like you, and strong princes like I once was. Do not cry, my dear. There is nothing to cry about. You are young, and we have much time."

But Kathryn held his hand tight with both hands and thought that she, too, might have had a miscarriage of her savior. If the king had died, she would, even now, be fortune's orphan, tossed about by fate and the whims of men. No. It must not happen.

"I must have a child," she said, crying. "I must have a Duke of York, for Your Majesty's joy and the peace of the realm."

"Well, then, my dear, you will have a Duke of York. Only you rest now."

She rested. When she woke up, it was full day, and Lady Rutland was waiting, cheerfully, to help her bathe.

It was three days before Kathryn was fully on her feet again, and a good week before she felt like herself. In the meantime, weak and slow, she found that Dereham, who had arrived sometime while she was unconscious, had been causing problems in her household.

Forty-five

"It is that Francis Dereham, my lady," Lady Rutland said softly, while Kathryn was getting dressed in the morning.

"What? What has he been doing?" For all this time, and though he'd arrived at court days ago, she had not seen him yet. "What does he wish?"

"He's been quarreling with Mr. Johns," Lady Rutland said. "One of your gentlemen ushers. You know what men are, very full of their privilege and clinging to their rights."

Kathryn didn't feel equal to judging disputes over privilege or rights, and certainly she didn't feel equal to considering anything that might involve Dereham. But she knew that she must, and she might as well do it now as ever. "What has been happening?"

"Well, as you know, Your Majesty," Lady Rutland said, probably knowing full well that Kathryn knew nothing of the kind, "lingering over their suppers is a privilege of those who are in the queen's council. Everyone else, all your servants and ladies must eat speedily, and leave the place, so the next set of servants and ladies can eat. As doubtless—"

"I remember well. I do. So pray go on."

"Well, my lady," Lady Rutland went on, "you know how Francis

Dereham came to join your household while you were . . . while you were . . ."

"Recovering, yes."

"Yes, while you were recovering. And Francis Dereham, being what he is, well, you know . . . I don't mean to criticize your having chosen him for one of your secretaries, but . . ."

"He was chosen because he's a protégé of my grandmother's," she said. "And my grandmother and the lady my aunt, the wife of the uncle who helped raise me, asked me most particularly. He was hired as a favor to them and not of my own accord."

"Yes, Your Majesty." Lady Rutland sighed. "I don't know if when those ladies knew him before he was the same sort of roguish kind of man he is now. I heard that he's been a privateer off the coasts of Ireland, and faith, that is a wild occupation and bound to change a man. But at any rate, he is not what I would call a polished gentleman, and as he was lingering over his supper, Mr. Johns, he got quite upset, and sent him a message demanding to know whether he was of the queen's council that gave him the right to linger over his supper in that way."

Kathryn heard herself moaning, and Lady Rutland nodded. "That is how I feel about it, too, Your Majesty. For what good is there to confront that kind of rogue in that way. When a man has no notion of his place in the world, not all the talk or the sermons will make him have it. But Mr. Johns would have his way. And Master Dereham answered just in the way I would have expected. He sent a messenger to tell Mr. Johns that he was part of the queen's council before Mr. Johns knew Your Majesty, and that he would be part of your council after he's forgotten you."

"What can he mean by that?" Kathryn asked, well understanding the implications of the sentence, but honestly wondering what Dereham meant. Could he mean to put her head on the block, even if he had to lay his alongside hers?

"Well, ma'am. And I don't understand it. We were hoping that you understood it. Was he then your friend and adviser at the Duchess of Norfolk's?"

"No, no," Kathryn said. "Or if yes, only in the way that children are in council. There was a group of us, all together, and we often took rides, and . . . and employed our games together . . . Nothing more than children games. We might have consulted him—we maidens—about what lace looked better in a bonnet. No more than that."

Lady Rutland nodded. "And I told Mr. Johns that was all it would be. Young men of Master Dereham's stamp are like that, always trying to make their wild boasts sound far more important they are. I told Mr. Johns how it would be . . ." She hesitated. "But perhaps Your Majesty will receive him with myself a distance away, so that if you need to give him a right proper dressing down, you will not be embarrassed by my hearing you, but so that I can testify you were chaperoned, and everything done all right and proper, so that no one needs think that the queen was alone with this rogue."

"Yes, Lady Rutland," Kathryn said, meekly, glad the woman had suggested it, else she would have had to try to find a time to be alone with Dereham, which, considering his mood, looked like a dangerous game. "I will see him, if you would call him in."

She received him in her antechamber, with Lady Rutland standing a little ways away.

At first she didn't recognize him and wondered how a little more than a year could have wrought such a change in him. Dereham, who had been considered by all the ladies at Horsham a very handsome man, looked smaller, as though he had shrunk in on himself.

That he was very thin couldn't be denied. Gaunt almost, his face showed sharp angles of bones through the stretched skin.

But there was more to it than that. He looked haggard, too, as though he'd been running from something for far too long. But more than that, he looked tawdry and tainted.

She couldn't really explain it any better than that. His eyes were as dark and sparkling as they'd been when he'd first fascinated her. His hair remained dark. There were, it is true, two vicious scars across his cheek on the left side, but Kathryn felt, in some obscure way, that this should have added to his charm rather than deterring from it. Why then did she feel as though he were not the real Francis Dereham? As if he were not nearly as important or handsome as in her memory?

He wore more expensive clothes than he had then—a beautiful doublet of green brocade that Kathryn would guess had been the duchess's gift—but they only made him look more like he was out of place. As though he were wearing the clothes of a more important man.

The way he walked into the room was just the way she remembered, too, head held high, his step long. But it had a way of looking, now, as though he were only trying to look confident, as though it weren't his true self, as if inwardly he were slinking and sliding into the room.

He approached her, smiling broadly, his hands extended to meet hers.

"Master Dereham," she said, sharply.

Something to her voice, she was not sure what, had the effect of bringing him to a standstill. "Kathryn?" he said hesitantly.

"Master Dereham," she said, again. "One doesn't address the queen in such a way unless one happens to be the king."

Dereham looked like he was about to speak, but the look on Kathryn's face—probably, Kathryn felt, made sterner by the fact that she was very tired and felt as though she were holding on to the very edge of sanity—must have quelled his ideas before they came to his lips. He bowed to her.

"It has come to our attention," Kathryn said, before he had time to think of something else to say, "that you have been causing trouble in my household, Master Dereham. It appears you have had a dispute with Mr. Johns."

"Mr. Johns, Mr. Johns, Mr. Johns," Francis Dereham said, mimicking her voice. "Everyone is so willing to lecture me about Mr. Johns that you'd think he was the king himself."

Kathryn made an effort to speak but lost, as she was seeing Francis for what he was—a shoddy, overconfident young man with a mocking voice and little else. This had seemed like maturity and manhood to her when she was at Horsham. How foolish she had been. Even Harry without the crown, with his clumsy hands, his hesitant ways, was much preferable to Dereham. And to Dereham she'd pledged her hand. Oh, she'd been very ill used when no one had given her a better knowledge of the world.

But beyond the shock of realizing that everything she'd once believed had in fact been wrong, ridiculously wrong, there was a deep tiredness from her not-yet-fully-healed body. When she spoke, she spoke in few words, afraid she could not command the breath or the ability to speak in longer sentences. "Master Dereham, Mr. Johns is one of the men who run my very large and very complex household. Every time you disrespect him, or cause him to have to enforce his perfectly right and legal rules upon you, you make my household run a little worse.

"I'll have you know that before, when my vice steward got drunk, the king himself took a particular interest in the case, scolded him, and told him he would not be drunk before me again and also that certain rules of sobriety and cleanliness would be observed in my household."

"I was never drunk," Dereham protested, his fine dark eyes flashing at her.

"No, Master Dereham, and that makes it worse, since you said nonsense about having been in my council before I married my lord the king. Nonsense that, badly interpreted, could cause my lord to think that I was less than honest with him or less than a pure maiden when I married him. Know you that the king had a friar arrested for speaking against my reputation? Why would you then wish to risk it?"

Dereham was looking at her, his mouth half open, as though he meant to protest but had been stopped by the very idea that he'd put his own life in risk when he'd spoken. And that was the worst of it. Kathryn realized that he had never loved her. He'd loved his own pride. He'd loved what he thought was his prowess in attaching the daughter of the Howards. Nothing more.

Had he loved her, he might have been maddened enough with jealousy to be willing to die to get his revenge. But the truth was that he hadn't known he was at any risk. He'd only thought to do her a bad turn because she had preferred the king to him.

In Master Dereham's own mind there was one person he loved, and that was himself. No one else even appeared to him as another person, much less as someone he could love.

"Do not say things of that kind again, Master Dereham," she said, tiredly. "The palace is large, there are many people in it, and some are bound to put quite the wrong construction upon your words. In memory of the carefree children we once were, I would fain not see your head separated from your body."

He pushed his lower lip forward in a petulant gesture and tried for a come back. "There are things I could say," he said, "if I wanted to."

"There are things all of us could say," Kathryn said, "if we wanted to. But the truth is, do we really want it? When it comes right to it, Master Dereham, think about whom it would hurt. We would fain not see you hurt."

He opened his mouth, then closed it, and finally pivoted on his foot and left, still walking in his broad stride, with his head held high.

"A very upstart sort of young man," Lady Rutland said. "Riffraff, as Mr. Johns said."

"And Mr. Johns was right," Kathryn said.

Forty-six

"SWEETHEART," Henry told her one night, after making his clumsy love to her and while he lay beside her, his great hand resting on her stomach. "Do you think you are now well enough to go on progress with me? I've been meaning to do it for years, you know, but first there was Jane's death and then . . . well, there have been a lot of reasons I haven't done it." He paused. "But I think that the country needs to see her king, and the North Country most of all."

"I will go wherever you command me, my lord," Kathryn said.

He patted her. "You see, there have been rebellions in the north, and now we need to go and show them our majesty and our power. It will be a very big progress," he said. "We'll assemble the whole court, and as soon as the road is dry enough—for you must know it has been unseasonably wet—we'll progress to the north with carts and baggage. I meant to do it when you fell so ill, and we had to wait until you recovered. But now we will go. There will be tents and carriages, and I will try to make it as grand and great for you as I can manage. Would you like that, Kathryn?"

Kathryn said yes, partly because she wanted to get away from the confined palace, where she had been so ill, and partly because she thought the king himself was longing to go, and she should join him.

In a few days they left, progressing north to Collyweston, the great country palace of Henry's grandmother Lady Margaret Beaufort. After four or five days, they crossed into Lincolnshire.

"The progress will stop resentments," the king said. "It will knit me and my subjects as a whole once more."

It seemed that way. They went into Stamford and Boston in procession.

For Henry and Kathryn it was a sort of honeymoon combined with a pageant—an extended coronation trip for her.

At night they slept together in whatever beds the local gentry made available—and those were often at least as good, if not better, than the one they had at home—and during the day the king often rode, or if his leg troubled him, he would sit in the litter with Kathryn. Together they would doze, or she would play the lute for him. Sometimes he told her he should compose songs anew—that he would compose her such songs as would amaze her.

And sometimes he told her about the country ahead—the loyal gentry and those that were not so loyal.

At other times, she taught her ladies new dances, which they displayed for the king when the progress was stopped long enough. Or she and her ladies would plan new and elaborate gowns.

All should have been well—it all would have been well. But Kathryn, though she tried very hard, could not forget Thomas Culpepper. In her mind and heart, he kept returning, like a dream from which she never fully woke and wasn't quite sure she wished to. Day and night she thought of him and imagined what he was doing.

During the progress, sometimes she leaned out and would catch sight of him riding beside the litter. The thing was that whenever she looked at him, always, she would see him looking back at her.

This is foolish, she told herself. *Queens don't develop passions for young men of the court like silly young girls do for men in their grandmother's household. I am the queen. And, force, Thomas Culpepper has caught my fantasy but I trow he's no great thing. At heart, he is no better than Dereham. Riffraff.*

No matter how often she told it, she could not believe it. She would catch sight of him, and always he was as he should be—a gentleman of manner and of fact, riding his horse or playing at dice; practicing his sword or perhaps dancing in the evening with one of her ladies.

One of the evenings, the king saw her looking and patted her hand. "Thomas Culpepper is a good dancer, is he not? I vow he is the most graceful of my gentlemen. He's been my page ever since he was old enough to toddle about court." He grinned. "When he was very young, sometimes he would get scared and crawl into bed with me during the night. Now I hear he crawls into the beds of half your ladies, the scoundrel. But perhaps I shouldn't say that to you, my dear. I see you're shocked."

Kathryn felt as though she'd been slapped. The idea of Culpepper sleeping with half her ladies made her throat close. She wanted to dance with him. She wanted to remind him of his letter to her—oh, she should have kept it!—she wanted to make sure he loved her as much as she loved him. That he loved her so much he would never forget her, and that no one would ever replace her in his heart.

She could not say that. Not to the king. She heard her voice, distant and even, say, "He seems like a very good sort of gentleman."

"The best gentleman that ever lived," the king said, and then cleared his throat, as though realizing that what he had just said contradicted his earlier statements. "And I'm sure if he ends up in any ladies' beds, it is as much their fault as his own. For he's a young and madcap creature, and at that age it is hard to resist a pretty pair of eyes or a fair smile. But . . . well, so it is at my age, is it not?" he said.

Kathryn nodded absently. Her mind was full of Thomas Culpepper, and she longed for him so much it hurt. And yet it must never be, never. Everything separated them, but most of all that she was married to the king. Even an ordinary man had the power to undo his wife, but the king's majesty could utterly destroy where it loved. If she crossed him, she would not rise again.

At the end of a long day, they withdrew to their lodgings at Lincoln Castle, where they had separate apartments.

As was customary, the king visited her, but he soon left to go back to his own apartments. Since his leg had stopped flowing for those few days, he seemed to have remembered his age. He would come to her every night, but often he would leave her, that they both might sleep undisturbed, he said. He did not want to keep her awake, he said, since her health was still fragile. And besides, he slept best upon his own bed.

Normally as soon as the king left, Kathryn fell asleep and stayed that way till early dawn. But this time, she could not. She kept thinking of Culpepper at the dance that evening, dancing with half of her ladies. Was he sleeping with them, too?

She got up and she paced her chamber, but it was too closed in, too hot, too confined. "Jane," she called, touching Lady Rochefort's arm, as the woman slept on a camp bed at the foot of her own bed. "Jane, I beg you, come."

Jane got up. She had that look in her face, as though she were once more seeing things that weren't there or perhaps only things that were not there to anyone else. She would jump at shadows and look around in confusion.

However, Kathryn thought, it was as well. She was taking Jane with her, and the fact that she had Jane with her should be enough—more than enough—for people to think she was well chaperoned. And besides, she meant to do nothing too dangerous, nothing too bad. If anyone asked, she would say she was going to the king's chambers to check on her husband's sleep, having been disturbed by a bad dream.

She was going to the king's apartments, that much was true. She was going to check on the whereabouts of Thomas Culpepper, king's gentleman and the most gallant man in the court.

Outside her chamber, there was a hallway, and at the end of the hallway a door, which led to a sort of terrace. Past that door was the other side of the palace, which was built as a mirror to this part—and in that other part the king's chambers.

As Kathryn started down the hallway to the king's chambers, she saw a gentleman come the other way, carrying something. Both of them stopped. She thought she recognized in the dimly lit gentleman the form and shape of Thomas Culpepper. She must be dreaming. But he had stopped at the same time and was staring at her.

"Master Culpepper," she said, at the very same time he said, "Your Majesty."

They looked at each other across the hallway. Slowly, slowly he came toward her, as though he were afraid she would vanish. Kathryn was conscious of Jane at her elbow, and she wondered what Jane would make of this all but was afraid to turn and see.

"You see," Culpepper said softly. "I was coming to your chamber in the hopes of finding one of your women who was still awake and who would relay my gift to you."

"Your gift, sir?" she asked, confused. For a moment she thought he meant his love or perhaps his heart. But he extended the thing he'd been carrying, which on second look was a round basket of the sort rustics carried around.

"This morning," he said, "while we were riding past a field, I saw the finest strawberries, and I remembered my promise to that little girl who grew up to be Your Majesty," he said. "I thought I should fulfill it. We all know how important promises are."

"Yes," she said.

He looked around. "I see you have your woman with you, so nothing could be more proper," he said, "than if we went out through this door and onto the terrace and ate strawberries in the moonlight. Would Your Majesty like that?"

She inclined her head. "I couldn't think of anything I would like better."

Forty-seven

THE strawberries were sweet, and so was the company.

Jane, perhaps sensing she was not wanted, or perhaps acting solely in response to her ghosts and visions and those half-formed dreams that seemed to be more than half of her consciousness, sat a little away from them while they sat on the steps of the ancient terrace under the moonlight, the basket of strawberries between them.

"You don't know how many days I spent on knees, in the chapel," he said. "Crawling to the crucifix."

"You did?"

"Yes, while you were ill," he said.

"For the king's health?" she asked.

"I love the king's majesty," Culpepper said. "And as God is my witness, I'd never wish any evil to befall him, but in truth, it was you I prayed for. When you came upon Charles and I in the king's chamber, seeing you like that, pale and wan with the blood pouring out of you . . . we thought you were dead, and that is the truth. And for days, even your women seemed to think you were dead."

Kathryn reached for a strawberry. Quite accidentally, her hand touched his. He did not remove his, but instead, he turned it upside down, so that her hand might rest in his palm, and then, slowly, he closed his palm, so that he was holding her hand, in the basket, over the soft, sun-warmed strawberries.

He looked ahead at the little wood that bordered on the terrace, as if he expected some sort of answer from the shadows and the trees. "Do you love him very much, then?" he asked.

"Him?" Kathryn asked, quite lost.

"The king. His Majesty. The way you worried about him . . . Then way you came running so fast and then were so distressed that the child must perforce leave your womb . . . I realized then . . . Kathryn . . ." He waited as if to see if she would object to the use of her given name. When she didn't, he inclined his head, as if this too were an answer. "When you came in like that, so anxious for his health, I realized what a fool I had been. Trying to spite the duchess by not answering her summons, I lost the opportunity at having for wife not only the most beautiful lady who ever lived, but the sweetest, too consumed with zeal for her husband's well-being."

"Should I not care about the health of my lord?" Kathryn asked, and then, more angry at herself than at him or even at the duchess or the duke of Norfolk, feeling that everything she must say and live and do was a lie, and it was all her fault, she charged ahead, "If it counts, Master Culpepper, I don't think you spurned the marriage. I don't think you'd ever have been given a chance at it."

"But the Duchess of Norfolk summoned me," he said. "She sent word to the court that I was to come and that she would have a message to my father about a very advantageous marriage for me."

Kathryn, who felt as though in the last year she'd learned far more of the world than she'd ever meant to, gave a hollow laugh. "Oh, I know that's what she said. But I think the truth was quite different. I think, Master Culpepper, that the Duke of Norfolk and the dowager duchess went fishing. And that I was that with which they baited their hook."

"You think they meant you for the king all along?" he said.

"I would lay a wager on it," Kathryn said.

"Well then," Culpepper said. "My guilt is less but not my regret. You were always, then, too dear for my possessing, but a man can dream."

Kathryn smiled. She shouldn't say it, but there was the moonlight on her, and Jane was far enough away that she could not hear them. And it seemed for once she must tell the truth, even if she might die for it. "A woman can dream, too, Master Culpepper, and I wish it had been an earnest summons and that you had answered it."

The hand surrounding hers clenched tight upon it.

Forty-eight

The progress continued, but something had changed. Outwardly, it all was the same. The king would visit the queen's bedchamber at night. During the day they would spend time together. She played for him, or they played at cards together.

But after he left her bedchamber at night, after most of her household was asleep, two hooded shadows would often come out of her room and meet with a gentleman similarly attired in whatever garden, chase, or preserve offered.

As romance went, it was nothing like what Kathryn had experienced before. Culpepper never did any more than hold her hand and once, in a transport of passion, kiss it.

Not for him the careful explorations that Manox had made upon her body, or even lying naked abed with her, the way Dereham had.

Instead they talked.

They talked of everything. Their childhoods, their dreams, even their hopes of heaven. Like two children dreaming of the future, they imagined what their life would have been together had they married. In their dream they picked their castle from one of those that his father held. They furnished it. They chose their horses. They hired imaginary servants. They dreamed up schemes to increase their fortunes, and they imagined what their children would have looked like.

Unspoken but clear between them, so clear that Kathryn herself could not lie to herself and pretend it wasn't there, was the certainty that they would do all this, should something happen to the king. Only, of course, Kathryn wasn't sure she would be allowed to do any of it—to leave court and marry Culpepper. It seemed more like a dream than something that could ever happen. And she knew, all too well, that it could never happen unless she were pregnant or had already born the Duke of York when the king died.

So was lost in a dream she walked with Culpepper night after night.

There were some scares. Once, in Lincoln, when trying to get back into her apartments, she'd found the door locked fast against her. Culpepper had been forced to pick the lock so that she and Jane could return to their beds without disturbing any of the other inmates of the household.

Another time, when she was going into her room, she'd met with Mr. Johns himself, who said he was coming around to investigate a sound. Kathryn had told him she was coming back from the king's apartments, and she hoped that he would not check.

And then another night in Pontefract, one of the finest castles in England, while they stayed there on an extended visit, after Kathryn had been out walking with Culpepper, Jane had looked at Kathryn as they were about to go back to their apartments, and she had said, "Pray my lady, do not take me amiss. I believe you know what love is now."

Kathryn was very afraid that she did know.

Forty-nine

THE progress continued. They moved to York by easy stages, and took a major detour to inspect the fortifications at Hull. At York, Henry lingered very long, showing Kathryn what a great domain their son would hold, should he ever decide to appear.

But after they returned to Hampton Court, once more, Henry's wound closed up and the humors pent up within the leg.

That night, Kathryn met Culpepper, and she was frantic. "My lord," she said, "will die."

They were in a little landing off the queen's apartments, a stairwell where no one ever went. They stood by a window. A cold breeze blew in, playing with her hair. She'd removed her hood, because he liked seeing her with her hair loose. She'd done it automatically. She had to do everything automatically because she could not think.

"My lord," she said, "will die."

Culpepper didn't reassure her. He did not, as he had those many months ago, tell her all would be well or that Henry would live. Instead he looked worried and the only comfort he could lend her was to touch her hair softly, his fingers like sparrows. After a long silence, he said, "I will take care of you, Kathryn. I will always take care of you."

She felt tears falling down her face. She wanted to tell him that he had even forgotten the strawberries, so why should she believe him now. But she also didn't want to. In a way, she dared not. Even if he were an inconstant man, she didn't want his inconstancy exposed to her and the world both. Let her dream; let her hold on to the dream as long as she might. It would not be very long.

"Aye," she said softly. "And you won't be able to. Had I a child, then it would be different. Were I carrying the Duke of York, then it would be different. But since that time, it hasn't happened at all, and more than half the time my lord—" She stopped, realizing what she was about to say was treason. But then, meeting Thomas out here was treason, aye, and what she wanted with him was treason, too. "More than half the time since that day, my lord proves incapable of performing what my grandmother of Norfolk called the office."

"Perhaps you are with child already," Culpepper said.

She shook her head. "Nothing has happened since my last flux that could make it so," she said, and realizing she sounded like Anne of Cleves laughed, her laugh tinged with a little bit of hysteria. Then her words came again, low, and she said, "If my lord left me with child, then my family . . . aye, they're powerful enough. Between them, I trow, they could manage to keep me safe. As regent or else with one of them as regent while I retired somewhere in comfort." She looked at him and frowned. "I still misdoubt I may ever marry or at least not till the child would be old enough or till his brother ascended the throne." She shook her head. "But I would at least be allowed to live."

"You'll be allowed to live," Culpepper said. "We'll find a way to take you far from all these court intrigues, away from people who might wish to harm you. I'll take you right away from all of this to where you may be safe and know you are."

She laughed at the back of her throat. "What?" she said. "Take me to France, perhaps?"

"Perhaps," he said calmly, as though this were perfectly reasonable. "If I must."

He couldn't know that he was, in his very different way, exactly replicating what Dereham had told her once. He didn't know how futile it all sounded. If Margaret Douglas, more resourceful than Kathryn—aye—and more forceful, too, could be separated forever from the man she loved, what would not happen to Kathryn.

In that moment she shivered, realizing it could be far worse than her death. She might live a long life in some desolate priory, some distant convent, never seeing Thomas again. Looking up at his face and thinking of never seeing it again made Kathryn's heart clench and her breath turn to a small, forlorn gasp. She reached out blindly. She took his hand and guided it, under her neckline, to rest on her breast.

At first he tried to resist, to pull back, but she kept his hand there, and little by little, as a child that learns to stand or walk, his hand started fondling her breast with slow, experienced movements. She bit her lip. She would not cry out. The slightest touch from Culpepper was better than the greatest pleasure from her other lovers.

Yet she must keep all her wits about her, and with her mind on it, she must make him want her enough that he'd forget danger and fear, aye, and loyalty and honor, too.

She worked as hard as she ever had, using all her artifice and all her power, pressing against him and begging him, then sighing and whispering. Enticing him. Telling him that only Lady Rochefort and Mary Tilney would be present. Telling him that he must save her life by taking her honor.

He asked if she knew the danger in it, and who better to know it? She had nodded and said, "I am my father's daughter." And to his quizzical look had answered, "For though I don't know it of my own accord, it is said that my father was a great gambler, always ready to risk fortune and livelihood upon the gaming tables."

He'd nodded but looked serious. "Aye, I've heard of Edmund Howard. An excellent hero on the battlefield, but you should never let him borrow from you." He moved his hand within her bodice, so that it cupped one breast and then the other. "But I pray you're not your father's daughter, madam, for he always lost."

She shivered but laughed brightly, a bitter laugh. "I must try, must I not? All my life has been one long gamble; let me rescue my last desperate chance with yet a new one."

Little by little, she coaxed him and convinced him up the stairs and into her apartments. In there she shooed Mary Tilney away, bidding her watch the door.

Jane Rocheford had walked, as one who is not quite present, to her bed at the foot of the queen's bed and fallen asleep in that way she did that sometimes made Kathryn wonder whether she were truly alive or if her will and her love animated what should long since have been a corpse.

Kathryn had pulled Thomas onto her bed and closed the curtains tight against prying eyes. And then everything had been different.

So many times, and since so long ago, Kathryn had let men take their pleasure with her, and sometimes she even had enjoyed their caresses and taken pleasure in their taking of them. She had thought it would all be the same. The undressing, fast or slow. The frantic caresses. And then, suddenly, the union, which always managed to be less than she expected or thought or hoped.

But everything was different and everything was new. The well-known actions could be described in the same way. They removed their own and each other's clothes. Thomas favored the slow method of undressing his lover, each piece of clothing removed, and each portion of the body beneath caressed with sensitive fingers and worshipful lips.

But his touch felt to Kathryn like no other touch. It was as though her whole lifelong she had never tasted anything but the weakest of weak ale, and now, suddenly, she were given distilled liquor, splashing headily into the glass, overwhelming all her senses.

She had to bite her lips together not to moan, and even then she was sure some moans escaped her. She didn't fear waking Lady Rochefort, who when she was in this state, would sleep like the dead, but she feared that Mary, outside the door, might hear more than was convenient. She trusted Mary Tilney with her secrets—but how many secrets can you put in a single repository before they must, perforce, overflow?

Reaching for Thomas, she undressed him in turn, undoing doublet laces, feeling the skin of his body beneath his clothes. He looked a little surprised, despite his own experienced movements. Did her touch also feel to him as no other touch on Earth? Or was he, perhaps, like Henry, unused to a woman taking what she wanted in bed?

Her fingers caressed his skin, and it felt at once all new and as if it had always been so—as though she'd known what it would feel like. As though this were not the first time that she had felt his skin, but as though they'd been born for each other and were only now consummating what had been a long-preordained union.

And this time, when their bodies joined, there was no feeling that it was less than she expected. Instead, it was as though their souls joined, too, even as their bodies did.

In that moment, her arms around Thomas Culpepper's body, as he took her for his own and made her his, Kathryn knew what people meant when they spoke of heaven and bliss. And she knew that all her gambles had been worth it.

Fifty

THE king recovered. As before, the dangerous humors started flowing out of his leg again. It took days for him to be on his feet, though, and when he was, he always used his walking stick and was more ill-tempered than before.

Yet his love for Kathryn continued; and his desire for her. And if he could only rarely perform the office, he still came to her bed almost every night. And he still called her his rose without a thorn.

Kathryn didn't dare, again, admit Culpepper into her bed. In fact, conscious of how much greater their guilt now was, fearful of their own sins finding them, both had agreed they must not see each other. Or not as often.

Once more, she dared not meet him in stairways and empty chambers, in forests and parks and gardens. Instead, she was bound to walk where she knew he'd be so that they'd casually meet; she tried to look out of windows when she knew he would be below. And still she ached at the sight of him and ached worse when he was not there.

When her flux came, as usual, the next month, she cried a little, and Harry, hearing of it from one of her maids or perhaps from one of his men who'd talked to one of her maids, had patted her awkwardly. "I know how much you wish for a Duke of York," he told her. "But if he never comes, we must be content. Is not our present happiness enough?" He'd kissed her face softly. "You are the best and most perfect of my wives, my rose without a thorn. After all these marriages that have been afflicted by all manner of strange accidents, I have finally found a wife that suits my mood and who loves me with an all-perfect love. I will be grateful, even if there are no children. Aye, we have Edward, and he's a lusty infant and full of life."

Kathryn had let him caress her and comfort her, but inside she raged: Knew he not what would happen to her if he died? Knew he not the danger she would be in? Or cared he not?

For the first time since her marriage, she'd felt rage and repulsion toward Harry with the crown and Harry without the crown as well. But she could say nothing. Saying anything would only bring danger not only to her, but to Thomas as well. For Thomas's love, she would hold her peace and simper lovingly at her ignorant husband, and contrive to keep him happy yet a little longer.

Fifty-one

All Hallows' Eve was one of the times when the king must be seen to attend mass and to take communion, and Henry decreed that it should be a day of rejoicing throughout the country for his most perfect marriage.

He had not, she thought, as he had with his previous wives, prayed that God send him issue from this union. No. He just sang praises and ordered the Te Deum be sung for this most perfect species of womanhood, his rose without a thorn.

And Kathryn, whose heart was full of guilt and of hatred even, sometimes, clenched her teeth and closed her eyes and willed herself not to protest. This would allow her to hold on to life a little longer. And maybe, by a miracle, there would yet be a Duke of York. Maybe God granted miracles to desperate gamblers.

He had never granted it to her father, but surely all that meant was that the Almighty owed her family a debt. As well pay it here as not.

That night she slept with Harry nightlong, and he held on to her as a frightened child will hold on to his mother in a storm. She understood, then, that she clung to him because it would allow her to hold her life yet a little longer, and that he clung to her for no very different reason. While he held to her, he could tell himself he was still young, and while he told himself that, he could see his life extending far into the future. As long as he loved her, he loved his youth.

In the morning he left her, bidding her "Farewell, sweetheart," just as he had, she thought, so long ago to Anne of Cleves. Only it was not all that long ago, it just seemed so to Kathryn—a long and elaborate journey at the end of which you arrive quite a different person. She understood now that her gamble might be lost, but she refused to leave the table and she refused to turn in her cards. Somewhere, somehow, there must be a way for herself and Thomas to be together. There must be a way to survive Henry's death and become neither a pawn, nor a corpse.

She lingered over her dressing, demanding that her maids make the fall of her dress just so. She broke her fast on bread and small ale, her appetites all quite sated.

And then, because it was past All Hallows,' and Christmas and New Year's would be around the corner as sure as day follows night, she felt heavy and not interested in anything, but forced herself to act normally. She took her ladies into one of the larger chambers and started explaining a complex dance she had devised, which she hoped would amuse the king's majesty.

They were in the middle of it, and the player at the spinet had finally managed not to stop in the middle of a movement.

And then the door was thrown open, and there stood Cramner and two guards from His Majesty's private corps, and he gestured that the spinet player should stop, and the boy obeyed.

Kathryn turned around, fear rising in her, but rage covering it and rising with it. "What is the meaning of this, Master Cramner?" she asked. "See you not that I am practicing a dance with my ladies?"

"No more dancing now," Cramner said heavily. He looked tired. "The time for dancing is all gone, Your Majesty. You stand accused of treason, of having deceived His Majesty about your state as a pure and honest maiden when you married him, and of diverse indecencies and breaches of honor."

Kathryn shivered. She felt as though she'd not only turned into a statue, but she'd turned into a statue of ice. "What mean you?" she asked, or at least believed she had asked it, because she heard her own voice come back into her ears, but it came muffled and strange, as if from a very long way away, and she could only frown and shake her head.

"Mary Hall, née Lassells, who used to be the Dowager Duchess's of Norfolk's chamberer has spoken to us, being burdened in her conscience."

Again her voice, though she did not feel her lips move, nor—she could be sure—had she thought of the words, came back to her ears from a long way off. "Mary lies. She was always jealous of me."

Cramner shook his head. "We have apprehended two men. Henry Manox, musician, and Francis Dereham, until recently Your Majesty's secretary. They have confessed."

"How dare you?" Kathryn turned on him, screaming, even though she felt as though the real Kathryn remained frozen, locked within her. "How dare you? How dare you take the words of these knaves, these villains—"

"If they be villains, then it tells against Your Majesty," Cramner said. "For both men claim knowledge of Your Majesty, and Manox knows of a mark on your body, which the king's majesty confirms is so."

The king's majesty! They'd talked to the king. The king knew.

Well did Kathryn know how Harry with the crown would react to this revelation.

She didn't think any more than she had thought about the words she'd heard herself say. She just felt her own body spring forward, instinctively ducking under the arms the guards reached out to hold her, as if this were a game with Charles and Henry when they were children and she were running to stay ahead of them.

And stay ahead of them she did, down the long corridor of Hampton Court, between her quarters and the chapel, where—at this hour—Harry would be listening to mass.

Halfway through the running, as she panted and her heart beat hard, her thought caught up with her actions. She realized that her body was doing exactly the right thing. If she could get to Harry, then Harry without the crown would surely forgive her. But she had to get to him.

The doors of the chapel were closed. She pulled at the handles, but the doors wouldn't open. Locked.

She pounded with her small fists, hard, insistently, demanding the door open and screaming for Harry. But nothing happened. The door remained closed.

And then the guards were there, their hands grasping her fast and pulling her backward, toward her chamber, where they threw her and locked the door.

Kathryn collapsed to the floor, crying. And all the time, as her body cried and screamed, her mind was working fast. No more time to dance now. Now the die had been rolled, the last stakes placed. Now was the time to fight for her life.

Tumbling Rose

Fifty-two

SHE stayed at Hampton Court with her ladies. She knew not what to do or what would befall her. She gave up all interests and all pastimes, and day and night she walked, like the caged lion, the confines of her meager enclosure.

She touched her neck now and then as she remembered Anne Boleyn's fate. What Anne Boleyn had proven, and proven well, was that adultery by a queen was treason.

But they spoke of Manox and of Dereham. And neither of those were adultery. She had slept with Dereham naked in bed. She had allowed his member within her. A sin that might be, but it was not adultery, for neither of them had been married at the time. And she'd allowed Manox to touch her and enjoy her body, behind the stairs and in the chapel. And, force, that had been shameless, and perhaps it made her less than a proper and clean maiden. But adultery it was not.

And if they thought her promises to Dereham were a precontract, well then, they were married. And that means she might have broken faith with the king by failing to tell His Majesty that she was contracted to another. But again, that would make their marriage null. And whatever she had done, not adultery.

The more she thought of this, turning every idea in her mind, the more she liked the last because if she was pre-contracted to Dereham, and all but effectively married to him, then she'd never been married to the king. Let things take their course, and let him send her to some country place, and then, in time, release her, shamed and forgotten.

Then could she get the duchess to help her divorce Dereham—she felt sure that even with Kathryn's reputation broken, the duchess would never want a Howard daughter pledged to Mr. Dereham. Let her divorce Dereham, and she could marry Thomas Culpepper.

They would retire to the country and furnish a castle as they'd meant to, and they would have beautiful children, whom they'd teach to stay away from court and its snares.

She spent many days, sitting, dreaming of this. Her state of mind, alternating between aimless sitting and passionate crying, made people look at her oddly, and they started removing from her reach such things as she might use to do harm to herself.

But Kathryn still had hope; Kathryn thought the roll of the die might still turn out all right.

Above all she must keep from mentioning Culpepper. She must forebear to even think of him, lest someone divine her thoughts. Even if she had to fall, let him go on living.

In this she found that she was very different from Lady Rochefort, who was her very constant and faithful companion now. She thought that if she must die, then let it be so, but let Thomas Culpepper go on living. She felt only a little pang at the thought that he would marry someone else, then, and have children with her, but it was nothing like the pain she felt at the thought of Thomas dead. Thomas forever gone. And all because of her.

Fifty-three

At first it all seemed right. At first they sent her to Syon, and there she stayed, with only three ladies and three chamberers. One of the ladies was Lady Rochefort, and it seemed to Kathryn that the poor lady was more distant from reality than ever she had been.

She talked daylong to walls. But all the same, sometimes she would see Kathryn thinking or dreaming, and she would touch her arm and said, "Oh, love is a great misfortune, madam."

Just knowing that someone knew, even if the name must never be pronounced, was a balm to Kathryn.

By some means, though Kathryn never found out how and was afraid to ask in case she should be told that Jane got it from the spirit of the departed George Boleyn, Lord Rochefort, Jane always knew what was happening in the outside world. Her statements on this were always proven true, and Kathryn had learned to ask her and to listen to her on the subject.

When Jane told her that the investigators were pressing Dereham close because they were sure his affair with the queen had continued after her marriage, she could only snort.

The more they asked Dereham, the more they'd only get that the queen had told him to obey Mr. Johns and stop saying foolishness. Aye, and no less than Lady Rutland to attest to that.

Only some days later, Jane said that Dereham had named Thomas Culpepper as the person with whom Kathryn's affections now lay and that Culpepper had been taken.

Now Kathryn could not sleep, for in sleep she saw the beloved body being tortured, the face broken, the mouth distorted by the choke pear. If perchance she slept, the dreams came, and then she trembled and woke screaming, only to sleep again, such was her exhaustion.

To keep herself awake, she would play. In the middle of the night, she'd rouse all her ladies and make them dance with her, to keep away the images of Thomas suffering, of Thomas being broken.

She wrote the king two letters accusing herself, trying to stop the investigation into her further wrong deeds. She told him she'd been pre-contracted. She told him that it was all her fault. She prayed that he would probe no further. That he would put her away—or kill her even—but cease looking for more signs of adultery. That he would let Thomas go.

She was half mad with lack of sleep and half blind with uncried tears when Jane Boleyn told her that Bess Harvey, a sometime shadow of the ladies of the queen—a member of Anne Boleyn's house who had lingered on at court and served even Kathryn, though Kathryn never appointed her—had told all that she had seen Kathryn and Thomas Culpepper meeting late at night and often. She clearly had been spying for she knew of when the door was locked and it couldn't be opened, and also of the other times she and Culpepper met.

Kathryn laughed, for she could not help it, and when Jane

Boleyn asked her why she laughed—for once the sober companion to one acting madly—Kathryn had told her. In one of their conversations, Thomas had told her of Bess Harvey, who had been Thomas's lover before he ever saw Kathryn. He told her he'd dropped the lady quite suddenly, not even giving her the customary gift he usually gave his lovers.

And Kathryn thinking it all a jest and thinking that Bess Harvey, like so many ladies at court, had merely been trysting to pass the time, had sent Bess Harvey a gift, herself: a costly brocade gown. She now saw how this present might have galled Bess if she'd been in true love with Thomas. "How marvelously rich this game is," Kathryn told Jane. "That we must all play blindfolded and never know the importance of each roll until it is well done.

And Jane, mad Jane Boleyn, had looked at Kathryn as though Kathryn were mad.

It was all gone, now, Kathryn thought, and nothing could save her. And with this certainty came a calm and a great exhaustion.

When everything is lost, there is nothing to fight for. When the game is over, it is time to rest, for you cannot retrieve the hand you lost.

Fifty-four

And so the Tower it was, through Traitor's Gate. The Tower, where she'd been so afraid of seeing Anne confined back when she was a mere child and had confused the ceremonies of coronation with imprisonment.

But it did not matter, for perhaps her soul divined even then that Anne would also enter that gate, and then Kathryn also.

She took residence in the Tower as though these apartments had been waiting for her, her whole life.

If she cried sometimes, it was only a little, as she thought of Thomas, whom she was sure was now doomed. Was there a paradise, she wondered, where they would meet and hold each other again? She couldn't think of one, because the paradise they told you about in church was too much like an earthly kingdom, and if it were so, then the king of all would not take kindly to someone who had betrayed his brother on Earth.

Though she still had three ladies to attend her, Jane Boleyn was her only companion most of the time, the one who would sit with her and talk to her.

Of course, Jane spent most of the time talking to the dead she had wronged and seemed to see as present as life. Kathryn wondered if Thomas was already dead. And if he was, would he appear to her as George and Anne appeared to Jane, who now seemed at long last reconciled with the long departed and talked to them as with friends or family.

In fact there was some excitement to Jane, as though she were preparing to go on a long trip, and George and Anne were helping plan it. It was all, "Yes, yes." And sometimes, "I will meet you, then."

This was perhaps because Jane had been condemned for aiding and abetting the queen's adultery and, as such, had been sentenced to die with her.

The slow-thinking Kathryn at the back of Kathryn's eyes, the one who tallied the world without fear or favor, thought that perhaps this had been what Jane had wanted all along, to die in the same way her husband had died and thus expiate her crime.

On the twelth of February, a Sunday, Jane told Kathryn that George had said they were to prepare to die on the morrow.

It was no surprise then, when Kathryn's gaolers repeated the message. Kathryn was then sure that Thomas was long dead, and only one thing occupied her—to finish as well as she could.

For after the game is done and you have lost, it is best to leave as cleanly as possible and to show that you are not a poor loser.

She asked that the block on which she was to rest her neck for the fatal blow be brought to her cell so she could practice laying her head on it, so her neck was supported. Thereby, when the ax fell, it would sever her head with one clean blow.

Fifty-five

THE morning of her death was very cold. Kathryn had her hair arranged so as to leave her neck free for the blow. She looked out the window of her tower prison at the sun covered up as though there were cheesecloth in front of it, and she sighed. She would have liked to have seen the sun once more.

The short walk to Tower Hill seemed like a never ending trip—like those she had taken with the king on progress. When you know the end is near, each breath counts, and each of them seems to last forever.

It seemed to Kathryn there were days that had passed more heedless—years to which she'd paid less attention—than those few minutes. By her side Jane was very quiet.

Kathryn climbed the stand where the block stood, her old friend the block, which she had laid her head upon last night in her cell. It seemed like years before.

It was very cold, and there were very few people in attendance. She searched in vain but did not see her uncle or her grandmother. She suspected anyone else she might have cared to see had long been parted from his head, and she shivered at the thought of that head rotting upon the bridge's spikes.

She started her speech in a fainting voice, asking the good people to take note of her just and fair punishment, and she thought that was right for it was fair to die for trying to avoid the death that fate has laid in store for you. If she closed her eyes, she could still see the lace falling upon the floor of the dormitory. She could still hear Alice Restwold's voice tell her she would marry a Henry. It had all been preordained, and folly it was to try to avoid it.

"I beg of the king's majesty only two favors," she said. "That he will not prosecute my family and kin for the crimes that are only my own, and that he will allow my gowns to be divided among my ladies, for I have now no other way to reward them for their excellent care of me."

She took two steps toward the block, having now said what she planned to say. She looked down at its bloodstained, ax-scarred surface. Had Anne Boleyn also died on this block? Kathryn felt sure she had. She felt sure she had been preordained to follow her elder cousin's fate.

But this would not do, and she was not done yet. Kathryn might have to die as had been prescribed, perhaps before she had first drawn breath. She might have to disappear into some afterlife in which she couldn't very clearly believe. And it was possible she was damned for eternity, if she were in the hands of a heavenly king who would feel keenly the offense to His earthly counterpart.

She stopped and stood straighter, instead of laying her head upon the block. She could see shifting among those who had come to watch this done, as though they were afraid of what she might do next. The executioner, beside her, spoke from behind his hood, "It is time, now, my lady. I will make it swift." From the tension in his body and the way he spoke, she could tell he was afraid that she would resist it and would have to be forced to the block. Others had had to be forced in the past, Kathryn knew, and she imagined the executioner would be reluctant to have to wrestle with someone so much smaller than himself. Afraid of how it would look.

And now she stared at the crowd and imagined they perhaps were uncomfortable, too. Perhaps that was why there were so few of them. She was so small and so young, and anyone who saw her death would be unable to imagine but that they were brutes, putting a period to such a brief existence.

Well, let them feel it then.

It is time now, my lady, her mind said. *No more time to dance.*

But she would not go without speaking. She straightened her shoulders and she threw her head back. She looked at the meager crowd, the pale sun—even itself hiding as though embarrassed for the work he must witness—and at the tendrils of the fog on Tower Hill. Beyond it, the city of London would be waking, and on the bridge the head of Thomas Culpepper would be rotting.

Kathryn took a deep breath and spoke, not so much to the assembly or to the sun or even to London. She spoke to fate or perhaps that heavenly king whom she now saw as a slightly larger version of Harry with his crown. That king, too, must hear sometimes, and learn that though He had the power of life and death over His subjects, He could not make them thank Him for His unjust treatment of them. And He could not force His subjects to love Him.

Her voice rose, small and young sounding, into the cold morning, "I want you to know that though today I die a queen of England, I would much rather have lived the wife of Thomas Culpepper."

And then she was done.